W9-BDR-634

ZERO GRAVITY

Other books by Richard Lourie

SAGITTARIUS IN WARSAW

LETTERS TO THE FUTURE

FIRST LOYALTY

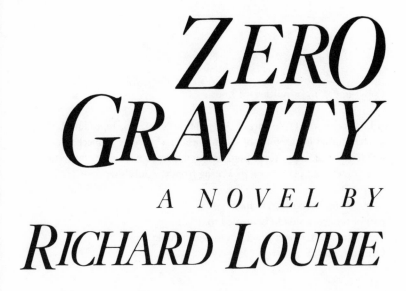

ZERO GRAVITY

A NOVEL BY

RICHARD LOURIE

HARCOURT BRACE JOVANOVICH, PUBLISHERS

San Diego ★ *New York* ★ *London*

HBJ

Copyright © 1987 by Richard Lourie

All rights reserved. No part of this publication may be reproduced
or transmitted in any form or by any means, electronic or mechanical,
including photocopy, recording, or any information storage and retrieval
system, without permission in writing from the publisher.

Requests for permission to make copies of any
part of the work should be mailed to:
Permissions, Harcourt Brace Jovanovich, Publishers,
Orlando, Florida 32887.

"My Prayer"
Copyright MCMXXXIX The World Wide Music Co. Ltd.
London, England.
Copyright Administrator for USA and Canada,
Skidmore Music Co., Inc., NY.
Copyright renewed. Used by permission.

Library of Congress Cataloging-in-Publication Data
Lourie, Richard, 1940–
Zero gravity.
1. Title.
PS3562.0833Z4   1987   813'.54   87-244
ISBN 0-15-199984-8

Designed by Camilla Filancia

Printed in the United States of America

First edition

A B C D E

To the sculptor,
the chef,
and the physicist

Come said the Muse,
Sing me a song no poet yet has chanted
Sing me the universal.

—WALT WHITMAN

PROLOGUE

The Polish general suffered severe gastric distress during the entire return flight from Moscow. Not because he had drunk too much vodka—he was used to that; and not because he was helping the Soviets oppress Poland—he was used to that, too—but because of a secret he'd been told.

The Russians were going to send a poet to the moon! Unbearable! The very thought of some Muscovite bard bounding from crater to crater bombarding earth with booming rhymed lies was more than the general could stomach. The night sky would be forever tainted.

The Soviets could not be stopped, but there was a chance to dilute the effect by slipping word to the Americans. They might think of something to eclipse this cultural/technical propaganda coup.

Then, by routes too circuitous and devious to detail, this information reached Europe and America, the "West" as they say in those lands where the sun sets early on unhappy cities.

PART ONE

Leonid Poplavsky was a busy man. Not only was he the Soviet cultural attaché in Washington, he was the KGB chief in charge of all espionage on the Eastern Seaboard, a position known in the trade as the *rezident*. Poplavsky believed in doing both jobs well, and not only because the more screenings, concerts, and readings he organized, the less likely the Americans would be to determine his actual function. He liked art because it was beautiful and had so little to do with life which, if the truth be told, was a clumsy business. Although he believed that art should of course serve the people and the party, it did so best by staying away from life. "Muddy boots are not improved by walking over a Persian rug," Poplavsky was fond of saying.

Busy though he was, Poplavsky usually found ten minutes each morning for the reading of intelligently written articles from the American press. He was determined to win a final victory in his eleven-year struggle with his linguistic arch enemies, the definite and indefinite articles. The conflict first erupted in his class at the special school at Gatchina where students were taught not only in classrooms but in a full-scale replica of an American town—supermarkets crammed with toilet paper, dog food, and chicken parts; gas stations with

Coke machines and Chevies with hand lettered, cardboard, FOR SALE signs on their windshields; and a McDonald's run by perky teenagers. "I want *a* box. I want *the* box. Why not simply—GIVE ME BOX!" Poplavsky had roared at his instructor who was running the checkout counter at the supermarket that day. Tearfully, she explained that not even the Soviet Academy of Syntax had been able to come up with a concrete rule that worked in all cases. "Then I'll figure one out myself!" Poplavsky had vowed with all the bravado of the youngish lieutenant colonel he was then; but now, as a middle-aged full colonel, he continued to struggle with those bedeviling linguistic will-o'-the-wisps.

"I don't think you want the 'the' here; I think you want an 'a'," an American had once remarked to Poplavsky after reading a Soviet-Embassy cultural press release.

"I don't want *a* 'the', I want *the* 'a'?" Poplavsky had replied, frowning in a consternation that was bordering on rage.

"That's right, a 'the' is not *the* right choice."

"But an 'a' is *the* right choice?" asked Poplavsky.

"Yes, an 'a' is *the* right choice."

"How can *an* 'a' be *the* right choice?" asked Poplavsky.

"A 'the' is right. The 'a' is wrong."

"Stop it, stop it!" said Poplavsky in a voice that managed to beg and threaten at the same time.

A soft, single knock at Poplavsky's door meant that Zivkin, the deputy cultural attaché, wished to see him. Setting his *Washington Post* aside, Poplavsky listened very carefully to the echo of that knock, for he knew that every human action betrayed more than it was ever supposed to. In the case of his deputy, what might be in the process of betrayal was none other than Poplavsky himself. And why shouldn't he betray me, thought Poplavsky. He does not think I will rise any farther, and therefore there is no reason to hitch his career to mine. And second, he considers me old-fashioned and doomed to the dustbin of history. He is modern and ambitious and knows as well as I do that the position of US Eastern Seaboard rezident can be a stepping-stone to enormous power. If he does not wish to betray and destroy, he has no business in the KGB.

"Come in."

"A cable for you, Comrade Cultural Attaché."

"Place it on my desk, please," said Poplavsky indicating his desk with a nod of his head. Keeping his gaze downward, he observed his deputy's hand come into view, watching for the slightest trembling of any ligament that would confirm his suspicions.

The fingernails were neatly manicured, and there was a light sprig of black hair on the first joint of each finger. Poplavsky didn't like the hand and could feel that the hand disliked him.

"Thank you," said Poplavsky looking up at Zivkin whose face was alert, official, admirably unreadable.

"Comrade Cultural Attaché, we're having a cash-flow problem," said Zivkin.

"Why?"

"There are so many Americans selling us technological secrets that we're in danger of not being able to make all the payments," said Zivkin who was in charge of technology procurement. Zivkin was so intent on the acquisition of dubious gadgets that he never bothered to attend a ballet—an oversight that, to Poplavsky, revealed poor taste and bad values.

"Do we need every last bit of everything they dream up over here?" asked Poplavsky.

"I don't believe I have to explain to you how important it

is that the Americans do most of the advanced research," said Zivkin with a touch of condescension. "The only other choice is to let our scientists travel abroad and attend congresses and read foreign literature, and you know what that would mean— ten thousand Sakharovs."

"Pay," groaned Poplavsky.

"I should also remind you that you have an appointment with Hartley Buckminister at ten o'clock."

"Thank you for reminding me," said Poplavsky in a tone that indicated their conversation was over. Everything essential had, after all, been communicated—the cable had been delivered, the payment question settled, the appointment noted. But most important of all was the tone Zivkin had adopted when speaking to him of science; it had contained enough arrogance to convince Poplavsky of Zivkin's motives. The man lived for nothing but Poplavsky's destruction and therefore had already doomed himself to extinction. Balding, big-eared, and old-fashioned though he might be, Poplavsky had no equal when it came to devouring those who would devour him.

He opened the cable.

TOP SECRET.

MANNED FLIGHT TO MOON SCHEDULED FOR EARLY AUTUMN. MULTI-NATIONAL CREW TO INCLUDE POET VIKTOR VIKTOROV WHO WILL READ POETRY FROM MOON. THEME OF PROJECT: HUMAN- IZATION, NOT MILITARIZATION OF COSMOS. TASS WILL MAKE OFFICIAL ANNOUNCEMENT ON MAY 1. SECURITY ESSENTIAL TO KEEP PUBLIC RELATIONS IMPACT AT MAXIMUM. RESPONSIBIL- ITY YOURS. ALSO YOUR RESPONSIBILITY TO WORK UP SUPPORT CAM- PAIGN (PRESS RELEASES, PHOTO EXHIBITIONS, ETC). DETAILS TO FOLLOW.

Unusual, thought Poplavsky, and therefore suspect. It was all too modern for his taste. Public relations. Stalin would have laughed. From the purges to public relations in a mere fifty years. Still, caution was required. Culture, though light-weight, could be a source of embarrassment. And besides, there had to be other reasons for going to the moon, other "hard" scientific and military reasons too delicate to entrust to a cable. Those details would come across the ocean safely locked inside a person's head, a "briefcase with two ears," as Poplavsky jocularly referred to such messengers.

Zivkin must be aware of the contents of the cable, not to mention the people in cryptography. Now there were two good reasons for trusting no one in his immediate organization. One, Zivkin may have already gotten to them. And, two, who can you trust?

Poplavsky crumpled the cable whose paper had been treated with a special chemical and dropped it into his wastebasket, which had also been treated with a special chemical. It was always a pleasure to watch as the paper fell into that little well of annihilation. As it touched bottom, the paper seemed to panic for a moment; as if everything that existed knew when its existence was menaced. The crumpled ball of paper immediately began losing substance, becoming transparent but retaining its outline. Suddenly, it was only its outline and then it was nothing, nothing at all, except for a few miniscule bits of chemical residue that, if accidentally inhaled, would not even be enough to make a person sneeze.

But why was that Hartley Buckminister coming to see him? And why did all those superpatriot ideological yachtsmen of the far right have the word "buck" in their name? Buckminister. Buckley. Make a buck. Pass the buck. The buck stops here. They should think a little less about money and a little more about their responsibilities to history and the world order. Americans were pursuing decadence with an adolescent, even athletic enthusiasm that was positively heartbreaking. America was the sweetest plum in history, and it would be a shame if it went bad before it could be plucked.

But what did Buckminister want? To complain about the Soviet Jews? Poplavsky had a few complaints on that score himself. He was absolutely opposed to allowing Jews to emigrate, not in the least because he was anti-Semitic, but because of his deep and realistic understanding of history in general and the history of the Jews and the Russians in particular.

Because of the Jew Marx's ideas, Russia had been turned into the Soviet Union. But Marx was like Moses or Isaac Newton, a prophet not the Messiah. Moses was superseded by Jesus Christ, and Einstein was the messiah of physics. But there had been no Einstein to replace Marx, so Russia was stuck with an outdated system concocted by an ill-tempered Jew suffering from carbuncles in the British Museum, or however it all got started. The point was that sooner or later some Jew was going to come up with yet another new idea that would cause the next great wave of history and he, Poplavsky, would just as soon be riding it as be drowned by it.

Poplavsky believed that Jews should be safeguarded and cherished, not killed as that idiot Hitler, who got everything exactly backwards, had decided. Jews were better than the best computer. They needed no spare parts and even reproduced themselves in large numbers if let alone and allowed to prosper. So, that stupid Hitler kills off the German and the Polish Jews, two very fertile sources that the world would miss sorely. So, what does that leave? The Jews of America, the Jews of Israel, and the Jews of Russia. Why should America and Israel have all the Jews? Especially when both countries are our enemies!

There was no way of predicting when and where the next Jew genius would arise. Maybe in the US, maybe in Israel, but maybe in Russia, too. Those stupid merchants, swapping Einsteins for grain that gets eaten and machines that break! If—no, not if—when he was the head of the KGB, he would push with all his influence against Jewish migration. Until then, he would keep his mouth closed on the subject, and give everyone the same line that he would give Buckminister later that day—that it was an internal affair, very complex, and presently under advisement. Meaning—nothing was happening and mind your own business.

Buckminister was almost an hour late because his private jet had run into some "weather" on his way back from addressing a group of jobless steel workers. His theme: The Price of Liberty. When he finally arrived, Buckminister apologized, but in a way that suggested that tardiness was but one attribute of his importance. There was something else in his manner—a hint of distaste at the very need to apologize to a Soviet, especially a squat and balding bureaucrat whose smile seemed to be tugged upward by invisible strings from large ears that looked as soft as an old catcher's mitt. Buckminister had a perfectly ridiculous desire to touch those large, soft ears, a desire he repressed at once with vigorous Yankee will.

"Please, please, sit down," said Poplavsky indicating the high-backed, tufted, leather armchair facing his desk. "You look tired. You need tea. There's a Russian saying—If you don't drink tea, where will you get your strength from?"

Buckminister, who did not like being told he looked tired, especially by an enemy of his nation, and who thought the Russian saying apt if moronic, was in fact dying for a cup of tea. But he wondered whether accepting tea after Poplavsky's comment about his looking tired might put him on the defensive to some degree. On the other hand, he *was* tired and refusing the tea would keep him from regaining his full natural bristle of confidence. For that reason it made better sense to accept the tea, where else was he going to get his strength from?

"Yes, a cup of tea would be very nice, thank you," said Buckminister after settling his long and angular body in the chair and crossing his legs as smartly as a new pair of scissors.

Tea was brought.

"This beautiful tea service," said Poplavsky as each man fixed his own cup of tea, "once belonged to Count Pantifleev of Tula and is now the property of the Russian people and is temporarily in the custodianship of myself, Leonid Nikolaevich Poplavsky, the son of a plumber. In a sense, you are drinking your tea straight from the Russian Revolution."

Buckminister felt his Adam's apple balk with abstract disgust, but forced himself to swallow. Was that little hydrant of a man running circles around him already, or was he imagining things?

"Then it's something of a historic occasion," smiled Buckminister. "Though I am a bit surprised that there's no blood in the cup."

Aha, starting already, thought Poplavsky. "Yes, Russia pays in blood, not in money," he said, "which is perhaps one reason that America understands my country so poorly, if you don't mind my saying so?"

"I don't mind," said Buckminister, "though I don't agree."

"You don't agree that you Americans don't understand Russia when statistics show that there are more *teachers* of English in the Soviet Union than there are *students* of Russian in the United States?"

"I believe the statistics on the number of English teachers in the USSR is a Soviet statistic," said Buckminister, "and, for that reason—how shall I put it?—is approximately as reliable as the Soviet pledge to abide by the Helsinki Final Act."

"You would like on-site inspection of Soviet teachers of English?" said Poplavsky with good humor that even forced the incision of a smile on Buckminister's face. "And, as for blood, at least Russian blood is not shed in 10,728 handgun murders which occur each year in America, and that, Mr. Buckminister, is *your* statistic, which *we* are perfectly willing to accept, and, believe me, with no on-site inspection required."

"Yes, in America we've always preferred to have our criminals in the streets. But, be that as it may, I am here today for a specific purpose, Mr. Poplavsky, and that is to present you with a letter signed by myself, and what may modestly be termed other luminaries of the American intellectual world, protesting the treatment of a single person, to wit, the great refusenik poet, Lev Brumsky."

"Let's go point by point. Great. Refusenik. Poet. Alright, I agree. Brumsky is a poet. At least he uses rhymes. I've read his poetry, in the original I might stress, and it could be called many things, Mr. Buckminister, but great isn't one of them. If Shakespeare, Pushkin, and Dante are great, then Brumsky is not. And if Brumsky is great, then Shakespeare, Pushkin, and Dante are not."

Buckminister regretted having used the adjective, but he would make up his losses on the next one, "refusenik." "Let's leave the question of greatness to the test of time. The real point is that a person wishes to leave his country, is not being allowed to, and so is, in effect, a prisoner."

"Well, as you Americans are fond of saying—that's one point of view. May I offer you another? How come there is no such word as acceptnik?"

"Acceptnik?"

"Yes. Tens of thousands of Soviet Jews left the USSR in the '70s," said Poplavsky, suppressing both regret and fury. "They applied and their applications were accepted. Therefore, they should be called acceptniks. But of course there is no such word because your press is only interested in bad news, about which many heartland Americans have also complained. So, if you don't want to acknowledge the existence of acceptniks, why should we acknowledge the existence of so-called refuseniks?"

"Are you saying that no Soviet Jews are being denied visas?"

"Not at all. That would not be the truth. But every state has to make up its own mind as to what to say yes to and what to say no to. Take the American Civil War which everyone in this country seems to have forgotten. The South wanted to secede from the Union. The Union said no. Therefore, the South became a Confederacy of refusenik states. Then, as I recall, force was used and the problem was solved. And so, we can truthfully say that the question of allowing Jews to secede from the Union, the Soviet Union, assumes new dimension when looked at in a broader historical context, isn't that so?"

"I don't accept your analogy between states and individuals. States and individuals are not the same thing."

"Alright, let's agree on that. States and individuals are not the same thing," said Poplavsky. "Next question is which is more important, the state or the individual?"

"We believe that the state exists for the individual, and Russia has always historically believed that the individual exists for the state," said Buckminister.

"In tsarist Russia the individual existed for the state. But in the Soviet Union the individual exists for the state only so that there can be a state to wither away for the individual. That's one thing. And let's look at Russian history. What do we see? Russian people are sitting home quietly drinking their tea, more or less like you and me, and then suddenly someone kicks down the door and comes rushing in and tries to kill us. It doesn't matter what the name of the person bursting through the door is, Ghengis Khan, Napoleon, Hitler. And, by the by, it should be mentioned that sooner or later all those invaders were hacked to bits!" said Poplavsky with sudden emotion.

"We're well aware of the invasion theory of Russian history, Mr. Poplavsky, but the fact of the matter is that in the twentieth century, the Soviet century, most Russian blood has been spilled by other Russians."

"We have admitted in *Pravda*, the central organ of our party, that certain excesses and distortions were committed in the period of the personality cult. But look at it like this. Russia has always had real enemies outside and real enemies inside. Say there was a person close to you who, you suspected, wanted to destroy you," said Poplavsky, summoning Zivkin's image to mind, which lent his words added sincerity. "There are three possibilities. You destroy him. Later it turns out that he in fact wanted to destroy you. In that case, you can rejoice in the health of your own instincts and in a victory over your enemy. This we could call an ideal situation. Or, you destroy him and it turns out that he wasn't really after you at all. Then of course you will feel terrible and remorseful, and experience what is known as moral suffering, from which people seem quite able to recover. Or, the third and last possibility, you suspect he wants to destroy you but you're not one hundred percent sure; you're afraid of moral suffering; you play Hamlet, and the next thing you know you're dead. So, it stands to reason that your own personal death is the worst-case scenario and that triumph over an enemy is best, and that the destruction of a theoretically innocent person is neither the best thing in the world nor the worst but somewhere in between. Undeniable or not?"

"There is a certain mafioso logic to what you say, Mr. Poplavsky, but let's stop taking refuge in grand generalizations and get down to cases, specifically, Mr. Poplavsky, the case of the refusenik poet, Lev Brumsky."

"The trouble with you Westerners is that you have lost all sense of destiny. Brumsky is living out his destiny. He went from being one of many to being the great refusenik poet as you yourself called him. Now Brumsky's poems are even translated into Norwegian. Somehow or other his foreign royalties reach him, and I am told that he recently purchased a VCR. Not only does he have a VCR, he has a place in the history of the Jewish people for whom I have unbounded respect. Most important, Brumsky has achieved what few men ever achieve—a destiny. Not just a life, but a life with a built-in meaning and drama. How can we deprive him of that?"

"That is the most absurd rationalization I have ever heard for a violation of the basic human right to leave and enter one's country freely."

"You think too rationalistically, mechanistically, and idealistically, Mr. Buckminister. Just think realistically for one moment of what will happen if we give Brumsky a piece of paper saying he can leave Moscow. He comes to the West. For two weeks he's a hero. For two weeks he's news. Then he's a depressed immigrant on the lecture circuit if he's lucky, and on welfare if he's not. His children start to speak a different language; all they care about are sneakers and music and cartoons on Saturday morning. American publishers don't like his new work expressing autumnal melancholy of exile from Russia. And worse, it turns out that he's not such a big liberal after all, and he starts taking positions very similar to yours, Mr. Buckminister, thereby alienating the little clique of East Coast liberals who control American culture and which, if I am not mistaken, Mr. Buckminister, you are constantly railing against yourself."

"What you continually fail to understand is that Brumsky, as a human being, has the right to freedom, and whether he uses it well or not is no one's concern but Mr. Brumsky's."

"That is the psychology of the lonely crowd, the famous American alienation which your sociologists have described well and in detail. The Russian tradition is more communal or, to put it more simply, in Russia people still care about each other. It pains our hearts to think of someone pining away in a distant and alien land where even the air smells wrong and the pleasure of one's native speech, so essential, by the way, to a poet, is nowhere to be obtained."

"Before handing you this letter, Mr. Poplavsky, I wish to stress that one measure of Soviet intentions in the upcoming period is going to be the treatment of Brumsky. To put it rather bluntly, the Soviet Union wishes Most-Favored-Nation trading status with the United States, and the United States cannot most favor a nation that is so unsure of itself that it feels threatened by people wishing to exercise the most basic of human rights," said Buckminister with a quick grimace as the letter changed hands.

"On behalf of the Soviet Union, I accept this letter, Mr.

Buckminister, and even though this is an internal affair, and a very complex one, I nevertheless can assure you that this matter is already under advisement. And I can also say that it was useful and interesting to have a frank conversation with a representative of the American right. The accepting of such petitions and protests is something which I treat very seriously, which is why I met with you today, for otherwise, simply to collect such material, the box would do very nicely."

"You mean *a* box."

"Ech!"

CHAPTER *2*

Rabin ducked the Frisbee. A radioactive, lime-popsicle-green, the Frisbee was being hurled with extra vigor by the students who, in the five minutes between classes, ran out between the barracks to shout, smoke, curse, spit, flirt, anything to feel alive before the next hour of having the Russian language crammed down their throats like grain down the gullet of a Strasbourg goose; and by a teaching staff of over one hundred DPs, defectors, exiles, political refugees, ship jumpers, WW II POWs, and emigrés, all of whom spoke Russian with native fluency even though some were born in Harbin, China, and others in the ruins of postwar Germany. Recently, the Defense Language Institute West Coast (DLIWC), America's leading military language school, had relaxed its standards and had begun to accept instructors who, though not born of Russian-speaking parents, had still mastered the language of America's nemesis well enough to teach it to young enlistees of both sexes. Eliot Rabin, who had just passed safely through the Frisbee free-fire zone and was pausing for a last cigarette on the barracks porch, was one of the Americans so honored.

Or so humiliated. For Rabin, the mal de mer green barracks stenciled with numbers, the students raw as new sub-

★   21

urbs, the thirty-hour teaching load, and his colleagues, most of whom stared off into places only they could see, made for a state of mind that only Hieronymus Bosch could have painted—the jibbering third-rate limbo into which those who fail to receive tenure are cast. In real geographical space it had been a fall of seventy-five miles, from the University of California at Santa Cruz at the north end of Monterey Bay to DLIWC at the south end. A fall from a private office with a secretarial and a swimming pool at his disposal, to not only an office shared with seven others but a desk shared with two others, a situation which gave Rabin a feeling not unlike that of the DLIWC men's room where, in the best military tradition, there were no stalls separating the toilets, which led to social encounters that could only be termed grotesque. Of course, Santa Cruz had not been a real university, more of a theme park—Knowledge Land. "They teach History of Consciousness but they have no consciousness of history!" one professor of European extraction had railed epigrammatically. But compared to DLIWC, it was the Agora.

The one-minute warning bell rang, breaking thousands of hearts. The Frisbees hummed with a last desperate intensity, the horseplay reached a fever pitch, and a few punches were thrown out of sheer unhappiness. And still, to Rabin, the smoke from his cigarette swirling in the sunlight was beautiful; the scent of sea breeze and eucalyptus was bracing, medicinal; and there was something oddly enchanting about the barking of seals in the bay as it mixed with the sound of artillery practice at Fort Ord, metallic popcorn in the air.

His bloodstream translated the sea breeze into hope. The future was still as large as the summer seems in early June. He would yet rise, return, and triumph. He would be vindicated and his enemies downcast. The hour of his glory still awaited him. Without that belief he would not have been able to perform the next three operations—grinding out his cigarette, turning on his heel, and entering the classroom for the hour before lunch when the students were at their unruliest and he, too, would find himself staring out the window, dreaming of cheeseburgers, freedom, another life.

Rabin heaved his briefcase onto the grey iron desk, which, like the grey iron chair and the grey iron wastebasket, was stenciled with a number, that had to exist and yet was without meaning to anyone. He walked to the blackboard and began erasing it, vaguely aware of the smell of chalk dust, which had been with him since first grade. As he erased the word *kosmos*, Russian for space, he wondered about the cultural effect of the two concepts—space, kosmos—on the minds of the young people in each society. Space promised the boundlessness that could no longer be found in America, where every square inch of land, every blade of grass on the prairie, was owned, either by private persons or by the government. But space was also a word that belonged to the basic vocabulary of modern physics: space and time, space-time, "spime"—there probably should be a word like that so the two mysteries could be seen melting into one another like the parts of the Trinity or like Thesis and Antithesis clashing and transcending in a Hegelian symphony. And then there was kosmos, the opposite of chaos, which the Russians feared in heaven as they did on earth. Did Russian youth—

The question was never able to achieve formulation because ten American youths, nine male and one female, had just entered the room all at once, squeezing protoplasmically through the door, their ten bodies bound loosely into one by military discipline and the whip of the final bell. Turning from the blackboard and without saying a word, Rabin managed to greet each of them as they passed. To McHenry, a little nod of encouragement to say that he hadn't washed out yet; to Sergeant Dubois a nod as well, but that of older men who had been around and knew the world a little, not like these kids; a squint of warning to the jokester Carullo. Rabin shot a sort of intellectual salute to Daniels, a boy from Tarwater, Alabama, who learned Russian as easily as if it were a game he had played as a child; and for Private, first class, Brown, the only girl in the class, who today looked rather clean-haired and brown-eyed in her Air Force blue, his gaze glinted with a male curiosity that made her smile and look down at the floor. He knew these students, and he loved them with that mixture of caring, irritation, and professional remove that is a teacher's love. He only hated them when they became symbols of his humiliation, and even then he fought with himself to keep the distinction sharp: to see them as people, kids, not as talking furniture in his room at Hotel Despair.

But why were they so well-behaved? Why were they taking their seats so quietly and so quickly? It wasn't like them at all.

Lowering his goatee to his chest in a buffalo-like attitude of menace, Rabin glowered at them so they would know he had noted their behavior and found it suspicious.

Homework was passed out. Faces shone, faces fell. They moved on to the drill, a numbing conversation that no two human beings on earth had ever had, and which seemed more of a mental survival test than an attempt at instruction. But everyone was still alert and awake, even McHenry who, in his milky innocence, would usually glaze out during the drill and sometimes even fall into a sleep that looked so blissful Rabin would hesitate before shouting him awake.

Poor McHenry had never really understood the Russian

alphabet. The questions he asked bespoke such nightmarish stupidity that Rabin always winced when he saw McHenry's hand straggling upward.

"I don't understand why their language doesn't have an *H*," McHenry would say.

"It just doesn't."

"But I mean they had an *H* but they called it an *N*."

"McHenry, to them an *H* is an *N*. They don't have an *H*. They have to say things like, Gerbert Goover studied Gegel at Garvard."

Feeling vaguely edgy, Rabin reached for the pack of Marlboros in his shirt pocket. Just as his fingers were pincering out a cigarette, his hand came to a halt. Smoking was not allowed in class, either by students or instructors. That rule, and the rule that no instructor could leave the grounds before five o'clock, forcing him either to obey or slink off, were the two principal measurements of his abasement. He who should have been advising presidents could neither smoke when he wished or leave when the day's mind-shredding work was done. A stream of angry sadness went through him, and in rebellion against his fate, he withdrew the cigarette. He might not smoke it, but at least he could have it in his hand.

But once it was in his hand, he wanted it dangling from his mouth, and once it was dangling from his mouth, he wanted it lit and alive, the sweet smoke in his lungs and nostrils, in that little smokey orgasm of happiness that nearly every cigarette gives. He'd fight the urge as long as he could but—fuck it, he didn't care anymore; if he wanted to smoke it, he would! Even the memory of his three months of unemployment could not stay the fury of his despair and desire.

"My military unit is now stationed at the outskirts of a major industrial center," translated Daniels.

"Quiet! American spies are everywhere!" translated Brown.

Rabin looked up to see if that attempt at avuncular jocularity by the unknown composer of the dialogues had elicited even the faintest of smiles. It had not. That was probably just as well. Why should they care about the whole idiotic world of spies and industrial centers? They were young and horny and dumb. But then why weren't they acting it? Why hadn't anybody been hit over the head with a notebook? Why had no goofy, dirty jokes been made? His left hand went searching for his matches.

But maybe he should hold out. Maybe he should make it a test of his will, that rope of iron he was going to have to climb if he was ever to hoist himself back into the land of the living, the brilliant, the rewarded. The matches were now in his left hand; the cigarette bobbed expectantly on his lips; some secret electricity flashed between the two points. No one in the world could stand it! You had to be a saint!

And Rabin was no saint, not even a candidate.

"Stop worshipping that cigarette," said his conscience in a voice that sounded like Moses.

"I don't worship it."

"You do. You give it power over you. You bow down to it. You are a willing slave to it."

"I'll quit when I get out of this job and I can live like a human being."

"Now you are lying and breaking another commandment."

"How can you live without lying? Everyone expects you to. People get confused if you don't."

"Now you are lying to yourself."

"Alright, I smoke, I lie."

"And you do not honor your mother and father."

"Who does?"

"Some do."

"Anything else?"

"You live outside of marriage with a Christian."

"Alright, then let me ask you this. If I cheat on her, is it a sin?"

"It is."

"That's not fair. If it's a sin to live with her, how can it be a sin to cheat on her?"

"A sin is a sin."

Suddenly, like a man who has forgotten that he was naked until he realized the window was open, Rabin now felt utterly transparent.

"Dictation!" he snapped, to break the spell. At the same time he broke the cigarette in his hand without quite meaning to. "Pencils out!"

Rabin immediately regretted the decision because now he would have to correct those dictations along with the stacks of other quizzes, vocabulary checks, and fill-in-the-blanks that had to be corrected every day, five days a week. And that would mean another twenty minutes stolen from his own work, another in a series of the pettiest of petty larcenies, that would, in time, take his life. He prayed for deliverance.

And deliverance came, at least from the dictation. It took the form of a brisk knock at the classroom door, a purely official knock that was only announcing itself and had not the least intention of waiting for any invitation to enter.

It was the new director of DLIWC making a surprise inspection visit and, right behind him, was Romanovsky, head of the Russian section, managing to look woebegone, compassionate, alarmed, hopeful, and demanding all at the same time. The new director wore Air Force blue and gleamed with insignia, but Rabin had no idea what his actual rank was, although he knew every epaulet and lapel badge in the Soviet military—KGB and Border Guards included. From the quick constriction of the new director's eyes, Rabin was aware that he had not, as usual, made a good first impression. The belly spilling over the belt was always distasteful to trim military types, as was his goatee, black, Hebraic, vaguely pubic. Rabin's maroon tie and his dark blue shirt suddenly made him feel like someone whose fondest dream is a green card. The director glanced at Romanovsky without saying a word, but none was necessary. All three of them knew what was being said: "This is one of ours?"

"There's been a lot of slackness around here," said the new director, his nose twitching as if it had detected the odor of Jewish brimstone in the air. "People leaving before five, instructors smoking in the classroom, sections falling behind schedule. We'll be running a tighter ship from here on in. Please continue with what you were doing."

Rabin shot a glance from the corner of his right eye at his students and knew they were with him. He could also see that their textbooks were still open.

"We were just finishing up a translation. And I believe it was Daniels' turn. Daniels, three lines up from the bottom."

"My military unit is now stationed at the outskirts of a major industrial center," translated Daniels even pausing for a moment before the word *major*.

"Very good," said Rabin.

"Sir?" said Daniels.

"Yes, Daniels?"

"Is *major* the best choice there, or would it have been better to just say *large*?"

"No, your first instinct was right. *Krupny* means major."

"*Spasibo*," said Daniels.

"That means 'thank you' in Russian," Romanovsky explained to the new director whose eyebrows rose slightly to indicate that he had understood and that he was even a little impressed with students who were both respectful and clearly well-prepared.

"And then, PFC Brown, the next line, please," said Rabin.

"One moment," said the new director. "Do you always go in order?"

Order, he would like order, wouldn't he? thought Rabin.

"Yes," said Rabin.

"Not a good idea!" said the new director. "A student can figure out what he'll have to translate and forget about the rest. My experience is that people have to be kept on their toes. Let's take someone else, let's take . . . McHenry, is it?"

McHenry's face darkened with a triple terror. It wasn't that he couldn't remember how Brown had just translated the line two minutes ago; he was terrified of being so terrified that he might do something wrong, that he was convinced he would.

I should have flunked him out two weeks ago! thought Rabin. This is what compassion gets you.

Then the Bronx-born Carullo came to the rescue, employing the one great gift nature had bestowed on him—the ability to cough and whisper answers simultaneously.

"Quiet! American spies are everywhere," croaked McHenry.

Now all the class chuckled faintly, patriotically, just enough to show that they had understood and appreciated the little joke but not loud enough to contain even a hint of rowdiness.

The new director, continuing to demonstrate that he was nobody's fool, turned to Romanovsky, not Rabin, and asked: "Is that correct?"

"Entirely correct and perfect," said Romanovsky with a nod of his enormous, grizzled head.

The new director did not respond in the least, demonstrating that he was not impressed when things ran as they should. With a last sniff at the air, he turned and left the room, Romanovsky following like a faithful old retainer behind the new tsar.

Rabin sighed audibly. "Thank you, Daniels, McHenry . . . and Carullo."

Everybody laughed, all eleven of them, united in the community that only laughter can create.

"Anyway," said Rabin, "it won't last long. A month, but not two. Once they discover the golf course at Pebble Beach . . . All social machines have something like a fan belt in them, and every so often it gets loose and starts flapping. Somebody comes by and tightens it up, but as soon as he walks away it starts getting loose again," said Rabin who had as much difficulty in refraining from digressions as from cigarettes. "Anyway, that took time so we better get right to the new vocabulary."

As soon as he saw the lesson number, 12, he understood everything: why they had come into the classroom so quickly and so quietly; why no one had glazed out during the drill. It was the infamous chapter 12 trap, and he had fallen into it unawares. The chapter was built around the verb, *atakovat*, to attack, and the noun, *ataka*, an attack. In the best pedagogical tradition, the noun had been linked with a verb, *otbeet ataku*, to beat off an attack, one of the basic military situations. Then, in all the innocence of the foreign-born, the unknown composer of the vocabulary list had felt it important to single out the verb *otbeet*, which he then quite logically rendered as "to beat off." Wave after wave of students taking the forty-eight-week Russian course had been grateful to that soul.

"Alright," said Rabin looking up at them, giving not the slightest sign that he was aware of anything, "repeat after me."

Backbones came to attention.

"*Atakovat*," boomed Rabin who had discovered that the louder something was said, the more easily it was memorized. "The verb to attack."

"*Atakovat!*" hollered the students.

"Good. Now, *ataka*, the noun, an attack. Say it, *ataka!*"

"*Ataka!*"

"Yes. And now, the expression, *otbeet ataku*, to beat off an attack. Why is it *ataku* and not *ataka* in that expression, Dentner?"

"Accusative case, sir."

"Yes. Alright, repeat after me, *otbeet ataku!*"

"*Otbeet ataku!*"

"And then we have the verb, the perfective verb, *otbeet*, meaning—"

"TO BEAT OFF!" brayed the usually silent Dentner.

It was more than the rest of them could reasonably be asked to withstand, and by any definition of military discipline, they went wild.

"Go otbeet your otmeet, comrade," Daniels punned bilingually.

Private First Class Brown's scalp flushed with shame.

"Boris Beetoff!" howled Carullo, barely able to get the words out, he was already laughing so hard.

"And the beat goes on!" chimed in McHenry who needed this more than anyone.

At last, one student was hitting another over the head with a notebook.

Rabin glanced at his watch: fifteen seconds to go. They had come through for him—the tricky little bastards, he hadn't even suspected that they'd gotten the stupid joke in the dialogue—and he was going to repay the favor on the spot. He blessed the chaos with his silence and his smile.

Then suddenly the bell rang, announcing the long lunch hour. Free as they all were at that moment, none of them would be truly free until he was out the door. The wisecracks and laughter diminished precipitously, the moment now as irretrievably gone as childhood or Egypt.

Rabin was the last one out, but only by a footstep or two, and his cigarette was lit before he hit the porch. He was free, but that meant making up his mind about what he wanted to do. The problem quickly resolved itself into a set of contradictory needs, the need for solitude and the need for a cheeseburger. If he could have had both it would have been perfect. To sit in pure contemplation with the taste of bun, cheese, ketchup, burger, and then bun again in his mouth would be all the heavenly solace he could desire. Unfortunately, things were so arranged that the only place to buy a burger on the base would also be filled with many other hungry people, not to mention several of his lugubrious colleagues who would invite him to their table with a heartbreaking gesture; they would have already accepted rejection but would look at him as if still praying for a miracle. He hated to refuse them, and he hated to lose the hour. On the other hand, there was an intimate relationship between the exact happiness of Rabin's stomach and the grace and power of his mind. He had never once had an idea that interested him after a meal of liver and onions.

There was a little place just outside the gate, which sold decent submarine sandwiches, but the bread was always a little tough, and sometimes they didn't put enough oil on the meat and peppers, and a can of Coke would fall just short of assuaging the dryness this produced. Irritating even to have to think these thoughts, thought Rabin. Deciding on the sub, he set off toward the gate, nodding as he passed his colleague Marya Antonovna whose light blue eyes were radiant with sorrow and the Russian Orthodox religion.

"Plenty of oil!" said Rabin watching the counterman dribble a few drops on his steaming steak.

Then, warm bag in hand, Rabin walked the two hundred yards to his favorite spot, a grassy slope overlooking the blue haze of Monterey Bay. Both the seals and the artillery seemed to be taking a midday rest. The moon, faint and white, was already out; a cloud if you didn't look closely.

The sub was a little too oily. And of course they had only given him two of those skimpy dispenser napkins which hardly sufficed for the greedy lips that lived in his goatee, not to mention his hands, which were rather small and delicate for a man of his general suet and girth. And so it wasn't long before his thumb left a greasy print on the page as Rabin read the conclusion of his paperback edition of *Breaking with Moscow* by Arkady Shevchenko, the highest-ranking Soviet official ever to defect, and in Rabin's opinion, no vital loss to the USSR. The book was one of the most boring he had ever read, which was saying quite a lot for a specialist in Soviet affairs. It was Rabin's postulate that Soviet boredom was as far from French ennui as you could get. Soviet boredom was brutal and aggressive, a way of lulling the enemy's vigilance through sheer stupefaction—boredom as a wall of secrecy, boredom as a jamming device. In fact, in the entire book only two sentences had quickened Rabin's attention. One was Gromyko's famous line, "I am not interested in my own personality." The other was a remark by Shevchenko to the effect that Soviet leaders felt insulted by the failure of Americans to appreciate the magnificence of Russian literature.

Was that so? Were they genuinely offended? Rabin wondered as a wave of oily, meaty, green-peppery pleasure broke over his tongue. After all, there was some sort of secret relationship between art and dictatorship that no one had ever quite adequately explained. Hitler painted, Stalin wrote poetry. Perhaps dictators were failed artists, and artists were failed dictators.

But what hypocrites! thought Rabin. They silence writers, exile them, imprison them, and then *they're* insulted! But maybe it wasn't hypocrisy. What choice did the Russian leaders have? They had to punish writers who were too free or told the truth, each of which was as bad as the other. Everyone had his role.

But the Russians hated to feel inferior because feeling inferior was the necessary subjective reflection of being objectively behind. What counted was arms. And there was no question that the weapons of the future would be space weapons, and there was no question that they were going to cost a fortune. In America they probably would almost pay for themselves in terms of the capital, jobs, and spinoffs created by the new technology—video wristwatch phones would appear on the market at exorbitant prices, and three years later even bag ladies would have them. But in Russia the money would have to come out of people's hides.

So Rabin could see it was in the Soviet interest to keep space demilitarized, and that seemed to have been the thrust of Soviet policy for some time now. Whether or not they were working at breakneck speed for some space breakthrough of their own was another question. They had a few orbiting space stations, but no Soviet had ever set foot on another world, and nothing could quite match that in the popular imagination. And so, if the Russians wanted to be smart, they should outdo the Americans by sending a peace delegation of children to the moon from where they would appeal to all mankind to stop the madness before it was too late. Or maybe the Soviets could try something cultural: Swan Lake in reduced gravity. Or, if they were so proud of that Russian literature of theirs, they could send up a writer, but it would have to be a poet, no one would want to hear a short story read to them from outer space. But which poet could they send? Rabin asked himself as he washed bits of meat and pepper from the grottoes of his teeth with a tide of Diet Coke. Yevtushenko and Voznesensky they could allow to New York but not to the moon. Pasternak and Akhmatova were the last of the giants; even Russia had no poet. It would probably have to be someone like Kornelchuk or Bezoblatov. Or maybe even Viktorov.

Rabin burped. He loved to burp. He was a connoisseur of burps. This one had substantial volume and a carbonated, Cokey aftertaste. It was followed by a few small aftershocks that resonated in his chest and throat, and a series of quick, light burps, skimming like a flat stone across lake water. Then, because the two dispenser napkins were already slippery with oil, he wiped his lips on the sleeve of his corduroy jacket; after all, one of the secondary pleasures of solitude was that it did not require good manners.

He knew his bad manners had not helped him in academia. But good manners wouldn't have helped all that much either, Rabin reminded himself. He was just wrong for the club. And that's all there was to it. If it had been a flush period, if the government had been scared enough to start squirting money their way, maybe he would have sneaked by into tenure. But it had been one of those periods when rich Republicans were putting on the squeeze for the good of the country, and Rabin had lost the game of academic musical chairs, which had turned surprisingly nasty at the end.

He grimaced as the next idea came to him. He would write up his speculations on the potential Soviet culturalization of space. Of course, culture would end up in space. Science, business and the military, the three main and most serious things, were already there, and so culture couldn't be all that far behind, especially if it could serve political purposes. That was the idea; the grimace had a different source. It came from knowing where he would send that little article—to the *Sunshine Supplement*, a daffy, eight-page weekly published in his most recent hometown of Santa Cruz. From time to time he wrote about the Russians for the *Sunshine Supplement*, and for two reasons, one healthy, one not. On the one hand, it was a challenge to put a little of the heavy matter of reality into those blond heads (though in another way it was almost a shame, and, who knows, maybe even dangerous, since that extra weight might cause some sudden mental tilt while they were out surfing). The unhealthy aspect was an inflammation caused by ingrown vanity: he would publish in the *Sunshine Supplement* rather than sign himself Eliot Rabin, DLIWC, in any scholarly journal.

But his book would save him. His book would reveal him as the man who knew Russia best. He would be swept back up to the heights, and the respect he received would be greater for its nuances of apology. Rabin would be a nobler figure for what he had suffered. He was, however, coming to some odd and disquieting conclusions in that book. He had perceived a new link between secrecy and tyranny in Russian history. It wasn't the obvious—that all malefactors prefer the cover of darkness. No, Rabin's work was revealing something else: the more unfree any system is, the more predictable it becomes. Secrecy is therefore a necessity to the Kremlin. Otherwise, the very predictability of the Soviet state might make it all too transparent, all too outguessable. Life and reality, no small factors, always clouded the issue, of course, but Rabin had nevertheless begun to observe certain regularities, certain periodicities. He had even reduced all Russian history to two basic rhythms, which he called the Ivan-the-Terrible contraction and the Peter-the-Great expansion. Russia was either closing in on itself, shunning the world, hating foreigners, purging the bad blood, seeking the dark sources of its strength; or else it was expanding, reaching out for the fruits of the West, the fruits of science, which, as bad luck would have it, grew best on the tree of liberty.

The phase of contraction seemed to be the norm. Russia always tended to be closed. Expansion, except in geopolitical terms, was the exception; when Russia expanded, it did so in order to acquire buffers, that is, to better isolate itself. So then what caused this alternation in the normal rhythm? The perception that Russia's enemies possessed some superiority in science, meaning technology, meaning weapons. Then Russian society was forced to reach out, expand, open. This was an instinctive survival reaction—the Peter-the-Great expansion. Thus, in some bizarre way, the arms race might be good for Russian society, and this was one of the conclusions Rabin was not happy to reach.

Or was that conclusion the result of a Republican administration producing a Republican Zeitgeist that caused his mind to think Republican thoughts? Or was it the Zeitgeist that kept electing Republicans to office?

Then, for a period of time, Rabin had no thoughts, intelligent or otherwise. Forgetting that he was unhappy, he became happy. Happy with health, lunch, fresh air, his final burps, his sudden awareness of the ants rushing in their Amazon of grass.

Artillery practice resumed at Fort Ord, and, perhaps in response, a few seals began barking in the bay. Far in the opposite distance, the first warning bell for the one o'clock classes trilled faintly like some new worry just arriving in the outskirts of the mind.

He got up to his feet and began heading back.

CHAPTER *3*

Moscow was furious. Five months before TASS was scheduled to make the Soviet mission public, the United States government had announced that it would be sending a poet to the moon. Now, not only had the timing for maximal public-relations impact been lost, but the Soviet government had been put in the humiliating position of appearing to be imitating the United States. Some ground, however, had been regained when the Soviets proposed the idea of a joint reading from the moon, which America had accepted. The Soviets had also fought for and won the rights to exclusive media coverage of the event. The Americans were more than willing to grant the rights—a first—since a Sunday morning poetry reading, even one from the moon, did not seem likely to distract significant numbers of Americans from church, golf, or sleep.

Washington was one place where the information could have leaked and Poplavsky, as the *rezident*, was taking the heat. The whole business was of little interest to him. That techno-cultural sideshow did not have the true weight of significance. Moscow's anger would pass. At the same time, he was not deceived in the least as to the secret significance of the leak. It was nothing less than a knife aimed at his throat and wielded by Zivkin's hand.

Zivkin kept insisting that the Washington group could expunge its shame with a brilliant technological coup. "Give them one first-rate guidance system, and the whole thing will be forgotten!"

Zivkin's latest mania was the so-called 128 Area outside of Boston, Massachusetts. Until now, all efforts had been concentrated in so-called Silicon Valley in so-called California— no, California was not so-called, it was just California. It was easier to raid 128 from Washington and New York, as it was easier to fit in with people who wore dark clothing and had long winters. In California a lot of valuable time had been wasted getting people tan enough to blend with the local environment. Many agents had tended to burn, and most of them never looked right in those sport shirts.

"The software for one code system and they'll be giving us medals!" Zivkin had said.

But Poplavsky knew that Zivkin had no interest at all in expunging their shame. He intended to take full credit for any technological acquisition of significance and to ensure that Poplavsky took full blame for any sloppiness. The point was to demonstrate that Poplavsky was slipping, giving the little signs of trouble that precede the big ones.

Poplavsky decided to assume a pose of slightly depressed forbearance when later that day, Zivkin knocked.

"I don't understand this at all," said Zivkin.

"What?"

"Here is a newspaper, if you can call it a newspaper, and look what it prints two weeks before the American government even makes *its* announcement!"

Poplavsky took the newspaper from Zivkin's extended hand, and next to an advertisement for vitamins and the single life, he saw a long narrow column entitled: "MOONSHOT."

"Not only does he say the Soviet Union will probably send a poet to the moon, he even names Viktorov as a possible candidate," said Zivkin as Poplavsky quickly skimmed the article for the gist.

The fury Poplavsky now felt for Zivkin was so cold that even bacteria could not have survived in it. No, thought Poplavsky, it was not bad enough that you had to humiliate me and the Soviet Union by leaking the information, but first you had to place it in some ridiculous rag. You didn't even have the decency to leak it to a respectable newspaper like the *Post* where even scandals have a sort of dignity. And no doubt a copy of this rag is already on its way to Moscow, proof positive that Captain Poplavsky had lost control of his ship and was taking on water in the most improbable places.

"And how would you suppose that this news reached all the way to Santa Cruz, California, where this thing is published?" asked Poplavsky.

"We would not have known about it at all except that one of our people at the army language school in Monterey happens to share a desk with the author, a man by the name of Eliot Rabin."

"And who is this Eliot Rabin?"

"We're running a complete check on him. I'm having our dish antenna in San Francisco monitor his phone conversations. However, the first indications are that he is an ordinary Kremlinologist."

"Jew?"

"Yes."

"Russian-born?"

"No."

"I thought their policy was to hire only instructors who were Russian-born."

"It was, but they changed it. They started running out of Russians."

"Another good reason to prohibit emigration," said Poplavsky, to give the impression of being so caught up in his old man's obsessions that he was missing the point that had been stuck so arrogantly under his nose.

Zivkin smiled indulgently.

"So," continued Poplavsky, "it would seem to me that there are only two possible ways to interpret this phenomenon. One, this Rabin is a genius who can read the minds of the Politburo. Two, we have a traitor on board."

"It strikes me as a security problem," Zivkin replied dryly.

"Me too."

"What steps should be taken?"

"I'll give that matter some thought right away. Thank you for your diligence."

For a moment after Zivkin was gone, Poplavsky's eye was drawn back to the article, to a portion of a sentence that read: "Kiev's two centuries of golden peace when Russian princes still had the luxury of warring with each other." Poplavsky wondered what Kiev had to do with the moon. He would read the article later. Now all that mattered was a working plan that would remove Zivkin from the picture.

There were various FBI people who were always willing to make a trade. Zivkin would be a good-sized catch for them. But how? Exactly how—that was all that mattered now.

As always in such situations, a proverb came to his aid— "The fishing's good in troubled waters." And no sooner had he remembered the proverb, than he became it: part of his soul was a patient fisherman, and another part, troubled waters. The murkier and more turbulent the water grew, the more alert Poplavsky the fisherman became. As always, it was a question of waiting and outwaiting.

Then he felt a faint twitch of curiosity at the far end of his line, then hesitation, then the first nibble. And it was only when some perfect sense assured him that the hook was pointing to the roof of the mouth, that he jerked the line upward and then reeled in exactly whatever was thrashing for its life at the other end.

CHAPTER 4

There were no words in his mind, not even his own name. He was a naked spirit in a naked body wrapped in clean sheets and the last morning dreams.

That grace lasted until Arthur Blaine realized it was grace.

Then it was a responsibility: to walk that grace safely through the minefield of the morning and to sit down with it at his desk where it would shine in the long vowels of his poems.

The two on the digital clock, its white plastic bandaged with duct tape, changed to a three making it 9:23 as his bare feet touched the floor. The morning coolness of floors, said a part of his mind where sensations echoed as words.

Now it was required that his robe be snatched from the chair and fitted to his body in two motions faster than the eye could see, the way it went around him able to predict something about the quality of the coming day. Snatched perfectly, the robe would infuse him with all the courages of its crimson. The crimson excellence of Harvard / the red-coat red of Boston's brick / the slash of art's again reopened wound / and the scarlet fever of the poet's pride—as he had put it long ago when the robe was new.

The robe did not resist him that morning, a good sign. He

tapped the right pocket. There were a few Camels left in the pack. Good. Nothing caused more inner commotion than looking for something trivial yet essential.

Pissing yesterday's wine with a tangy vigor, he was tempted to shift his head fifteen degrees to the right to the mirror. The face always wants to be seen. Except when face is lost.

But he did not want to see his face, he did not want to be that person yet.

His face jumped into the mirror, trying to startle him into seeing it. But all he saw was thickish, snarly, brown-gold hair brushed forward like one of the madder Emperors, the bristle-specked space between his nose and upper lip always much too large, looking either aristocratic or simian, today, fortunately, inclining toward the lordly. But why was there always something vaguely reddish about his lips?

Now it was required that he walk at a certain pace through the book-lined hallway. Today, the blue and gold of *The Collected Poems of T.S. Eliot* reminded him of the smell of steamed milk in the Turk's Head cafe, in those last years of bohemian Boston before the new world took over and Gauguins began deserting Tahiti for the stock market.

The black and white City Lights edition of *Howl* was right next to Eliot, not a chance arrangement but there to remind him of his incomplete allegiance to both. And though he kept meaning to, he had not gotten around to rereading Kerouac, afraid to find a Dreiser on benzadrine.

But those days, those few years, when life was exactly right!

The world that he wanted to live in no longer existed and would never exist again. And he hated the world he lived in because it was at once so flimsy and so lethal. A world that believed in nothing, cared for nothing, truly valued nothing but itself, and that none too highly either. There was no more art, and there never would be again. There were only products for a cultural market. The world was a store. It was over.

Davis had not left her dishes on the table, a good sign. Dishes left on the table could say—you're taking me for granted. A half-drunk cup of coffee could say—I'm important, too. Bedfellows make strange politics.

Though he adored everything about Davis, from her last-name first name to her toes, she was also capable of using expressions like "he's a hunk" and watching television while having her morning coffee. Very bad.

Davis had left him plenty of coffee, which saved him from a whole series of mechanical operations, and he blessed her for that little gift of love. She had also brought in the *Globe* and the day's mail.

There were two letters, and a flier. One letter was from his publisher which, from the time of the year and the size of the envelope, he knew to be his royalty statement. The other was from Glass and Vincent, Developers, no doubt awarding him a junky toaster oven to be presented upon his visiting their eye-sore development in some scraggy Cape Cod town. Hunks, punks, junk—the era of the "unk" words. But the words

Arthur Blaine
237 Marlborough St.
Boston, MA 02110

typed on the letter from Glass and Vincent, and printed out on the one from his publisher, turned him into something he did not want to be, a citizen, a resident, an addressee. He slid the two letters under the paper.

Sipping black French roast, he glanced at the headlines, dreary as flood shots on the news. Iranis and Iraquis were still killing each other. Let them! Official indicted. Toddler missing. Remarks spark controversy. Three alarm Chelsea blaze claims seven. For a moment he could hear screams in flame. Dollar plummets as yen skyrockets.

On the off chance of seeing his name in print, he turned to the "Arts and Living" section where the recipes had long since outflanked the book reviews. He did not have to look for his own name; it would spring to him like his face in the mirror, but today's mirror was blank. He did have to focus, however, to check for names that were almost as important as his own, the names of his rivals whose talent, through some grotesque yet entirely predictable misunderstanding, had been confused in quality with his own. Theirs were not mentioned either. No changes in official status, as on those days when no teams play and none can surge ahead, or slip behind.

Enough nonsense, he could feel his clarity of mind being sucked into a blotter of newsprint. He stood up abruptly and then, cup in hand, he walked the last few feet to his final destination, his study, a room which had the stillness of a side chapel.

Pausing on the threshold, Blaine wrapped the robe closer around him, even clutching it closed at the throat for a second. He had a sense of awaiting himself in the plain wooden chair at the plain wood desk, both bequeathed him, along with a few faded Orientals and a small trust fund, by his Uncle Henry, Mummy's brother.

Just as he was sitting down, a voice behind his right ear whispered "darkness with the weight of snow." Since this beginning of a new poem might just as easily turn out to be the next to last line, he wrote those words about a third of the way down on a sheet of pale blue paper, which he preferred to the formal finality of white. Yes, winter was coming, the

Boston winter, which could be loved if only because it yields the resurrections of April—the college girls' arms bare again, the Charles sculling out to sea. Darkness with the weight of snow. But winter had its own beauties, its days black and white as pages, old-world frost on the windows, the bright cave of the evening. Rooms lit with lamps and the light of faces as people spoke to each other of their lives. He wrote that, too—the bright cave of the evening.

But there was something wrong with the line, nice as the two *v*'s sounded. But what? It couldn't be clearer. And the only word that could possibly be removed was the second *the*. bright cave." But that was too much like "twilight's last gleaming."

Then he understood why the line didn't ring true. Because it wasn't true! The cave of evening was not lit by lamps and faces but by television sets. People staring glassy-eyed at a glassy eye, in training for the dentures and laxatives so exclaimed of in prime time. Didn't Americans have teeth? Had they even lost the most basic ability of all?

The world was not a battlefield of darkness and light, but of light against light. The light that had lit the paintings of Fra Angelico had been opposed by the radiance of technology. The outcome was no longer in question. These were the Bright Ages.

None of that mattered, nothing mattered, all that mattered was darkness with the weight of snow.

But though he sat and sipped his coffee and puffed gently on the first Camel of the day just as he was required to do, no more English came singing into mind.

Was that going to be all? Two measly phrases? Had he lost that magic, sparkling clarity somewhere along the intricate line between waking and writing? But a day without poetry was a dental appointment.

A little more coffee never hurt.

Half way to the coffee machine, also bandaged with duct tape, he threw the *Globe* aside and grabbed the two letters. He opened the royalty statement first, the printout-cardiogram of his career. In the previous six-month period his most recent book of poems, *Rookies of Existence*, had sold an additional eleven copies, bringing total sales to 997. This had earned him a royalty of $1.08 per copy for a total of $11.88 which, subtracted from what was still owing on his advance of $1,100, netted him a grand total of $oo.oo, a familiar figure in his life.

Infected by arithmetic fever, Blaine figured in the margins that, at a thousand volumes sold, he would be reaching 1/240,000 of the American population.

And what could be more alienating than your own alienation expressed as a fraction!

Should he open the letter from Glass and Vincent while he was at it? The quality of the envelope seemed too good for junk mail, unless junk mail now had a first and second class.

After skimming the letter, Blaine lowered himself onto a kitchen chair. His landlady had died six months ago and he had never known it. Paying rent to a ghost, he had continued to make his checks out to that saintly old Boston intellectual who in twelve years had never once raised his rent—now as out-of-date as the five-cent candy bar. And that, without her ever saying so, was her gift to his art. The good woman's estate had turned the Marlborough Street building over to Glass and Vincent for development as luxury condominiums, and Blaine, as a tenant, had the option to buy his apartment at the preferred price of $270 thousand. He was exactly $270 thousand short. Aware that he would be grieving for himself in a minute, Blaine, a spiritual gentlemen, grieved for her first, since she had done that greatest and strangest of things—died.

He was going to have to pack up his life in brown boxes begged from grocery and liquor stores; he would be barred from his own city because he lacked the invisible grace of credit; he was going to have to scour the rentals, every bit as pathetic as the personals. The fourth estate and real estate had triumphed! The worst were full of passionate intensity!

A monumental drunk was mandated. He dressed quickly— dark green corduroys, an army-navy store black turtle neck, cordovan Wellingtons. The dime, nickel, and three pennies in his pants pocket, crumbs of a five lent him by Davis, reminded him that he was broke, and would be until the next trust fund installment came dribbling in. A frantic check of other pants, jackets, shirts, seat cushions and kitchen counters proved thirty-eight cents more lucrative than poetry had been in the last six months.

He was momentarily heartened by the balled-up paper in one pocket of his herringbone topcoat, but the fingertips, fluent in the feel of currency, were quick to report the bad news. Then a scarf—an even deeper crimson than his robe—around his neck, he was out the door and into the blue-grey chill of an October morning.

His body tilted slightly forward like his handwriting, Blaine stomped down Marlborough Street toward the Commons. Though his pace was brisk, almost manic, he had no destination at first, wanting only the soothing balm of the city's age.

He turned right on Exeter, a mistake. The Exeter Theatre, a jumble of cream-and-truffle stone, where he had first seen

The Seventh Seal, *The Lavender Hill Mob*, and *Grand Illusion*, was now, like nearly everything else in the city, in the process of being turned into something else. A bar and restaurant had already emerged from its side like some hi-tech tumor filled with singles seeking to exchange illusions and infections. One night, blind drunk on Dago red, he had stopped in front of a line of people freezing on the sidewalk, waiting to get in, and told them what he thought of them: "You characterless twerps have ruined a noble city. And you do not even have the sense to know it. Attila would have at least taken pleasure in destroying something so beautiful. I hate your Silly-Putty faces. Fuck you *and* your therapist!" As best he could remember, he had also attempted to rescue a young woman from that line, that restaurant, that fate, then it all faded out in a flurry of punches strobed by the blue light of a cop car.

Now the Exeter shimmered with insubstantiality just as Paris had that last time. Two days before he was due to return home on his cheapo charter, he had been walking down boulevard St. Michel, aware mostly of the iron gratings around the trees and a vague aroma of urine and Gauloises, and when he looked up, Paris was shimmering, the way the air does on too hot summer days. Paris had shimmered because it was disappearing from his life. And now Boston was shimmering that same way!

He focused his mind on the matter at hand, what he referred to as Blaineonomics, the art of plucking small sums out of nowhere. His first stop was a Newbury Street art gallery where he attended openings in search of something he had once had and had not yet found again—a painter friend.

The gallery owner, a man of complex European origins who spoke several languages imperfectly—English because he had learned it late and the others because he never used them any more—had always been after him to write a press release.

"Your timing is perfect!" said the gallery owner. "I am about to launch a very important career and we will need all the ink, as they say, we can get. Come. I show you."

In the back room, a grand sweep of the hand indicated a series of large, hinged panels. "Triptychs by triplets! The Vogel brothers, very hot, from Germany. Each one does his own panel. But they all reject art in the name of art. And therefore I am calling their show: Three Times Three Equals Nein. Good title, yes?"

"As inkable as I've ever heard," said Blaine, leaning forward to examine a panel, stick figures in a fire-bombed café. "The sensibility of dementia out of Grosz."

"Use that! Write it down. In five years the Vogels will bring a fortune at auction, this I know," said the gallery owner withdrawing his checkbook. "I pay twenty for a press release, ten in advance, ten upon delivery. And we leave the criticism to the critics."

"The poor beggars have to have something," said Blaine, taking the check by one corner so not to blur the ink.

After waiting more than ten minutes in line at the bank, Blaine was told by the teller that the check would need to be approved since he did not have an account with them. The sole bank officer was on a call, the phone settled comfortably between her ear and her shoulder. Smarting with a variety of indignities, large and small, Blaine retained his composure out of sheer defiance. He kept waiting and waiting so that he could have enough money to pay for boilermakers at a South Station dive and, with luck, finally weep. When his presence had become sufficiently annoying, the officer took the check and his driver's license, looking at it before him, and scribbled approval with her initials. Rejoining the line, which had grown in the meantime, he looked through the plate-glass window and saw Clive Hammond, a black saxophone player he'd known for years. Blaine gestured him in.

"Give me five, Arthur," said Clive.

They shook hands.

"And can you give me five more, the five you owe me?"

"My pleasure," said Blaine.

Half a block down Boylston, alone again, Blaine was accosted by a street person with watery blue eyes and a red beard who extended his hand and said simply: "I'm homeless."

Accosted as well by a superstition that told him not to refuse, Blaine said: "Me too," and handed the man a single, having netted four dollars on the entire transaction.

For a moment he was tempted to walk over to Beacon Street and up to his brother-in-law's investment firm to convince his brother-in-law to buy the condo as some sort of write-off, letting Blaine pay him off over time. But, Arthur, they don't give eleven-thousand year mortgages.

And did he really want to live there any more, now that its nature had been violated to the quick? But where could he go? Maybe one of those sea-coast towns that had too many Portuguese welfare recipients to have been worth spiffing and hypeing. But the very thought made the city shimmer, and he turned on his heel, heading for the South End apartment of someone who, for a change, owed him money. The debtor in question, a video artist for whom Blaine had once written thirty dollars' worth of soundtrack, pleaded cash flow but provided

Blaine with a ham sandwich and three beers. It wasn't a free lunch, though; Blaine was invited to view his host's latest video.

The first two minutes were fascinating; the next three were interesting, while the remaining twenty-five were not only moronically repetitive, they proudly declared that content-lessness is the content of the empty and lack of talent their aesthetic.

"It's better if you're stoned," said the video artist as Blaine was leaving.

"I'm sure," said Blaine with a smile of his best pity.

While in the neighborhood, he called on a former lover, Miriam Brandis, who had retained several of his art books on loan. Their amicable separation had resulted from her insight that theirs was an inverse *Annie Hall*-type relationship, making her Woody Allen, and she'd be damned if she was going to wait around for him, Arthur (Diane Keaton) Blaine to walk out on her.

"Sorry," he said, "I need these books back now. I've been commissioned to write a little something on art."

That, of course, was not only somewhat true, it sounded much better than saying he was going to take them at once to the used book store in Harvard Square that paid the best prices. And it was more effective, too, sparing him the sympathy and disapproval always given to people in need along with whatever else they're actually requesting.

But, inevitably, as soon as he was in the Square, he made a bee line for the Folio, a store devoted exclusively to poetry. As always, the front window was shingled from within by tatty Xeroxes—readings, workshops, contests, announcements of new journals that would live for an issue or two like some species of insect failing the hard test of evolution. And, as usual, those announcements were being tragically scanned by an ill-kempt young man in a dirty down jacket past whom Blaine swept into the only place in the world where he was a hero.

The owner was on the phone, but she covered the receiver with her hand and smiled a happy, honored welcome. Empty, the store did not seem to want customers at all, preferring its own silent, vertical privacy. Blaine marched immediately over to the B-section where he found three copies of himself in the very good company of Blackmur and Blake. He took out his pen, knowing a signed copy had a better chance of being sold— if not to a lover of poetry, then at least to one of those crafty oddballs who bought signed first editions and ended up making more money than the writer.

Arthur Blaine. Arthur Blaine. Arthur Blaine, he wrote, hearing the name each time, remembering yet again that he could doubt anything but himself.

He flipped over one copy of *Rookies of Existence* and glanced at the forever-chattering and still-embarrassing blurbs: "In this sonnet sequence on baseball, the thirty-four-year-old poet Arthur Blaine has produced a work that is both classical and American, sophisticated yet accessible. Witty metaphysics . . ." He opened to the back flap and the photo of himself, the pretention not in the pose but in the very fact of that photo's existence. The space between the nose and upper limit was decidedly simian. But the eyes were still so hopeful then! That was to have been *the book*, he remembered, smiling down at himself with the fond sarcasm of an older brother.

Bio, photo, flap and blurb. Shakespeare would laugh at us all. Though, who knows, that single small earring of his would be horrendously hip today.

As he did only at key moments, Blaine opened the book at

random, intending to treat the first lines on which his eye alit as prophecy, a higher fortune cookie of the mind.

On Deck

In a halo of white lime, the rookie
longs for the long, violent triple to left,
astonishing fan, fielder, and bookie . . .

"Arthur, how especially nice to see you," said the owner, her chopped hair greying, her voice cheerful but weary with the effort required to make a living at the very margin of the cultural margin. "How are you?"

"Never better, Marjorie," he replied, snapping the book shut and replacing all three copies. "And yourself?"

"Fluish."

"I never get it. The Blaines have strong constitutions. Hale and hearty till the day they drop dead."

"We sold a copy of *Rookies* just last month," she said, glad to report good news.

"Excellent."

"Has it broken a thousand?"

"More or less."

She gathered her purple Peruvian shawl about her, looked around the store, and sighed. "You've read Mary McCarthy's book on Venice, of course?"

"Of course."

"You remember the part about the stingy Venetian woman who put coins in her fish tank to keep the fish alive on the minerals the coins give off?"

"I do."

"That's this store."

Noticing that she had begun attaching Scotch tape to what appeared to be a poster of unusual elegance, Blaine went over for a closer look.

"What's that?"

"The announcement for that poet-to-the-moon business."

"I thought I read they were going to send up one of those reporters who thinks style means piling on the adjectives."

"Apparently they changed their mind."

"Quite a handsome poster. Let me see."

"Arthur, I thought you eschewed government contests."

"I eschew my espinach," said Blaine with a Spanish accent.

They both laughed.

Blaine's eye picked out the key information at once. The winner of the Apollo Prize—decent choice of name he thought—would receive an award of twenty-five thousand dollars and a gold medal, one side of which depicted the god of poetry and the other, the *Conestoga I* blasting off from Cape Canaveral, bearing the winner to the moon where he would read his poetry to Earth.

"But Marjorie," he purred, "I'll simply win the goddamn thing!"

CHAPTER *5*

"Rabin, every time I call you, I hope I'm going to get a recording saying the phone was disconnected at the customer's request."

"And what you get is me. Tough, Howard, tough."

"What I'm saying, Eliot, is when the hell are you going to get out of California? Before you come down with avocadoization of the brain, or after?"

"California isn't the problem. California is fine. It's the job that's killing me. It's a structural humiliation."

"Any prospects?"

"Some. But nothing definite. Hey, how come there's always a siren going by in New York?"

"You can hear it?"

"Yes, I can hear it."

"With ten million people, what can you expect?"

"Maybe they should invent sirens that play a medley of the top Broadway tunes of the season, or at least the 'I-Love-New-York' theme."

"Very funny."

"You want to make cheap anti-California jokes, I'll make cracks about heart-attack city."

"What's the weather like out there?"

"Perfect. It's always perfect."

"We got slush here like you wouldn't believe. Freezing rain. For the first time in my life I thought about where I should retire to. I love the city, but I can't see being an old man here."

"Like my friend Sidney says, we'll all end up playing gin rummy in Miami. With wives that look like Jewish sea serpents. Howie, you schmuck, you played the ten?"

"How can you stand it out there, it's so un-Jewish."

"Wherever I go, it's Jewish enough."

"By the way, I'm reviewing a book for the *Times* called *Jerusalem of the North* about the Jews of Lithuania. You should read it."

"What, your review or the book?"

"Both."

"All you guys do back there is read each other's reviews in the *Times*."

"At least we read."

"Meaning I don't?"

"No, nobody reads more than you do, Rabin, but that still isn't going to prevent avocadoization because the culture you live in, the people you talk to—that makes a big difference."

"I know they have minds like drive-in movies out here. Not that I don't like the drive-in myself once in a while. Besides, if you want my opinion no intellectual culture is better than ersatz intellectual culture and that's mostly what you have back there. People reading the same books, seeing the same movies, giving their little opinions. Who fucking cares?"

"There's more to it than that, buddy boy. There are people here who really strive for excellence; out there they think achievement is a mental illness."

"Who knows? Maybe it is."

"Another stupid remark."

"It's not stupid, and I'll tell you why. The whole mind-set back there is basically eighteenth century. Rationalistic with a little hedonism and divorce thrown in so it doesn't get too boring. It prides itself on not being metaphysical, as if that were a sign of maturity, whereas, in fact, it's just the other way around. And in California at least there's a little metaphysics in the air. I mean, in the end it's religion that counts most. Or whatever relates our lives to the only question that really matters—what happens when we die?"

"Metaphysics on that level is one thing, and then there's the head-shop level. And what was the name of that class you were starting the last time I called? What was it? Oh right, Scuba Yoga."

"OK. I understand. To you Scuba Yoga sounds ridiculous. But, if you think about it a minute, it makes perfect sense. In scuba diving, breathing right is the most important thing. You breathe wrong and you get the bends or some fucking embolism explodes in your brain. It's serious. And yoga is the science of breathing; some of those guys can control their breath so they go into suspended animation. So, it's a natural combination, scuba and yoga. My teacher studied at Scripps Institute and some ashram in Benares."

"Now I remember. Weren't you getting a little hung up on her?"

"I'm totally hung up on her. I've never been so fascinated by any woman. Everything. Her ear lobes, her ankles, even her clavicles—"

"So, what are you going to do?"

"I'll tell you. I don't like to talk about these things, but I'll tell you. I'm going to go for her. The guilt is going to be monumental. It may even break up my thing with Janey. I can't take that anymore anyway. I wasn't cut out to live with a woman who's got a kid by another marriage. I can't connect up right on the level of the blood. My blood is never warm enough in that house."

"You don't have to break it up. Have your little whatever with the instructor, and that's that. She doesn't sound like anybody you want to live with."

"I don't know. I hate the power you get over someone else's life when they love you. It's not just that it makes the woman sad when you say goodbye. It's that, when they get to a certain age, you're almost exiling them to some fucking Siberia of being alone. Who wants a thirty-eight-year-old woman with a hostile adolescent?"

"You did for a while."

"She was thirty-five then, and he was eleven."

"Are you going to leave her?"

"I don't know yet. Sometimes I think the only thing to do is chuck everything and move to Mexico. Make a few dollars somehow, and live the life of the senses, just fucking live for a change."

"I'll lose all respect for you, Eliot, if you do that. California is bad enough, but Mexico is the end."

"Let's not fight about it quite yet. How's Sylvia?"

"Sylvia's fine. She's giving a paper in Denver this month and Berlin next month. To tell you the truth, her income's going to make life very sweet when the kids are through college.

"Is that another siren?"

"This time it's a fire truck."

"I'll tell you something. I love California because it's the future. You wake up in the morning and it's really tomorrow. But I will say this for New York. New York is the present; New York is today. Europe is yesterday; that's why I love it."

"And so what does that make Russia?"

"Russia? Russia is a week ago Thursday. They'll never catch up. Democracy is the best medium for developing technology and for making money, too. If the Russians want to keep up with the West, they have to have a free and open society, not because those are the highest human ideals, but simply so that their society can be quick and flexible enough to develop technologically. That freaks them out. And so they'll do anything but the one thing they have to do. And besides, some of them may not be so crazy about technology. Look at the KGB. They still believe in the man in the field. Those guys who got caught at 128 were out working in the field."

"That whole setup reminded me of an FBI sting, you know, the hotel room, the hidden video camera."

"Sting, schming. Those guys were out shopping. And one of them was even the deputy cultural attaché. You've still got your anti-anticommunism going. Part of you still thinks Joseph McCarthy was worse than Beria."

"He was, for America."

"Anyway, maybe it was a sting. Maybe they were set up by somebody inside their own organization. Maybe there was a power struggle going on inside the American outpost of the KGB. Or maybe I'm just getting paranoid."

No, not at all, my dear brilliant Professor Rabin, thought Poplavsky as he clicked off the recording of the tap on Rabin's phone, which Zivkin had so efficiently arranged before his career came to its unfortunate end. Don't doubt yourself, Professor Rabin, you are even more wonderful than you know.

CHAPTER 6

Exhilirated with the self-confidence that is the natural condition of genius, Blaine set to work at once.

But there were real reasons to worry. Tin-eared judges, entranced with the latest *ism*, might not be susceptible to his music. Critics might be terrified by a clarity that threatened to eliminate the middleman.

After a few fitful starts, he could see the bright ghost of an idea: Earth and the Stars. The stars had once belonged to poetry and myth. Now the stars belonged to science. Man would never be complete until the stars belonged to both science and poetry. Man is sad without poetry, and stupid without science.

But Arthur Blaine would reunite them. Arthur Blaine would marry Earth and the Stars, Reason and Imagination, Harvard and MIT!

But nothing of real interest would happen without the grace of the muse who did as she absolutely goddamn pleased. Sometimes, in loving justice, she would respond to his faithfully performed devotions of pure superstition. And sometimes she could be tricked by a performance that was not altogether sincere, though he couldn't help feeling that she was aware of that insincerity and took a perverse pleasure in it. But there were also stretches when every prayer was a failed rain dance in Apache dust.

And then one day out of the blue at a bus stop she would sing English to him.

Her relationship to actual, living women was bewildering. She seemed to feel a certain sisterly solidarity with the women in Blaine's life and would coldly withdraw if he so much as came close to breaking any of the universally known rules of love. She even seemed to have a hand in the women he chose, and in some way she was able to inhabit their flesh, parade through life in their bodies, smile in their smiles. But a human life can not be amusing for very long to a god, and she'd get bored and want new eyes, new hair, a new story.

Blaine had slipped into solitude as easily as a man slips into deafness. Davis, who had not been with him long enough to recognize this state, took his withdrawal as withdrawal. Wanting to be clear on this point, he explained that when he was writing, the world was cleanly divided into work and interruptions, and even a meteor streaming a six-hundred mile tail of flame as it ploughed into the Boston Common would still have to be classed with the interruptions.

"I don't interrupt you when you're working," she said.

"If I'm lucky, I have two stretches of real poetry in a year. It's like an emergency, it's all you can deal with."

"But what about love?" she asked.

Wondering if he should even say it, then curious to know how she would react, Blaine drawled in a Bogie voice: "I'll tell you, kid, it's like somebody said, every orgasm is a sonnet lost."

"Fair price, I'd think."

When having her coffee one morning after another evening alone with her dismal poet, Davis turned on the television even though, or especially because, Blaine had asked her not to till he was done with the poem. The talk show's guest that morning was a Manhattan call girl whose Ph.D. thesis had just been published in somewhat popularized form ("for the layman, and laywoman," she said with a wink, and the audience loved it) as a paperback original entitled *Your Sexual Thermostat*.

The wisdom she had distilled from her years in lab, library, and field was that if the house gets chilly, turn up the heat. Passing directly from theory to useful example, she revealed that in her experience there was hardly a man alive whose sexual mercury did not rise at the thought—not to mention the actual sight—of a woman in a black bra, black garter belt, black nylon stockings, and high heels. Science, she said, had not yet determined exactly why this is so, but, speaking nonprofessionally, who cared?

That evening Davis watched Blaine out of the corner of her eye as he sank into a stupor, drinking wine as he watched wrestling. She did not find it amusing in the least that he knew all the wrestlers' names and was actually a fan of André the Giant.

He looked like he was sitting there waiting for her to come home. And she was home!

"I'm going to take a shower," said Davis, checking for his response to that erotic signal.

"Good," said Blaine, with the irritating delay of a satellite-transmitted call.

Her lips twitched inward at the corners. Defiantly turning off the television, she left the room, trailing indignation, not even looking back to see if he was angry.

He was, but not very. He closed his eyes. The white blur of the after image continued to wrestle in his mind. Instead of fading, it suddenly acquired the fascinating brilliance of a miniature hallucination. A thrashing, radiant, möbius strip. The main event. Jacob versus the Dark Angel. The dark angel of a vision as yet unseen.

He would never be a great and full poet until he had his own master vision of the mysteries and the facts. It was a fact that he was on a chair in a room on a planet that was spinning around a gigantic blazing star, making a sound that he had once heard. It was a fact that he had not been here before a certain date and, after another equally definite date, he would no longer be locatable for even the quickest of quick drinks. Those were the facts but they were also the mysteries.

But could he take the whole thing? Could he take the dryness and constriction of waiting? Could his nervous system stand the voltage of revelation? Or would he go mad as Cousin John?

Yes, he had the monk's strength of dry patience, yes, he could take the constriction of waiting, and yes he would stare greedily into that jewel when its last rags were unwrapped.

Opening his eyes, Blaine saw Davis approaching him from across the room, an unlit cigarette pointing back across her shoulder, her flesh especially white and glowing in the spaces divided by black straps.

Oh God, Davis, he thought, what a childish cry for attention. And those absurd, overpriced strips of cloth, stitched together by some illegal alien mother of six . . .

"Could you give me a light, Arthur?" said Davis, pressing her fine auburn hair to the left side of her head as she leaned forward.

"Davis, it's just that . . . of course, I'll give you a light but . . . it's Tuesday."

"Thank you," she said, after his thumb spun the ridged wheel on his old Zippo twice before making flame.

The proximity of her breasts to his eyes was transforming him into a pure mammal whose very essence is defined by its life-long desire to suck nipples. To feel nipples graze his eyelids. Sliding from one corner of his lips to the other. The breast filling his skull.

But Arthur Blaine was no wriggling sexual seal, he was a poet who could fly above the storm of the flesh. If only she would walk away a little, that would give him the distance he needed.

"I think I'll get a wine glass, too," said Davis, blowing smoke.

Good, she's going to walk away. But no sooner had she turned and taken the first two steps, than he thought—bad, she's going to walk away. Bad, because this view of her sent him instantly back to the bliss between gorilla and citizen when the sight of female buttocks retreating into the leaves was an invitation, an imperative, and all the introduction required.

It's nothing, it's nothing, it's just where she sits down.

It wasn't that she didn't look quite adorable, but once they got started they'd drink two bottles and the better part of a third and he'd wake up the next day with a brain chirping like Cockneys in a London fog.

Strips of cloth, sold in a store.

But what exquisite strips of cloth, he thought, recalling the black mesh over her nipples, a pattern like the score for music from another world. Instinct encoded as design. Where was she? Why was she taking so long in the kitchen?

He thought he could hear sparks of nylon static fly from her inner thighs as she strode toward him. To his surprise, disappointment, confusion, she walked right past him.

Davis pressed the power button with the tip of her index finger, the stereo already tuned to their favorite, golden oldies station. There was music at once, music that changed the lighting in the room.

> When the twilight is gone,
> And no song birds are singing,
> When the twilight is gone,
> You come into my heart.

Now Davis came around the other side of his chair, her complete revolution enclosing him in a magic circle of moving flesh, smoke, and a smell like apples from the cellar.

"Could I please have some wine, sir?" asked Davis.

When Blaine picked up the bottle from the floor, Davis handed him her glass with a gesture that said: "Holding my glass as you pour is the least you can do, considering what I am doing for you." No sooner were both of Blaine's hands occupied than Davis fell to her knees, a Saint Theresa struck by ecstatic need.

She kissed him through chino, feeling him extend along her cheek.

"Don't, Davis, I can't pour like that."

A splash of wine dampened her hair and a red tear ran down the side of her face. She caught it at the corner of her mouth with her tongue and wet her lips with it.

Thanks to the invention of the zipper, it was only a matter of seconds before Davis was greeting Blaine like a hostess in a receiving line who, after exchanging small talk with distant relatives and acquaintances, is genuinely delighted to see the face of a beloved friend.

When the twilight is gone,
And no song birds are singing . . .

It was the greatest thing in the world. He had forgotten that—what a fool. It was the greatest thing in the world, and nothing finished a close second, and all the visions and honors and poems were nothing if you didn't have this, because this was life, because life was sex and sex was life and best, best of all, sex was sex.

As if they knew the instant he would choose to open his eyes, Davis's were waiting for him, damp opals.

Blaine gasped from astonishment, among other reasons, for he had recognized that combination of humor, mischief, and passion in Davis's eyes as not only Davis's but *hers*.

Then suddenly everything was so inside-out and backwards that even sonnets went speeding back to the muse.

CHAPTER 7

There was every indication that Zivkin had been pathetically devoid of higher ambition; that is, he had not been scheming in the least for Poplavsky's downfall. Rabin continued to turn out startling articles, some of which were written in response to events that took place after Zivkin's departure from the scene. Surveillance of Rabin and the monitoring of his phone demonstrated that he was not being fed information from any outside source. Yet he continued to astound and disturb Poplavsky both with his general theories about Russia (the Peter-the-Great expansion, the Ivan-the-Terrible contraction) and by his ability to detect historical currents just as they were brimming from the potential to the actual. A careful reading of Rabin's earlier published work showed this to be nothing new for him.

Poplavsky wanted more hard evidence before taking any concrete action, but, intuitively, he had no doubt that Rabin was the man he had always known would come around the bend some day—the next Jew genius, the Einstein of history.

But just how fundamentally important was an Einstein? Poplavsky asked himself. Alright, let's say it's before World War II, the '30s. Einstein is working away. If you abduct Einstein, you have the most advanced mind of the times working for you. Why steal the plans when you can take the entire person? He might have eight great ideas left in him. But suppose he won't work for you? Alright, at the very least, he's not working for your enemy, which is good in itself. But why shouldn't he work? What else is he going to do? A singer isn't happy unless he's singing. A thinker isn't happy unless he's thinking. What does a person need anyway? Some nice food, a soft bed, a woman, a few friends, and work. A man needs work. A man is not a man without his work. To a man, his life and his life's work are almost one and the same. And that's even more true for types like Einstein and Rabin.

So, that wasn't the problem. And the logistics of abduction were simple enough. The only real question was how to play the Rabin card if it proved to be an ace.

In the meantime Poplavsky decided to mount a two-pronged operation. One, make preparations for Rabin's abduction and, two, seek verification that what he was thinking about Rabin was not beyond the pale of possibility. But that meant dealing with other people. Nothing was worse than other people. Not that he was worried any longer about any conspiracies against him. No, the problem with other people was simply that they were other people. With other desires, other ideas. A whole world full of other people. Bad enough that they had to be there in the first place taking up tables at restaurants and clogging public transportation, but actually entering into any serious dealings with them was always an unpleasant prospect. But nothing of magnitude could be done alone.

Fedya Ulovkin was their specialist in abduction, and the man to talk philosophy with was Sergei Lazar. Each of them operated out of the Soviet-owned building on Connecticut Avenue, a gracious mansion across from the Hilton. From time to time, the Washington press and diplomatic corps buzzed with rumors about what went on in there. Their guesses were always too colorful, thought Poplavsky. All people did there was talk.

But what could be more dangerous than talk? Talk was the most dangerous thing in the world. Everything starts with talk.

Poplavsky was still pulling on his light topcoat as he went out his office door, announcing: "I'll be out for the rest of the day. Beep me for emergencies."

No one needed to know where he was going, although there might be an interested party or two waiting outside. It was early spring; it would be nice to walk. It was the sort of weather that was neither quite cool or warm but something in between that everyone interpreted according to his metabolism and style. Women in fur passed young men in T-shirts.

Over the years Poplavsky had developed a sort of proprietary feeling for Washington and would experience a local's irritation when the tourists arrived in droves at cherry blossom time. He liked the city's sweet Southern slowness and the general friendliness of the black population. And today he felt benignly inclined to the city because it was, after all, the setting for one of the most important chapters in his life.

Odd that it should be here, he thought. But, then again, not so odd.

Poplavsky found Fedya tinkering about in his small lab. Fedya, whose eyebrows were the special shade that comes when blond turns to grey, beamed with pleasure and curiosity when Poplavsky said: "Let's go to Room 3."

Room 3 was considered the most secure room. All five secure rooms had been given the designation: ABSOLUTELY SECURE. And yet, people, being people, somehow felt that Room 3 was more secure by an extra little bit. All the rooms were protected by special materials imported from the Soviet Union.

In fact, every plank in every floor was from the Soviet Union, as was every nail in every plank. Aside from these physical barriers, the secure rooms were surrounded by a triple zone of interference. A wall of jamming. A wall of white noise. And, in the unlikely event that any sound happened to escape, there was the code zone. Ingenious engineers had created a system that keyed certain Russian sounds to tape recordings of speeches by Franklin Delano Roosevelt. The most American intelligence had ever gleaned from the mansion on Connecticut Avenue was that we had nothing to fear but fear itself.

Still, as a rule, Poplavsky kept his voice low, even in Room 3. Machines break. Systems fail.

"Yes?" said Fedya with the insinuating certainty of any person who serves but a single purpose. His movements were fine and quick, and even though he had lived his entire life in big cities, he had the deeply distracted air of a man who spent too much time alone in nature.

"Yes, we may have some business, you and I," said Poplavsky with a sigh.

"May?"

"Yes, may."

"And what sort of business might that be?"

"The usual."

"Local?"

"No."

"US?"

"Yes. West Coast."

"Southern California?"

"No."

"Too bad."

"Why?"

"I'd like to see Marine World."

"Another time. Fedya, here's what may have to be done. A certain person may have to be picked up and sent back with the diplomatic mail. What we will need is some sort of container that he can be kept in so he doesn't freeze to death in the cargo hold."

"Something will have to be built into the plane, but that's just a matter of hardware. I'll see to it. But the interesting part is picking him up and getting him on the plane."

"I know."

"Tell me this, is it a man?"

"Yes."

"Under sixty?"

"Yes."

"Married?"

"He lives with a woman."

"For how long?"

"Three years."

"Is he engaged in any illegal activities? Drugs? Anything?"

"No."

"Is he in desperate need of money?"

"No."

Fedya crossed his legs and grabbed his chin. "I would say that after three years most Americans tire of their wives, sexually, I mean. You can see how much more powerful Russian women are, Leonid. I tired of mine in six months."

Poplavsky laughed. The only thing Fedya ever joked about was his wife whom Poplavsky had met once and found a perfectly pleasant person.

"So," continued Fedya, who did not laugh at his own jokes, "he must be ready for another woman."

"He is. Listen to this."

Poplavsky withdrew a cassette tape from his inside jacket pocket and inserted it into the recorder on the table.

"This came in today," said Poplavsky, pressing PLAY. "First our man speaks, then the girlfriend."

". . . I know, I know, believe me, I don't like it either."

"Well, Eliot, I am glad you have a conscience."

"Of course, I have a conscience. I wish I had less of one. My problem is that I have a strict conscience but no character, so I'm always doing things that make me suffer."

"So, like, don't do them."

"I can't help it. I can't help it that I find you absolutely entrancing."

"I'm glad that you do, Eliot. Like, I really am."

"Could you not say *like* quite so much?"

"What?"

"Forget it, forget it. I like you just the way you are. Don't change an adverb for me."

"Eliot, sometimes I don't know what you're talking about."

"It doesn't matter; it doesn't matter. I'm sorry I said it."

"I think we're too different."

"Of course, we're too different. That's the beauty of it. Who wants anybody the same as themselves? One of me is too much as it is."

"But, Eliot, the karma in this kind of thing can be really heavy."

"I know, I know."

Poplavsky clicked off the tape.

"What's karma?" asked Fedya.

"I don't know."

"Sounds promising, but she's still refusing him."

"I wish she would give in already. He wants her very much; he's not happy with the other one."

"You sound like you care."

"I want him to be happy."

"But you also want him in the diplomatic mail, on a regularly scheduled flight out of San Francisco, I take it?"

"Yes."

"See this?" said Fedya, withdrawing from the pocket of his lab smock something that resembled a TV remote control. "It's my latest. We could make money selling them to terrorists. Good money. Watch."

Fedya held the device closer to Poplavsky who now saw that it contained a small screen. He thought there must be a miniaturized TV camera inside the device, because he could see the image of the room moving in the screen as Fedya's hand shifted back and forth.

Fedya pressed a button on one side and a red dot appeared on the screen. "That's the lock-on laser guide."

"What does it do?" asked Poplavsky.

"First, I choose a target, that armchair at the far end of the room, for example. When I have the red dot where I want it, I press this button and the dot locks on target. Then, within a certain range, I can fire one of the five darts this device contains, and it will automatically hit the target selected. Automatically."

"And the darts, what do they do?"

"The darts are furnished with a triple-action narcotic that first anesthetizes the little puncture it makes, then causes an instantaneous mood elevation followed by profound unconsciousness."

"And how long can you keep a person out?"

"Give me his basic physical data, and then you tell me how long you want him out. And that's how long he'll be out."

"With no danger to his system, his brain? Even, say, for twenty-four hours?"

"With no danger at all. But there is one problem."

"I knew it was too perfect," said Poplavsky. "What's the problem?"

"It's the propellant. It makes a terrible sound. Listen."

Fedya aimed the device ten feet away from the armchair he had targeted; then he pressed a button marked with a small arrow. The air was immediately rent by a sound like an old pillowcase being torn in two: PfffffffffffffffffffffffffffffffffffffffT!

"Keep working on it," said Poplavsky, rising from his chair.

Thank God, Rabin's love problems were at least normal, thought Poplavsky strolling back through the soft twilight. The sight of two young men, both with mustaches, had reminded him how many homosexuals there were in America. And their mustaches never looked like anyone else's; you could always tell them by the mustaches, and a certain look in their eyes, a look there was no word for, at least not in Russian. Maybe the homosexuals had their own special word for it. A Jew had once told him that he could always tell another Jew by the eyes. And Russians could also tell other Russians just by a certain sharpness to the gaze that was forever taking measure. For Jews the look was not so much distrust as apprehension.

Poplavsky wondered why were there so many homosexuals in America. The American intellectuals never wrote about such things because they were always afraid of giving offense. But it was a question of world historical significance. A superpower, the leader of the West, the bastion of capitalism and so-called democracy, and one man out of every six likes it up the ass? No, that was a serious subject and deserved serious thought. Was it a form of moral decay caused by too many civilized comforts? Or was it the result of some essential disruption between man and woman in this society where anything goes but nothing stays?

The only solid explanation he'd seen was in Rabin's essay "The Smerdyakov Principle." According to Rabin, every new force in society is conceived on a high level but invariably settles to a low level, just as the Karamazov brothers' secret will was carried out by their deranged half-brother, Smerdyakov. Sex, too, had been Smerdyakovized. After World War I a great surge of energy had been directed toward liberating human beings from sexual repression and superstition—Freud, Joyce, Lawrence, Miller. Important court cases had been won, and the end result seemed to be peep shows and bad marriages. Of course, said Rabin in conclusion, this is a paradox, but paradox is the highest level of consciousness, the mind's last effort to make sense out of what is in fact a mystery.

Poplavsky almost came to a standstill on the sidewalk, magnetized by the power of the thought that had just occurred to him. He was beginning to see the world as Rabin saw it. He was becoming a disciple of Rabin. Here he was making plans and traps for Rabin, and it was he who was in Rabin's power. On another level, to be sure, but power was power, and there is no power like the power over another person's soul. And Rabin had power over Poplavsky's soul. Even at a distance of three thousand miles, like Rasputin who could cure the Tsar's son of hemophilia from Siberia just by closing his eyes and entering into a trance with the universe.

He had been too crude. He had worried about the wrong things. The abduction would probably be no more difficult than pulling a tooth. The threat lay in the paradoxes, that universe of magic danger where the hunter is simultaneously the prey.

It was, in several ways, a new Poplavsky who, three and a half weeks later, entered Room 4 (the ambassador had reserved Room 3, and, except in certain circumstances, the ambassador took precedence over the rezident). He had become more thoughtful, and had even acquired some of the melancholy gentleness that usually comes with knowledge. This did not, however, blunt his ambition; on the contrary, it only whetted it by showing him that the contest was ever greater than he had suspected.

Poplavsky had come for a drink or two with Sergei Lazar, who had a Russian mother and a Jewish father, a tasty and appropriate combination given the situation at hand. Lazar was in charge of propaganda, which was a government function, not KGB, as was disinformation. Since, however, the two tended to merge, Poplavsky and Lazar had built up a working relationship that, from time to time, also included a little recreational drinking.

They had been fairly open in those sessions, and Poplavsky had sensed that Lazar had worked out some worldview of his own, that somewhere in a few thousand secret cells of his brain, Lazar allowed himself to be philosopher. Lazar, on his part, had come to be interested in Poplavsky's mind and personality, but Lazar was always slightly edgy with Poplavsky. Anyone who made a career with *them* had to be somehow disturbed. And the fact that Poplavsky had chosen a secure room for their conversation indicated that, for all the vodka and appetizers on the table in front of them, this was, essentially, business.

"You don't look too bad," said Poplavsky.

"Please. No compliments that I can't return."

Both men laughed, addicts of sarcasm.

"Let's drink right away," said Poplavsky. "I'm so dry, you can't imagine. Alright. I want to drink to the Jews and true knowledge."

"You're starting on a high note," replied Lazar, pouring himself a bit less vodka than Poplavsky had taken.

"Why not? A dying man once told me, 'Leonid,' he said, 'life is not even one second long.' "

"To Jews and true knowledge."

Their heads shot back like the bolts on old-fashioned rifles. They grabbed appetizers, tore at them with their teeth, and only then did they exhale.

"Mostly we run around; mostly we are busy," said Poplavsky as he settled into a chair. Lazar took the end of the couch nearest him. "But sometimes, all of a sudden, you get this angry feeling that you want to know what the hell is really going on."

"And what is really going on?"

"The specifics don't matter. It's the principle that counts here."

"Alright, what's the principle?"

"It takes the form of a question. Can we have true knowledge?"

"Or are we doomed to have a series of murky ideas and then die?"

"Precisely. What do you think?"

"I think the question itself represents an incorrect formulation."

"Alright, Sergei, then what is the question?"

"The brain has certain jobs to do, like the knee. One of its jobs is to invent questions. This is a necessary and important function. Because man is in part an animal. Therefore, he needs food, shelter, protection from danger. So, the brain asks, how can the shelter be made better? And then before you know it, you have architecture, castles, the Taj Mahal. But then the brain gets overheated and starts asking stupid questions like a child, questions that don't have any answer to them."

"So then, you are denying the objective existence of true knowledge?"

"No. Not in the least. We want true knowledge. We need true knowledge. And we have been given a means of acquiring true knowledge."

"Namely?"

"I don't know the name of that part of the mind, perhaps no one has even given it a name yet. It's the part of the mind that can hear the music of history, the music of reality."

"Is that an original idea of yours?"

"No. I got it from the poet Alexander Blok, who said he could hear, actually hear, tsarist Russia coming apart. It was he who taught me that time was not to be understood but heard. Yes, I admit it, I'm a Blokist."

"Just make sure you stay a Soviet Blokist," punned Poplavsky.

Lazar grimaced in appreciation.

"Still," continued Poplavsky, "there is such a thing as evidence, patterns."

"All music is pattern. All pattern is music."

"I understand, but I want to take a different position. If someone is able to hear history and then translate what he hears into useable ideas, such a person would be of great value, wouldn't you say?"

"There are such people," said Lazar. "Dostoevsky, for example. Many critics have pointed out that his obsessions turned

★   81

out to be the obsessions of the next era. Dostoevsky is much closer to Soviet Russia than Tolstoy. Tolstoy outlived Dostoevsky by thirty years, and yet today he seems to have died long before him. Tolstoy even made a recording, did you know that?"

"No, I didn't. Have you heard it?"

"Not yet. I keep putting it off. Something about the very idea disturbs me. It somehow diminishes Tolstoy, makes him one of us."

"Let's drink to Tolstoy and Dostoevsky."

"Good idea."

"To Tolstoy and Dostoevsky!"

"Tolstoy! Dostoevsky!"

The room, the air, their chests and throats echoed with the greatness of those names, which sent the second vodka speeding on its way through the blood stream.

"Yes, but Dostoevsky was too elevated. I am curious to know whether more detailed knowledge could be obtained by some genius whose nervous system was tuned to what you call the music of history. Do you consider such a being hypothetically within the realm of possibility?"

"Interesting question," said Lazar, puzzled by the bizarre turn the conversation had taken. Poplavsky seemed to be getting to the point, but could this be the point? Since this was business, better play it safe. "Strictly from the point of view of Marxism, reality can be understood and, once understood, directed toward its inevitable goal. I accept that basic principle, and I have no problem in resolving it with my Blokist outlook. History has a dynamic. It moves; it makes patterns. The patterns can be heard intuitively like some form of music, and there is no real reason why some genius could not notate that music."

That seemed to be the answer Poplavsky had wanted, because he suddenly relaxed against the back of the chair, although that might also have been the vodka starting to take effect.

"But then what about the Jews?" asked Lazar.

"What Jews?"

"In the beginning, you drank to true knowledge and the Jews. We've spoken about true knowledge. But what do the Jews have to do with anything?"

"My dear Sergei, as you well know," said Poplavsky, "if there's anything important going on, the Jews have something to do with it."

CHAPTER 8

Light always travels at the same speed, but fame travels at dozens. It travels at the speed of sound, carrying the Apollo-Prize winner's voice through the air and, then, humming on the fine tympanies of ear drums, it is converted by the Rube Goldberg apparatus of the inner ear into the voice of Arthur Blaine, speaking, laughing, reading. Fame traveled at the speed of light bearing the ethereal technicolor likeness of Arthur Blaine into millions of kitchens, living rooms, parlors, bedrooms, rec rooms, bars, and Greyhound bus stations, so that, at the same instant in time, twenty-seven million optical nerves and cerebrums process and perceive the same image—that of Arthur Blaine. His fame traveled at the speed at which magazine pages are flicked in beauty parlors, though it caused more than one woman to stop and say to the woman beside her: "Isn't he cute?" His fame traveled at the speed of jet liners, and of cabs, cabs, cabs, bearing the source of all the sounds and images to one particular place that alone would be graced with his actual presence, to those who alone would see the original, while the rest of humanity would have to be satisfied with reproductions. His fame traveled at the speed with which checks clear, and there were more and more checks in his life now, although he did suspect that there were fewer balances. And Arthur

Blaine's fame traveled with the velocity of gossip and envy which, in the world of poets, may even exceed the speed of light.

"You represent your country now. You ought to get a haircut," said the Secret Service man.

Two other Secret Service men were debating whether Blaine should be frisked.

Blaine was busy telling himself not to be nervous, not to compromise his dignity with any stammering awkwardness. The President of the United States was just a person like anybody else and, as far as Blaine could remember, he didn't think he liked his foreign policy very much. But, he noted, words seemed to have greater power to alarm than to soothe; at least he had come up with nothing that equaled the force of the simple declarative sentence: "The President will present you with the Apollo Medal in ten minutes."

"I say a quick frisk."

"The guy is a national figure."

Checked by a metal detector but unfrisked, Blaine was led to his spot, premarked with masking tape on which his name was printed in bold black magic marker.

The President seemed to burst through the air surrounded by a heavenly host of agents who looked everywhere but at him. Blaine, too, could barely look at the President let alone see him. And when the President looked at Blaine, they both disappeared in a cloud of numinous silver like that in the unfinished portraits of George Washington. But Blaine was brought back to the Rose Garden by a hearty handshake. The President's flesh felt more like flesh and less like flesh than any flesh he had ever felt.

"All Americans are very proud of your accomplishment, Arthur," said the President.

"It's an honor to represent my country on the moon," replied Blaine, suddenly aware that here, on the highest level, words were of as little meaning as they were at a funeral; here only the most perfect cliches could be spoken, as if to mark the fullness of the reality itself.

"And you show that Rooskie we can hit the long ball in poetry, too," joshed the President, with a little wink that said: "You can quote that one to your friends."

Then more words were spoken, clear and empty as the sky, and once again Blaine's hand joined the President's, this time in holding a corner of the box containing the Apollo medal. Flash bulbs, cameras whirring like a locust storm.

The light of presidential reality seemed to magnify and flare and then suddenly Presence became Absence. As he was whisked away from his masking-tape "X," Blaine tried to fix the moment in his mind. But it had been an experience too charged to be remembered. He could only recall pictures of the President, shots on TV.

But now he was an official angel of the glorious and, as a true sign of his exaltation, a stretch limo was waiting in front of the White House to take him to his next stop—a reception at the Russian embassy.

"Our guest today is Mr. Arthur Blaine," said Poplavsky who was glad to be fulfilling his function as cultural attaché, there being no better relief from serious problems than pressing trivialities. "Mr. Blaine will read with our poet, Viktor Viktorov, on the moon. The very idea is so beautiful. Our nations, which were great allies in the struggle against Hitler's fascism, and which have drifted apart in the postwar period, now have the opportunity to express mankind's loftiest feelings and greatest technological achievements in a demonstration of peaceful cultural intentions in space. Yes, let space be a theater of art, not a theater of war."

The audience applauded, then rose to its feet, still applauding. Poplavsky, already standing at the mike, turned toward Blaine and began applauding him. Blaine rose and started applauding, too. But then, not sure whether he might be applauding himself, he stopped and began bowing slightly in various directions.

"And now a special treat," said Poplavsky.

The room went dark and screens at either end of the room, unapparent until then, were lit by the flickering light that precedes the image.

"By closed-circuit TV, from the American embassy in Moscow, Mr. Arthur Blaine and ladies and gentlemen, it is my pleasure to introduce to you the Soviet poet-cosmonaut, Viktor Viktorovich Viktorov!" said Poplavsky richly into the microphone.

Viktorov's smile had all the confidence of an athlete being awarded the gold. Blaine immediately drew himself up in an attitude that left no doubt that a double gold had been awarded in the Poetry Olympics.

But then Blaine caught himself in that gnat attack of vanity and envy, more unworthy of him now than ever. They were not rivals; they were compañeros.

"Reading from the moon is an honor and adventure," said Blaine, slowly, with a natural sense of how the interpreter would want the phrases fed to her, "but the mission is to return life to poetry, and poetry to life."

"I agree with my colleague, Mr. Arthur Blaine," said Viktorov in English, then he continued in Russian, his voice full and inky. The personalityless voice of the interpreter said in pure interpretese: "It is difficult to present oneself with the idea that we are indeed bound for cosmic travel and shall stand on the lunar surface and look down at our blue home."

Of all that pulp, grey as a hornet's nest, the only phrase which enlivened Blaine was the one that came at the very end, "our blue home." That was a dash of poetry. It gave him the joy that only poetry can give. Now he loved Viktorov.

"I wonder," said the American ambassador who was sitting next to Viktorov, "will you be looking down at earth, or up?"

A chuckle of wonder and appreciation rippled through both closed-circuit audiences.

After a thirty-second technical glitch, a great many more well wishes were exchanged, becoming doubly disembodied in translation. The evening concluded with champagne and caviar in the sort of upbeat atmosphere that occurs whenever an occasion is risen to. And the greatest elation was naturally felt by the person who was both the occasion itself and the one who had risen to it, Arthur Blaine.

At the very end, the Russian in charge of the event came over to him. Blaine had forgotten the man's name, though he recalled that it sounded like a washerwoman dropping three heavy bundles of laundry into a tub. "Well, once again, on behalf of the Soviet people, I want to thank you for being here with us today, but now, unfortunately, the embassy requires this area for other purposes."

"They've got this limo booked for you until nine," said the limo driver, a woman, who had a mysterious self-contained air.

"Nine?" said Blaine.

"Yes, and it's ten past eight."

Was she daring him with that blankness? Suddenly, he

didn't care. Suddenly, all he wanted was peace and solitude. There had been too many faces in front of his face that day. "Take me back to the hotel," he said.

Still, as they drove through the streets, which were dark and light at the same time, he felt a desire for another hit, a nightcap of celebrity.

"Let me off here," he said as they passed a bookstore which he had spotted earlier. "I'll walk the rest. Thank you so very much for doing your job so nicely." He looked to see if her eyes lit up. They didn't.

Blaine whisked into the bookstore and allowed himself to be beheld. As naturally as he possibly could under the circumstances, he went directly to the poetry section which, as always, was deserted. This caused a momentary fall of spirit, which was at once overcome by the sight of a thick, fresh slab of *Rookies of Existence* looking cover-out and eye-level at the world.

The new Blaine would now read the Blaine of the previous incarnation; as always he opened the book with Delphic randomness.

Don Quixote on the Mound, Panza behind the Plate

A wonderful title. He had always loved it. Now his eyes were drawn all the way down to the last line:

For his gift Don is forgiven at bat.

But how did that metric I Ching apply to his current situation?

"I saw you on the news tonight," said the attractive young woman at the counter in a tone that suggested there was no point in pretending she didn't know who he was.

Blaine nodded and smiled. "I see you have fresh copies of *Rookies*."

"Yes, we got them right after the announcement was made. The computer automatically orders a certain number of copies whenever anybody wins a prize."

"And are people . . ." How exactly does one ask that? thought Blaine.

"Buying?" she said. Her reflexes honed on the realities of commerce more quickly than Blaine's.

"Yes."

"Not actually."

"I see."

"You may be interested in this," she said, pointing to a paperback that had a bit of a rushed-into-print look.

"Ah," he said as he read the cover: *Mayakovsky's Suicide and Other Poems*, by Viktor Viktorov.

Instinctively, he checked the price: $8.95. But then he remembered he was no longer at the stage where the price of any paperback was an issue. You sign a slip and it's yours.

But none of the money was coming from the poetry itself. No one was actually buying the actual book and actually reading it. *The New York Times Magazine* was paying him twenty thousand dollars to keep a "Space Journal." Maybe he could smuggle a few lines of his poetry into it.

"I'll take it," he said pulling out his American Express card, not so much signing as autographing the slip.

He chose a secluded spot in the hotel bar, far from the action and the television, and, sipping a Heineken and dragging on a Camel, he read the translator's introduction to Viktorov's poems. Overly fussy, the introduction provided Blaine only with information, not with the pleasure words could give.

The translator pointed out that Russia had a long tradition

of respecting and punishing poets, but it cautioned readers not to think that all Russian poets were persecuted at all times. Some were in favor during their own lifetimes, though most came back into favor after death. Viktorov was a poet whose natural bents did not so much coincide with the system as not clash with it. Still, Viktorov had not been afraid to look behind the official myth of Mayakovsky as the bard of the revolution. Contemplating Mayakovsky's suicide, Viktorov had risked the following, quite unorthodox conclusion:

> *As the bullet leaves the barrel,*
> *it makes a horizontal exclamation point!*
> *Better that as a poet's last punctuation*
> *than a question mark, or the dot dot dot*
> *of a failed, genteel expiration.*

Blaine admired the translator's use of rhyme and thought that writing out "dot dot dot" was a stroke of genius. But he was not sure about the word "genteel." Could anything Russian really be "genteel"?

But Viktorov was absolutely right—the essential punctuation mark of poetry was the exclamation point! Question marks were for philosophers and lawyers, and periods were just the nails of prose.

As he looked up he saw a young, happy, and not entirely unfamiliar face.

"Do you remember me, Mr. Blaine? I took your poetry workshop when you were at BU."

"Of course, of course," said Blaine, glad to meet someone from "before," although he had no idea who this person was.

"Gil Allen," said the young man, not assuming for a moment that his name had been etched on his teacher's mind.

"Yes, now I remember," said Blaine. "You wrote that nice satire on the Cliffies."

"I feel very honored that you remember; I really do."

"Come on, sit down, have a beer."

"Thank you very much."

Blaine called over the waiter and ordered another Heineken. Switching immediately from the inferior student to someone who knew his way around waiters, restaurants, and the world in general. Gil Allen ordered a Tequila Sunrise.

"So, how's it been going?" asked Blaine, slightly regretting having asked him to sit down. There was nothing worse than being stuck with a student tongue-tied with admiration.

"Fine, really fine. Do you mind if I take a cigarette? I quit, but I still like one once in a while. Do you always smoke Camels?"

"I have for about twenty years," said Blaine, "but just six or seven a day."

"It's great that you can control it. Wow, I never could. But I remember you always telling us to use the classical forms to discipline us."

"It's interesting the classic and the masculine are defined in very much the same terms," said Blaine, glad to be talking literature again.

"I can't tell you how invaluable everything you taught us turned out to be in the work I went into."

"I'm glad to hear that. What sort of work did you exactly go into?"

"Well, sir, the thing is, I realized I didn't have the patience to sit around waiting to get rich and famous, but I have to say you paid your dues, and nobody deserves it more than you do, but I said to myself, Gil, do something of quality, but make sure it pays. That's when I founded Integrity Marketing."

"Integrity Marketing?"

"Yes, here's my card."

Blaine read it aloud: "INTEGRITY MARKETING. We market integrity, with integrity. Shouldn't you market with Integrity, too?"

"Could you explain a little further what this means?" asked Blaine, leaning back, his eyes narrowed slightly by suspicion.

"It's one of the great concepts. Alright, you know how when you're watching television and somebody comes on, say an athlete or a movie star, and they try to sell you orange juice or a car, you know that they don't drink the stuff or drive anything like that; they're only doing it for the money. But what if people with integrity came forward and only told the truth about what they really liked? I mean, isn't that a fantastic gimmick, I don't mean gimmick—gimmick isn't the right word—a fantastic way of eliminating the conflict between culture and the marketplace? For example, you smoke Camels and you drink Heineken. If you came on and said, 'After a day's writing, I like to sit down and have a Heineken,' you'd only be telling the pure truth. If you said you drank Bud, that would be selling out, but if you came on the screen and said you drink Heineken, you'd be making upwards of ten thousand dollars just for telling the truth."

Well, I do drink Heinekens, thought Blaine, but only for the most micro of micro-instants. "I've had a very long day, and I suddenly feel very tired," said Blaine in a voice whose contempt was only in its dryness.

"Sure. I understand. Anyway, keep my card; think it over. I know it sounds a little funny at first—"

"Good night."

At last alone, the lights out against all stimuli, Blaine lay in bed waiting for the distaste of his last encounter to wear off. At the brink of sleep, he was yanked back by fear. Now he understood that line from *Rookies*: "For his gift Don is forgiven at bat." Poets and pitchers were singular beings because they were beings of a single gift. They were excused from the world of action that was symbolized by hitting. Yes, the arm of a pitcher throwing a fast ball made an exclamation point, too. But it was also a warning: Beware of action, beware of the world when you are not on the mound but at the plate.

Hope for a walk not a homer. But Homer was the first poet, he recalled, and he, Blaine, might be the last. The last to inherit the mantel. The Mickey Mantel. He wrapped the sheets around himself as if they were fine, golden Hellenic cloth and could in fact protect his skin against the cold of that overly air-conditioned room.

CHAPTER *9*

Poplavsky was alone in Room 3 with all the lights off. The sound of his own breathing was faint and distant, like surf breaking far below.

He had come to the most secure place available to him in the Western Hemisphere, so that he could withdraw to the most secure chamber within himself.

He was doing this because Rabin had given him a very hard piece of evidence, in an article entitled: "Whose Idea Was It?"

In the article Rabin had asked why TASS had announced the Soviet moon-poet project one day after the Americans had announced theirs. Rabin doubted that the idea itself was American-born. At the very least, it had to have been the brainchild of some vengeance-seeking State Department official of East European origin. But even if that official had access to important ears, wouldn't his proposal of sending a poet to the moon before the Russians got the idea have simply sounded outlandish and elicited a pitying smile for the poor klunky foreigner who never got it right?

That aside, argued Rabin, the very idea looked like a Russian idea, smelled like a Russian idea, and had the heft of a Russian idea. So what the hell else could it be?

The question was how did a Russian idea end up in an American head? If the poet-to-the-moon business had originally been a Russian idea, it would have either been made public on the brag-about-the-good principle, or it would have been kept secret on the anything-worth-doing-is-worth-keeping-secret principle.

But was someone in the Soviet administration trying to mock and humiliate the new leadership? To make them seem culturally pretentious, panting after the West? But what Russian was going to risk everything for that?

It was also possible that the leak had occurred through a non-Soviet conduit. There would be a Hungarian, East German, and Polish cosmonaut aboard the *Tsiolovsky I* along with the Soviet poet. And that meant there had to be some high-level military contact between the Soviets and the respective countries. An East German leak was possible. Who knew what they really thought? The East Germans might hate the Soviets the most because the other Eastern European states had fallen to the Russians as the spoils of victory, whereas Germany had been the defeated enemy. And the Hungarians might have a bone or two to pick for all the success of goulash communism. Being run over by a Soviet tank makes for a lasting memory. But somehow, concluded Rabin, the whole business had a Polish tartness to it, as distinct as the taste of the local pastry. The Poles were Romantic existentialists, believing in acts, not odds. And it was always important to the hand-kissing, liberty-loving Poles that the Russians be revealed as sinister oafs.

Poplavsky had ordered a quick computer check on all high-ranking Polish military personnel connected with the moon flight. Various procedures reduced the list to seven names.

They were all called in for questioning, and one Polish general admitted that he might have mentioned it to his sister-in-law who, unbeknownst to him at the time, had turned out to have connections with the Solidarity underground. Since the military was such a key factor in running Poland, the general was only demoted to sergeant and transferred to one of the less ideal posts.

Under Stalin he would have been shot! Under Stalin he wouldn't even have dared to think about doing it!

"Not even have dared, Leonid," said Stalin, whom Poplavsky experienced first as a voice in that dark room and then as a pulsing shimmer, yellow as a tiger's eyes.

"Where are you?" asked Poplavsky.

"In your heart of hearts. That is one mausoleum they haven't removed me from."

"May I ask you one very important question?"

"Here you can ask me any question, and I will give you the most useful truth as my answer."

"What should I do about Rabin?"

"Kill him."

"Why?"

"You are too involved with him already. Living men produce unforeseen circumstances."

"But he will be of no use to me dead."

"His death will serve you well. It will keep you out of serious trouble."

"Does that mean he doesn't have any special gift?"

"No, the man has a gift. That's another reason he has to be killed. Our enemies may make use of that gift."

"But if our enemies can make use of that gift, why shouldn't we?"

"Because you will have to jeopardize your security in procuring that gift. Take no risks. That's what I learned from being Hitler's ally."

"But—"

"There are no buts when Stalin speaks. And do you want to know why, my dear Leonid Nikolaevich? Because I live by the most terrible truth. The truth no one else can stand to have inside them. The truth of reality and power and murder. That is the source of my power. I can face the terrible truth. And so there can be no buts."

"Yes, Comrade Stalin."

"You are a brave man, Poplavsky. You are becoming more and more able to face the terrible truth. Though I doubt that you will ever be strong enough to face the terrible truth behind the terrible truth."

"The terrible truth behind the terrible truth?"

"You don't want to know."

"Tell me, tell me, I can take it."

"You can't. I know."

"Then let it destroy me."

"Perhaps I should. There is something in the familiarity of your tone that does not please me in the least."

"I am sorry if—"

"Still, your heart has been loyal to my person, and I take that into account. I am going to tell you the terrible truth behind the terrible truth. Perhaps you know that my father was a drunken shoemaker who beat me unmercifully. I was always cowering in fear and wishing he would love me until one day I even stopped wishing that, and that's when I became Joseph Stalin. But now that death has cleared away the confusion of life, I can see that I really do wish he had loved me. I really do wish that I didn't have to be Joseph Stalin.

Papa! It's all so pathetic, so human. Isn't that the most terrible truth you've ever heard?"

"Please, stop, don't do it to yourself, stop, stop, I can't stand it! You really are destroying me! I should have listened to you! You were right! I wasn't strong enough! The truth is too terrible!"

Poplavsky stopped and waited for a response. But all he heard was his own quickened breathing in the ordinary darkness of Room 3.

CHAPTER 10

I still say it was a Polish leak, thought Rabin as he watched a news piece on the two poets training for space. The Russian was reported to be doing fine, while the American was experiencing some "weightlessness discomfiture."

The whole enterprise struck him as a pilot for a space comedy by Plato. Hadn't anybody in the American or Soviet administration ever read *The Republic*? Didn't a single person remember Plato's argument that poets are too irrational to be a part of any well-ordered state? And now the two greatest superpowers of all time are going to send not one but two poets to the moon! Serves them right if something goes haywire.

He snapped off the small black-and-white TV like an irked god snapping a universe out of existence. He was sick of the whole US-Soviet world. All he wanted to think about right now were the hours that lay ahead. At 6:30 he would meet his diving instructor, Vikki, at Pacific Grove Beach. They would go for a sunset scuba dive, build a fire, eat, drink California wine that tasted of everything but time, and, then with a little luck, would find themselves in the place that exists only between a man and a woman.

Or, to put it in plain English, swim and eat, drink and

fuck, said a part of Rabin's mind, which he immediately recognized as conscience, infiltrating this time in a macho disguise, a rather good disguise, Rabin had to admit, but not one that had fooled him. Conscience didn't want him to go and so was trying to make the whole evening appear in a vulgar and tacky light.

But now the sound of Janey banging a pan against some white enamel kitchen surface was like the cry of an angel heartbroken in heaven by the crime Rabin was about to commit. And the angel was doubly stricken, not only because of the crime itself but because a good man would be committing it.

Alec must have had a friend over. Rabin could hear two boys' voices talking nonstop, and for a moment he tried to remember just exactly what it was that boys always discussed with such ease and excitement.

That was life, drab and dear. The sounds of people you don't quite love enough moving close to you. The peace that comes at the end of the day. The sock in the corner. The mail in the hall.

That was one truth. The human truth. The truth we try to lose ourselves in because we are all too aware that life is not human. Humans are the ones who build a life apart from life.

But there was always that other truth. The truth that we belong to life itself. That was clear if you looked hard at the very beginning when your head enters this world from the walls of a bleeding vagina, and at the very end when your body is placed in a box that is then lowered into a deep hole in the ground.

Rabin began gathering the energy to rise. There was resistance to overcome because once he was standing, he would be, in fact, on his way to Vikki, and that would mean everything he said and did until he was out of the house would be a perfect lie.

"Eliot," said his conscience, now employing a voice of sad and gentle wisdom, "nothing has actually happened yet. Just stay where you are and the whole thing will pass."

At the door he turned for a last look at his study—the heavy volumes opened on his desk, a black pen at a windshield-wiper angle on a yellow legal pad, a chestnut he had picked up on his last trip back east. The view reminded him of apartments that had been turned into museums, rooms that had been preserved "just as they had been left." It was then that he noticed the half-eaten apple on his desk and had a strong feeling that he should at least throw it in the wastebasket. Why "at least"? And why did he have such a stupid urge at such a moment?

He strode angrily across the room and snatched the apple from the lean-to that had been formed by the cover of Chaadaev's *Apology of a Madman*. He was about to drop the apple in the wastebasket when he had a more playful and interesting desire to which he decided to yield, since yielding to desire seemed to be the order of the day. He resolved that the accuracy of his toss from across the room would be an exact measure of the rightness of his intended actions. Simultaneously sportscaster and basketball star, he gauged the distance. Rabin is back, Rabin turns. It's a hook shot by Rabin and it's—no good! But Rabin grabs the rebound: he's going in for the layup and it's—no good!

"Meaningless!" puffed Rabin as he lobbed it in the third time around.

"But you said—," said a voice from within.

"Shut up!"

For an instant in the hallway he seemed to have forgotten how to walk. The impulse to run and the impulse to tiptoe collided in his nervous system and produced paralysis. How did he normally walk out to the car? And the very idea of calling out a goodbye, with the cheerful casualness that only daily life, in all its unimaginable wealth, can afford, seemed utterly beyond his powers.

And how about coming back when it was all over, what would that be like? Coming back to the sleeping house with the smell of another woman on him like the smell of wine on his breath. That aroma could come back to you for days, and you'd never know whether it was some stray molecules freed from under a fingernail or simply a trick of memory.

"See you later, Janey," he called out, stumbling forward both into motion and speech.

"Where are you going, Eliot? Dinner's almost ready," came her voice from the kitchen.

"The sunset dive and the cookout with my scuba class. Don't you remember?" He had told her three times, but how could she remember something that didn't exist? He may have deceived her, but memory could detect what was real, and that information had passed through Janey's memory like a breeze through a sieve.

"I forgot. Stupid of me. OK, have fun. Be careful."

"Thanks."

The sight of Alec's bicycle leaning against the wall, nonchalant in matter's perfect trust of matter, halted him just as he was almost to the door. Alec had been so happy when Rabin had bought him that bicycle—exactly the bicycle he had wanted—because Rabin had remembered how important the right daring accessories could be to a boy. Janey had been so happy to have someone who understood what a boy was and what a boy needed. "I never would have known the right kind to get him," she had said, taking Rabin's arm and pressing the side of her face against his shoulder, a gesture he seemed to feel again for a moment as if the muscles had a memory of their own. Even Alec had thrown his arms around Rabin without any of the dutifulness or hesitation that usually marked his expressions of affection toward that man who was not his "real daddy." The three of them had been happy that day in the park in the golden California sunshine, happier than they had ever been meant to be.

The only thing that could stop Rabin now was Alec; if Alec fell off his bunkbed — that bunkbed where no brother or sister would ever sleep, only friends sleeping over — then Rabin would not go.

I'll give it all up for you, Alec, if you fall and hurt yourself and have to be rushed to the hospital for stitches or a cast. I'll do it for you even though I would really rather be with Vikki at the beach. And even though we never loved each other enough, Alec, I would do it for you. So, if you're going to fall, do it now, Alec.

But Alec didn't fall. What he did was open his bedroom door just enough to expose one cool blue eye that seemed to regard Rabin will full knowledge of what that man was about to do to his mummy. Rabin remembered lying in his own room as a child and listening to the adults' conversation, able to pick up every shade of deceit, boastfulness, and offense; why shouldn't Alec have been able to do the same when hearing Rabin's voice, falsetto with falseness?

"Going diving, Alec," said Rabin, needing to say something but hating to lie to a child, for he knew that in some situations even the truth was a lie.

No expression registered in Alec's cool blue eye, unless its indifference was itself a form of hatred.

After what seemed an unnaturally extended pause, Alec asked: "Where?"

"Pacific Grove."

Did the knowledge of corruption dim Alec's gaze for an instant? Was a poison injected into his soul by Rabin's voice?

Alec seemed about to reply but then just slowly closed his door.

The suffering began to lift as soon as Rabin was out of the house and under the sky whose blue was now being enriched with the first cobalt of dusk. And by the time his key was growling in the ignition, there was a completely different weather in his mind. For a moment he marvelled at the shiftingness if not the utter shiftlessness of things, himself included.

As he drove, the white stucco walls softened in the six o'clock light. With nearly no traffic to asphyxiate them, the grey and ratty palms seemed to perk up a little, which must have made Rabin's noxiously flatulent Saab all the more unwelcome.

After five minutes, Rabin thought he could feel the sea mist on the side of his neck. He was always fine-tuned to the presence of the ocean, which was always there, just as the stars were always there behind the blue of the sky. And, as he pulled into the parking lot at Pacific Grove Beach with a squeak of his brakes that for a second reminded him of the world of brake jobs and postage stamps, he may have been desiring the ocean even more than he desired the wine and the camp fire and her.

As he waved to her, he lost a few degrees of balance, tugged to the left by his equipment bag, heavy with his weight belt and tank. She was at the far other end of the beach, and he liked the intimacy her choice suggested. From that distance she was only another blonde citizen of sunshine and sand. Memory supplied the details, the usual three or four. Her Pacific-blue eyes, her hair tawny as the hills in dry summer, the sharpness of her clean incisors, the tendons in her feet playing under clear skin. And certain ways she had—tossing her head up and back when she laughed as if signaling to someone behind her to join in the fun, her purity which would have been laughable if it were not so genuine and if it were not a spiritual perfume to which he was always susceptible. If only she didn't say 'like' so much.

He walked past a young man playing Frisbee with a dog then skirted a gypsy camp of bikers relaxing from hell-raising. To avoid a couple of men in gaudy short-sleeved shirts whom he feared might be colleagues, he wriggled his way through a small tribe of surfers, blond seals suddenly called en masse back to the sea.

"Vikki, you look like a dolphin who went to heaven," said Rabin, letting his equipment bag fall to the sand at the edge of the Navaho tan blanket she had spread.

"You do say wonderful things."

"But only when I mean them."

"You better get your wet suit on if we're going to get a good dive in while it's still light. But, like, could I ask you a question?"

"But, like, why not?" said Rabin struggling into his top.

"Do you know what Kundalini is?"

"Kundalini with a little parmesan is always good."

"Eliot, be serious."

"No, I don't know what it is."

"You remember what Prana was from the class?"

"Prana is the life force in the air."

"That's right," she said with teacherly approval, "and Kundalini is sexual energy which Eastern religion says is a golden serpent asleep in our genitals. Tantra Yoga is the yoga that wakes that serpent. But, like, the trick is not to leave that energy there."

"It would seem like a fairly good place for it."

"That's a very unenlightened thought, Eliot. What we're supposed to do is take that energy and bring it up along the chakras, which are spiritual nerve centers that run along the spine. First, we draw the golden fire from the genitals to the solar plexus, then to the heart where we begin to experience love, then to the throat which can now speak new languages, then to the third eye or the pineal gland as Western science calls it. When the third eye is open, you'll have a revelation about the universe. But here's the great part. All that energy can go streaming out of a part of your higher mind called the Gate of Brahmin. And that's when you achieve mystical oneness."

"The whole thing sounds terrific to me."

"The very first second I saw you, Eliot, I said to myself, I could do Tantric scuba with that man. Then I was a little put off by some of your habits, the smoking, the red meat, the white sugar. But the vibe is always right."

"The vibe is always right," he repeated with a smile that was almost a laugh. He loved those sayings which were somehow both undeniable and idiotic.

They sat and regarded each other for a moment. Then she closed her eyes and he closed his as easily as if he were leaning back into his own pillow. He could hear her voice echo in his mind—breathe deeply and easily, the air, your lungs, and

★   107

your mind are all one and the same. And of course they were, if only because she was so innocent every word she said had to be true. Now his body was a silk shirt on a hanger.

They opened their eyes almost at the same moment, something trance-like about their gazes now.

They stood and stretched. Then, in silence that was perfect because nothing was going unsaid, they began moving toward the ocean.

Walking backwards, Rabin watched his hard black flippers stamp parallel descending fans on the damp sand. He liked the tug of the weight belt, the first shock of the ocean at his ankles, the exact tingle of life.

Vikki was bent slightly forward as she rinsed out her mask with saliva and sea water, and her pose reminded him of the sprite, magically bare-breasted, on the soda bottles of his youth.

"You look like a sprite," said Rabin.

"And you look like a root beer."

Rabin laughed, telling himself that cultural allusions were not important and he was with her exactly because she had none of the complexity of the great comediennes.

They turned and looked upward to the sky's arched miles of blue. But their eyes couldn't stay away from the waves, forever the same, never the same.

He felt close to her again because they were loving the same thing at the same moment in the same way.

But now it was business and the nods they exchanged meant that they were ready to submerge.

She dove, and he followed a second later. The top of his head registered the chill as he entered a dimension where light and water were one, not light and air.

For a few seconds he hated the rubber taste and gasping sound of the regulator, but then he was a dolphin, happy to be home from the diaspora of the land. He was charmed and gladly hypnotized by undulation. Everything undulated—water, light, vegatation. She undulated. He undulated, his body free of chairs and posture.

He kept her in his view. Sight was a lifeline here. Rapture had to be blended with sobriety as carefully as the air in their tanks had been blended.

She pointed to something white half-buried in the sand, and they both dove down, thinking it was an abalone shell whose coloring sometimes struck a perfect balance between mother-of-pearl and Neptunian green. But it was a piece of a white plastic bleach bottle. She let that shard of the economy fall from her hand with such sorrowful disappointment that he would have put his arm around her shoulder if it had not been for the tank on her back.

But all that passed as quickly as anything else they passed or passed them. Fish glinted past, ideas in the mind of the sea. A large crab regarded him with the frank equality of one creature to another. The crab's absurd bravery made Rabin laugh a cloud of bubbles. She looked back at him inquisitively, but he shook his head to say it wasn't worth bothering about.

Suddenly he found himself at the outer edge of a vast school of finger-sized silver fish, striped an iridescent blue. The fish fled from the waves he made, but were just distancing themselves, not panicking for their lives. Rabin noticed that when he moved his right arm, the fish fled to the right, and to the left when he moved his left arm. Now, hovering in midwater, he let the school reform. There were tens of thousands of them and they glittered past the limits of visibility.

Arching his stomach like a porpoise, Rabin moved toward that galaxy of silver fish. Then, with a quick lurch he was in its center surrounded by silver fish fleeing left when he waved his left hand and fleeing right when he waved his right. He wove them in silver scarves around himself, conducting them like a submarine Toscanini!

He could see her face laughing through the mask as he emerged from his minnow symphony. Skirting a kelp forest, rubbery, iodine-brown, they swam out to deeper water. A jangle of adrenaline went through his body as it felt the tug of the depths.

But then in a crater lake of warm light she began to swim around him, first her thighs above him in the water, then her face looking over her shoulder at him from below. He dove down and past her to come up from beneath her, arching so that their chests almost touched. Now even time was only water to swim through.

Twilight came to the ocean, not all at once, but a little here, a little there, just as it does on land. They turned back.

Then, startlingly, he was waist deep near the shore, the tank on his back suddenly a burden. Another beautiful hour was gone. But there were more beautiful hours to come.

He built a fire, the sole outdoor skill he had acquired in California and of which he was quietly proud. After digging a pit in the sand, he surrounded it with stones and used the smaller pieces of driftwood that could be broken by hand or over his knee for kindling.

When the fire was going, Vikki took a bottle of red wine from her equipment bag.

He felt a touch of guilt for asking her to bring the wine.

"You shouldn't smoke," she said when, after a few tastes of the California Zinfandel, he lit up.

"The first cigarette after a dive is one of the best. You'll never know that. Even if you smoked, you wouldn't be a smoker."

"There's no such thing as a smoker. There's only people who smoke and kill themselves with cigarettes."

"But did you ever notice that whenever they discover some Stone Age tribe living in the jungle, if there's anything to smoke in the vicinity, people will be smoking it. Rolled anything leaves."

"I don't understand how a person can, like, consciously clog his own Prana."

"I'll just smoke one, just this one."

With a disbelieving look in her eye, she handed him a pocket sandwich filled with tahini.

"Do you like tahini?" she asked in a tone that suggested his probity was also being examined.

"I like it, I like it. It's not something I'd order, but I like it."

They ate in silence, enjoying the feel of the fire as it met the chill of the ocean still on their skin, and they passed the bottle of wine back and forth without quite looking at each other.

Then, when she held out the bottle to him, he moved over to her instead of extending his arm.

The first kiss was a long and complex code they made up as they went along, finally breaking it at the end when his tongue could no longer wait to read the braille on the roof of her mouth.

As they rose to their feet, he took the blanket by one corner and pulled it over them like a poncho. They stopped three times on their way to the cove they had both spotted earlier.

She was naked under her wet suit; he had a bathing suit under his, and removing it was the last act that bound him to the vulgar civility of pants.

After a confusion of knees, sand and blanket, after the bones

★   111

had located their ease, and trust had become a pleasure, they were together in another undulant ocean, another dimension where everything was exactly as she had said it would be. There was a bulb of glowing fire at the tip of his spine that suddenly leapt behind his navel spraying golden heat through his stomach. His heart was immediately grateful to her for that temperature, and no sooner had gratitude opened his heart than he spoke in tongues. At last his mind admitted that life was a glory.

But now some invisible dome of fear was preventing him from streaming through the stratosphere of higher mind. Far below, their swaying hips bellowed the fire that shot again from groin to heart to mind, and now he could feel the subtlest casing of his psyche being rent open, seeming to make an actual sound, not unlike that of an old pillowcase being torn in two: PffffffffffffffffffffffffffffffffffffffffffffffffffffffffffffffffffffffffffffffffffffffffT!

PART TWO

CHAPTER *11*

He was rising through a darkness heavier than water. Had Vikki and he gone in for another dive? Had they gone too deep and run out of air? Was he now rising through geologic plates of pressure, having to exhale all the way up so that his lungs didn't explode like balloons? The bends, he was going to get the bends!

Don't panic, don't panic now, you can panic later all you want.

Almost there, almost there. A round splash of light on the surface of the water. The moon. No, not the moon, a face looking down at him. Vikki, to the surface ahead of him, looking for him, her mask catching then losing the light as her head turned. Yards, only yards to go. He could make it. He could make it! He would even swim right to her face and give her a scuba kiss of mask and mouthpiece, in the joy of being alive.

But it wasn't her face! Some hideous magic had transformed her into a balding, big-eared, middle-aged man.

Oh my God. There had been a traffic accident on the way home. Of course, this was his punishment, and he deserved it. How long had he been in the coma—days, weeks, years? Was anybody killed? Were there any children in the other car?

★ 115

Yes, he could sense the violence of the impact, but could not recall it to mind.

The face of the doctor who was bending over him was smiling a little now. Did that mean he was all right? Did he have all his parts?

He closed his eyes and sent his awareness to his toes. Drawing consciousness slowly back up over him, he felt his feet, his ankles, skipped the hard-to-feel calves and shins and went right to his knees. The thighs were there as sheer bulk, the precious penis as a lazy tingle. His fingers played a little riff of jazz piano; then his mind was back in his head feeling his face, which did not seem maimed. Suddenly his attention was drawn back down again to a sting, faint yet distinct, in his right buttock.

What could that be? Did it matter? What mattered was that he was alive. What mattered was that he had done terrible things. Now it was his spirit that fell back into the darkness through which he had just struggled upward. He did not want to face the world, people, and the truth of his criminal human negligence. It was better in the darkness.

But the darkness didn't want him anymore. Now it was squeezing him up and out. Or maybe it was the life in him, which rushed to break the surface and bring him back to that face, the face of someone who belonged to the world: a doctor, a lawyer, a policeman. He was someone's case now.

He opened his eyes. The face was still there. Sadder, more concerned.

Then he had the eeriest certainty he had ever had. It had something to do with the shape of the nose on the face looking down at him. It had something to do with the pale blue of the sky in the window behind that face, and it had something to do with the curtains on that window. He knew he was in Russia.

A jolt went through his body.

The face above his seemed to be able to look into his face and read his thoughts. The face could speak to him directly without using words like a lover's face. The face told him that what he was thinking was true but not to worry.

Rabin wanted to speak. He wanted to be back where people talked. But he could not remember any words. They had all been knocked out of him the way your breath can be knocked out of you.

"Am I in Russia?" asked Rabin, his voice very soft.

"You're so brilliant, I can't stand it! Yes, of course, you're in Russia!" said the face, which was likeable when it was sad but frightening when happy.

"Who are you?" asked Rabin.

"Perhaps the one person in the entire world with a true and full appreciation of your gifts," said the face.

Rabin could not understand. There were too many words. The words made him want to go to sleep. But he had caught the tone. The tone was one of profound admiration. The admiration that he had been seeking all his life. The admiration that was recognition. At last, he had been recognized. Someone knew who he was.

But he didn't know who he was. The face knew who he was, but he didn't. He was just himself, the same self he had always been. He was just himself lying in a bed in a room that smelled faintly of Mercurochrome and starch. Except that it was in Russia.

Then all of his faculties locked in at once, and, except for a dizzying hangover of amnesia, he was back on the common ground.

Rabin sat up, an action which convinced him he did not want to do any more than that.

"Who are you?" he said, but this time with a finer sense of what that question meant.

"Poplavsky, Leonid Nikolaevich," said the face. "And this is a great honor for me."

"I'm sure," said Rabin. "What happened?"

"It's a little complicated. But perhaps you would like some breakfast first?"

"How long have I been here?"

"Not long, a few hours."

Somehow that was a relief.

"Yes. I'd like some breakfast," said Rabin, and his mouth clicked with saliva.

Poplavsky pushed a button. Something buzzed on the other side of the wall. The door opened. A hefty, older woman, her eyes slightly averted, appeared in the doorway; she carried a tray of encrusted, silver dishware. Poplavsky picked up the bed tray and placed it with a nurse's solicitude over Rabin.

The woman set the tray on top of the bed tray, then turned and left the room with an air of fear and disapproval.

Rabin lifted the cover of the main plate.

"Smoked fish, kasha, and salad for breakfast?" he said with invigorating repulsion, feeling exile in the stomach first.

"Call it lunch then," said Poplavsky. "It's half past three."

"Get it away from me. The smell's making me sick. I'll just keep the bread and the tea."

"Very sensible, very sensible. No cheese?"

"No."

"Fine, fine, I'll take it right away."

Poplavsky hurried to place the teapot, teacup, and plate of rye bread on Rabin's bed tray then scurried to a distant table with the remainder of the breakfast. Watching him, Rabin wondered why this man seemed ready to cater to his every wish when it was also quite clear that he was Poplavsky's prisoner.

Smoked fish and salad for breakfast!

Rabin poured the dark amber tea into his cup, its steam and aroma crisping his senses.

The bread was good, dark and sour, moist enough to eat without butter. Poplavsky sat down by the bed, taking a grandmotherly pleasure in watching Rabin eat. Rabin scowled. He had not liked that even when it had been his own grandmother doing it.

"So," said Rabin, speaking with his mouth full, "how did I get here?"

"I'm glad you asked how first. How is simple. A powerful and entirely safe drug, I assure you, was shot into the upper rear part of your right leg at a moment when you were experiencing maximum distraction."

"It's disgusting to watch people."

"I agree. But it was a sort of civil disobedience in reverse."

"Meaning?"

"Meaning that sometimes the higher law has to be broken for the good of society."

"But what about Vikki?"

"She was injected with a very mild version, effects lasting twenty minutes maximum. Then she wakes up groggy but happy, reads the note you left, and goes home."

"What note?"

"A very gentlemanly note expressing gratitude for memorable hours and other such sentiments. You can read it later if you like; we have a copy on file. And I think you'll be amazed by the reproduction of your handwriting."

"Then?"

"Then mostly boring and regular except for one interesting technological detail. You went on an Aeroflot flight, San Francisco to Moscow, over the pole, except that you weren't in the passenger compartment. You went into the cargohold with the diplomatic mail and then were placed in a special pressurized, padded container. I am told that, except for a little wobbliness of the legs and a certain dizziness of disorientation, you'll feel fit by tomorrow afternoon."

Poplavsky was right, thought Rabin. *How* was simple. *How* was a wagon going from one place to another. The complications came with the *why*. But Rabin was afraid to ask that question because the answer would also reveal the exact nature of his fate.

"And what about my job?"

"You hated it!"

"That's not the point."

"You resigned."

"I had money coming."

"It's being sent to Janey. She needs it."

"And what about Janey?"

"You called her."

"I called her?!"

"There's a machine we have called the Parrot. If you feed it enough tapes of someone's voice, it can stitch them together so fast that it sounds like they're talking. Sort of like what you have on your telephone information except much better. How it works, don't ask me. Technologically I am an infidel."

"What did she say?"

"Needless to say, she was very upset. Names were called."

"For example?"

"It's too personal."

"Oh, now it's too personal."

"You can hear the tapes."

"I want to know now."

"Please, don't make me; once was bad enough."

"You're right. I can see your point. But I know Janey. She won't be satisfied with a phone call. She'll want a confrontation. She'll come find me. But where does she think I am?"

"Mexico."

"Mexico? Doing what?"

"Traveling. Finally finishing your book. Reassessing your life. Drinking tequila."

Rabin saw that it could not be avoided any longer. He took a breath, closed his eyes for an instant, turned toward Poplavsky, and asked:

"Alright, why?"

"Where to begin, where to begin. Let's start with the Polish general. The one you thought had leaked the secret about our poetnaut, as your press called him. You were right. We checked. He confessed. Real confession, not the old kind."

"And what happened to him?"

"Nothing so terrible. Demoted, transferred, nothing."

"And what else?"

"What you said to your friend on the phone—that the Russian official caught in the FBI sting in the 128 area may have been set up by his own people. That was on target too."

Rabin paused for a moment to take in what Poplavsky had said, and saw that this was still not the real *why* itself.

"But exactly why?"

"It's difficult and even slightly embarrassing to say, but I will try because it is of extreme importance that you and I have a perfect understanding. To put it in the simplest way, I consider you the Einstein of history, the smartest Jew alive."

"Oh my God," exclaimed Rabin, "that's exactly how I think of myself."

"And you know how rare it is for a person to be seen the way he sees himself."

"I know but—"

"But this is not the way you imagined it happening. So what? The important thing is that your dream has come true. You wanted to be acknowledged as a great genius; you wanted to have a chance to influence the course of events. I acknowledge you. I give you that chance."

"What does that mean, the second part?"

"My plan is straightforward. I will go to the Politburo, tell them what I have, and ask for a chance to put your mind to work for us."

"And what makes you think I'll work for you?"

"Your very own intelligence."

Rabin didn't like the sound of that. "Yes?"

"I personally am upset by even thinking of the alternatives. For both of us."

"I see," said Rabin, his tone as neutral as possible.

"So, what do you think the Politburo's reaction will be?"

"They'll throw you right in the nuthouse!" barked Rabin without meaning to but having an instinctive need to answer attack with attack.

"Don't say that!"

Noticing a minute crescent-shaped scar just below the corner of Poplavsky's left eye, Rabin could not help wondering how he got it. "Does the Politburo know you're coming?"

"Not yet. Certain arrangements have to be made first. Some of them involve you."

Good, thought Rabin, the sooner this thing came to the Politburo's attention, the better. They were practical, sober-minded men and wouldn't want any part of it. And he had a better chance of being released by them than by this man whose opinion of him was both flattering and suffocating.

"What's the first step for me?" Rabin asked.

"The first step for you is to go to the department of Special Disinformation or, as we call it, SPETSDISINFORM. You have heard of it?"

"Yes."

"Under Stalin you wouldn't have! Under Stalin things happened that will never be known for the entire rest of time! That's what I call security."

"I'll finish my breakfast and then we'll go to SPETS-DISINFORM."

"Today? You don't want to rest?"

"No, I feel fine. Let's get on with it."

"Amazing recuperative powers!"

But as soon as Rabin's feet were on the cool floor, the darkness, which he had struggled out of earlier, claimed him again, blackening the blood in his brain.

"Tomorrow, tomorrow," said Poplavsky, swinging Rabin's legs back onto the bed. "Tomorrow is time enough."

Dreaming a memory, Rabin was in his hospital crib after his tonsils had been taken out. The smell of ether went from his nostrils to the roof of his mouth, and there was a patch of soreness at the back of his throat. Without even trying, he knew he couldn't talk. For the first time in his life, he chose to think. He thought of great adventures: jungle safaris; himself in a diving suit and helmet searching for treasure on the ocean floor. Then his parents came in the door, both wearing hats and smiling with happiness and love. They had brought him vanilla ice cream to soothe his throat and make him happy, too. Ooooo, vanilla ice cream soothing his throat. Ooooo . . .

When he awoke the next morning, he did not even remember where he was because the feeling of the light on his eyes was so beautiful. Light and air, God was only light and air. We were wrong to give God so many attributes; God was only light and air.

But as soon as the door clicked, he remembered everything, and his mind was again lit by fear that came on like a yellow gas flame.

Poplavsky was just a touch brisker that morning, a man with appointments pretending he has no other interest but you.

Rabin was ready to get going too.

"You will find your jeans and shirt freshly laundered in the wardrobe," said Poplavsky. "But at some point, you may have to wear a suit. You should pay special attention to people's suits here. To you Americans all Negroes and all Russian suits look alike. I don't know about Negroes but I do know about Russian suits. The differences are very subtle. You have to pay close attention. I can tell an alcoholic collective-farm chairman just by his cuffs."

Aha, thought Rabin, now he's talking to me like we're already a team. His spirits were bouyed by the old familiar feeling of pulling on pants, buttoning a shirt and tucking it in.

"Do you think I can start getting some coffee? I only drink tea in Chinese restaurants," said Rabin breezily as they went out the door. He hoped the comment would remind Poplavsky that he, Rabin, was the genius, and that Poplavsky's hopes and fate were riding on him and not vice versa. And apparently Poplavsky had gotten the message, because he did not allow the chauffeur to open the door for Rabin but insisted on doing it personally. The small limo was in a courtyard of dark brick, several stories high. Grey metal stairs went up to grey metal doors. A man in a blue uniform came out of one door high up, and for a moment Rabin and he were aware of each other.

The windows in the rear of the limo were tinted a very dark blue, and Rabin could see nothing through them. The barrier separating them from the driver was the same dark blue.

"Why can't we see out?"

"This limo is for prisoners, I should say detainees, of the very highest level."

"But still why can't they see out?"

"If they see something that's good for them, that could be bad for us. If they see something that's bad for them, that could be bad for us, too, because we're trying to keep them in the best possible condition. As long as they're on that level, of course."

The highest level of prisoner rides in limos but is not allowed to see out, thought Rabin. Very Russian, very codified. What an education it would be if only he survived!

Since he couldn't see anything, Rabin summoned up images from other trips to Russia. A drunk pissing into the chrysanthemums from the broad, palatial, stone steps of a Black Sea health resort, at night, under a southern moon. The power of Russian eyes. The intensity of those eyes seen from an escalator descending into the Moscow subway. His friend Tanya crying as they said farewell. The tears splashing over her cheekbones and running down her face. Even her throat was wet with tears!

"We're here," said Poplavsky.

Rabin detected a note of worry in that voice and felt a second's worth of sympathy for Poplavsky.

Very small, this courtyard was made of yellow brick and seemed to be part of an annex to a building. They went directly to an elevator, which Rabin thought rather large for one that only went up four floors.

"We'll be meeting with the head of SPETSDISINFORM, Ivan Lunin, in his consultation room. A very interesting man. Very intelligent. I am certain you will enjoy your conversation with him."

The corridor was long and a whitish blue. Poplavsky seemed to be hurrying. Were they late? Or was it that he didn't want them to be seen?

"He also loves Jews," said Poplavsky in a confidential and reassuring whisper as he ushered Eliot Rabin into a good-sized office furnished in Scandinavian tan wood, glass, and steel.

Impulsively, Poplavsky strode right over to Ivan Lunin before the head of SPETSDISINFORM had even come out from behind his desk. They hugged and kissed, and Rabin thought he heard the expression "so many summers, so many winters" that Russians use when they haven't seen each other in a long time.

Although his taste in furniture ran to the modern, Ivan Lunin cultivated a vaguely nineteenth-century image and manner. He had a neat goatee and eyes that flashed with a doctorly sharpness behind glasses that could just as easily have been pince-nez.

Rabin didn't like the moment when those eyes were inspecting him.

"It is my honor to introduce Professor Eliot Rabin. Professor Rabin, this is Lunin."

Rabin shook Lunin's surprisingly springy hand and muttered the customary, "A great pleasure."

Now Rabin could see that Lunin's brushed-back hair was

greying but just at the tips. He judged him to be intelligent, as Poplavsky had said, but less well-disposed to him, of course, than Poplavsky.

"I have many things that need doing, and I'm sure the two of you can manage very well on your own," said Poplavsky smiling at his two friends.

"I'm sure we can," said Lunin, "and I'm sure you have plenty to do."

At that instant Rabin caught a whiff of the career politics that had to be involved in all this. The two men were allies and, by definition, their goal couldn't be to seize positions of less power.

Poplavsky left. Rabin and Lunin took seats around a glass table, and various offers were made—cigarettes, coffee, tea, something stronger?

"I'd like coffee with a little milk. And what kind of cigarettes do you have?"

"Anything. Kents."

"I hate Kents. How come they have Kents all over Europe?"

"We have Marlboro, but only soft pack. I have the suspicion that when the Americans are angry at us, they don't send us as many flip-tops."

"Marlboros would be fine."

Rabin hoped that the coffee and cigarettes would appear with magic totalitarian ease, but they didn't, and in the meantime it was diffficult to talk to that man who, Rabin knew, saw him mostly as a case and a chance.

"Don't worry, the coffee will be right along. So . . . ," said Lunin.

"So, I'm here," said Rabin.

"Yes, I can see. Very daring on Leonid's part, I must say. I only hope he has made the right move. He always has. Do you mind if I ask you a few questions?"

"No, but I could answer them better after some coffee."

"I'll keep them simple, yes or no questions. For example, do you know what Leonid thinks of you?"

"Yes."

"Do you agree?"

"Yes."

"Do you know what his plans are?"

"Vaguely."

"But are you willing in principle to help him?"

"Yes."

Rabin knew the politics of yes and no, the difference between the yes that was the truth and the yes that saved your ass.

He caught a glint in Lunin's eye that seemed to say, Of course, you're lying to some degree and that's good. Of course, of course, lie to us, but do it in the right way, so that we know where we stand.

"Aha, the coffee," said Lunin, rising.

Rabin watched as Lunin went to the door to get the tray. Lunin didn't want to be seen with him either. So far, Rabin had been seen only by two people: the woman who brought him the horrible breakfast and the man who came out of the door in the courtyard; the chauffeur probably hadn't gotten a real look at him. It made him feel unsubstantial, transparent, like a jellyfish in clear water.

Then, for a minute, Rabin was not in Moscow but in the world of coffee and cigarettes, which was the very taste of existence to him. Except that the coffee was a little thicker than he would have liked, and the milk tasted of foreign cows, which in turn may have affected the flavor of the Marlboro he lit after the first three or four sips.

Still, fairly quickly, he could feel the focusing effect. Now he was not only conscious but had his wits about him.

He offered Lunin a cigarette.

"No, I gave it up," said Lunin with a melancholy but resolute shake of the head. "And I'll tell you, health is a poor substitute."

"I know, I'll probably have to give them up one day, too," said Rabin with a certain sociable warmth, realizing it was inevitable that he and Lunin find some common ground, but also warning himself not to get too close to Lunin on that common ground either.

"I believe that quitting smoking is entirely a function of the degree to which we have realized our own mortality," said Lunin who seemed glad to begin a real talk.

"So you say it's automatic?"

"In a sense. Like taking your hand off a hot stove. Except on a more abstract level. But every bit as real."

Was that a philosophical concept, Rabin wondered, or a threat? Or both? Was he being reminded of his own mortality, of how easily his life could be terminated in some sub-basement? After all, no one even knew he was there.

"Though my background is more scientific than artistic," said Lunin, "I think that art has a major role in real life. So much of everything is invented, imagined. Which brings us to the subject of your life in Mexico."

"What about it?"

"I mean, it's a tabula rasa, a blank canvas. My department is in charge of creating the legend of you in Mexico. I wouldn't want your life to take any form you might find offensive, and so that is why I am requesting your cooperation in this very interesting and unique venture."

"Look," said Rabin, "I'm perfectly willing to help Poplavsky. But I don't want anything to do with that Mexico business."

"But why not?"

"It's not my life."

"Who else's is it?"

"Then have me killed there. There's plenty of things to be killed by in Mexico—earthquakes, scorpions, banditos, whatever you like; just get it over with."

"That's criminal; it's so brutal. It's like an abortion of the imagination. Just think of the possibilities. You could have a love affair with a divorcée who has a little drinking problem and is studying art in San Miguel Allende where you spent a few months, when was it? '73? '74? Or, even better, how about a radical Mexican folk singer with beautiful black braids and a terrific temper!"

"I'm not immune to the attraction, but I find the entire exercise basically disgusting. I prefer a fictional death to a fictional life."

"There is something attractive about a tragic early death," said Lunin pensively. "You're spared all the indignities of the old age, failing eyesight, lack of bladder control, all the funerals. And, to tell you the truth, I'd prefer that myself. I mean fictionally, of course. In reality, I intend to hang on as long as I can."

"On second thought," said Rabin, "maybe you better keep me alive for a while. I don't want people grieving over me, though they might as well."

"Have you been to Oaxaca?"

"No."

"It's supposed to be absolutely beautiful. But for the sake of a little humor and realism, your postcards could make reference to Montezuma's revenge just so your friends won't envy you too much."

Oddly, that remark made Rabin very sad. Suddenly, he missed the envy of friends, that sharp pimento in the salad.

"Yes, friends can be envious, and envied," said Rabin.

"But before you absolutely close your mind to the question, take a look at these," said Lunin, leaning back from his desk as he opened a drawer. He handed Rabin a stack of postcards. Flamingoes in flight, pink as cotton candy. Aztec stone calendars. White beaches. Pastel adobe cathedrals. Indian eyes, obsidian. "So, just imagine yourself in a little room here, drinking a nice bottle of Dos Equis, eating a burrito which our institute has stocked in its freezer, and listening to a record of mariachi music while dashing off postcards to friends, family, and former lovers. An extraordinary opportunity in itself. What man hasn't dreamed of living two lives? In fact, you were living two at the moment Poplavsky picked you up. So, this would just be a continuation of what you were already doing."

It had a certain bizarre metaphysical tang to it that appealed to him. And he definitely disliked the idea of having his postcards written by them—them; of having them attribute thoughts and sentiments to him, which, by definition, could be no more than a crude parody.

"No," said Rabin with a sigh. "I'm a prisoner. And a prisoner has certain rights, and a certain dignity that only prisoners can have. And that is proven by the fact that no one expects a prisoner to cooperate voluntarily.

"But I'm surprised that you have rejected an opportunity to exercise your free will."

"But the choice was not of my making."

"When is it ever?"

"Still."

"We can manage perfectly well without you. This was a courtesy we were extending to you."

"Yes. I understand. Thank you."

There was really nothing left to be said, and Rabin filled the vacuum by lighting another cigarette. Who knew? They might decide to take the cigarettes away.

Exhaling upward and to the left, Rabin found himself studying Lunin's suit for a second. Dark blue, almost to the point of black, it was much like Poplavsky's, except for a slight sheen in the material of Lunin's, which seemed to bespeak both a certain moral uncleanliness and a weakness of character, neither of which were present in Poplavsky or his suit. It was not an entirely honest suit. It had a hint of an allegiance to the illusory and the perverse. What! thought Rabin. Was he becoming a Soviet suitologist?

A quick knock preceded Poplavsky's entrance.

"Well, and so?" he asked, smiling broadly.

"Professor Rabin prefers that we handle this matter ourselves," said Lunin in a tone whose very neutrality expressed its disappointment.

The look of worry that softened Poplavsky's face was the most frightening expression Rabin had seen on it yet.

CHAPTER *12*

At the last minute the countdown had been delayed.

Arthur Blaine had hoped that he would be torn from earth like bandaging off a forearm: One quick shriek and it's over. But the bandaging was being pulled off very slowly, and he was feeling every hair plucked by its nerve root.

Worse than that was the fact that all this empty time made a perfect vat for the containment of dread. And there was no way that he could tell himself that the dread was merely the product of fearful imagination. It was not. It was the real thing, because in a matter of minutes he would either be blasted out of this world or out of existence altogether.

Blaine had been close to death before: a swerving car, an undertow, twenty seconds of passionate confusion. But he had never had the experience of being seated on the rim of obliteration.

He looked at the three others he could see. Each helmet was like a bionic mollusk shell, hard globes gleaming with the perfection that comes only from technology, never from nature.

Blaine thrashed for an instant in his chair, bound — arm, leg, and chest — by straps that would be released automatically when the *Conestoga I* had broken free of earth's gravity.

He thrashed because he had just realized that the sensation he was now experiencing, some rapid molecular disintegration of the very self, had not begun when he boarded the craft and had his first keen inkling of extinction. No, it had begun precisely when he looked out his front window on Marlborough Street and seen the two men in business suits coming up the front walk. At that instant he had been pierced by a fine two-pronged intuition of danger. And, he now realized, he had only been wrong about the details. He had known instinctively that those two men were coming to see him, and that they were none other than Vincent and Glass, the fiendish destroyers who called themselves developers. Their briefcases undoubtedly contained contracts, agreements, waivers, provisos, all written in that insane form of English which, by some magic, lost more meaning the closer you read it. They wanted him out. He was an impediment to the health of the golden calf of the economy whose rectal temperature was held up before the nation each day in the form of the Dow-Jones average. For the first time in his life he felt a passionate impulse simply to be done with the whole goddam thing and, had there been a pistol handy, he might even have blown his brains out before his fingers had the common sense to mutiny.

But, trained to respond to certain bell signals, Blaine was immediately snapped from his suicidal trance by the brisk, manly ring of his own doorbell. It was a ring that said serious men have come calling on you, men who are forceful but not unpleasantly aggressive unless, of course, forced to get ugly. A ring that expressed an adult certainty about life that would have no truck with immature nonsense. Was he going to end up like one of those little old ladies on the evening news, sitting in her rocker on her front porch with a .22, refusing to let the new interstate go through her living room?

134   ★

But it had not been Vincent and Glass; it had been Adams and Bourke. The two nicest guys you ever met. Adams was more the All-American kid, from some town that continued to turn out Jack Armstrongs for a dwindling market. Bourke was a little more subdued, perhaps as a result of lifelong complexion problems. And instead of telling Blaine that he was a real-estate orphan, they informed him that he had won the Apollo Prize and was invited to the White House to be awarded the medal itself by the President himself.

Now, strapped and trapped, he understood that Adams and Bourke were simply Vincent and Glass operating on another level. Vincent and Glass were physical demons, in charge of violating the living architecture of the city, but Adams and Bourke were devils of a higher order. They were responsible for destroying the very architecture of the self. They didn't even know what they were doing! Clean-cut angels, they thought they were the bearers of glad tidings!

Then, at a speed even faster than that of light, Blaine's despair turned to a wild, exhilarating hope. This was only the death of an old soul to make room for the birth of another. The birth of the full poet in him, who would speak to all mankind from another world, his iambic pentameters pulsing through the void's glinting dust, through heavenly cumulus cities, through an ocean of blue air with oxygen enough for billions of creatures to breathe all at once, his words finally entering the ears and minds of human beings, to reemerge on their lips as common expressions.

Yes, but perhaps he had disgraced himself too unutterably. For there was no mistaking the taste of disgrace, like globules of cheap fat in his bloodstream. How did he lose his integrity? How could he get it back? Should he trace the route of the error? Or was that just a continuation of the error? His mind responded to that barrage of questions by supplying him with a quick exact sense memory — drinking fresh-squeezed orange juice during his whirlwind television tour. He remembered wondering at the time why New Yorkers were so fond of fresh-squeezed orange juice. Was it their cells crying out for the vitamins that are also present in sunlight and which in Manhattan had proved expendable in the name of vertical growth? But why was his mind supplying him with a pulpy, orange, citric memory when it should have been seeking answers to the questions it had just been asked?

He had a moment of shame as he realized how far he had strayed from the path of the poet. Like the dreaming self, the poet thought in living images and not with geodesic modules of logic. His soul had given him the answer, and he was so out of tune with himself that he could not understand the message. He was caught in a crazy updraft carbonated with infinite questions. Everything became a question. Now he had to ask himself what he meant by what he thought, and whether the memory of the orange juice was in fact a profound symbol or yet another sign of a mind going berserk.

Or could all this be the effect of sitting perpendicular to reality? Was the blood moving in a slow tide across his brain, enriching areas that had long lain dormant? Was this the hidden family madness drinking his brain-blood like a vampire? He had to get level, he had to be on an even keel!

Then a voice which sounded like a robot cleverly supplied with a slight southwestern accent, said into the receiver in Arthur Blaine's helmet: "We have countdown."

A sacramental pause was followed by an irksome squall of static, a foretaste, he felt, of the entire enterprise.

"Ten," said the voice of NASA.

Suddenly, Blaine was in two time dimensions at once. In one, seconds were counted like pennies. In the other, time was as thin as the air is to a man who has just departed a window ledge. Blaine was falling through a bright void where symbols opened above him like gaudy parachutes. Now he understood why Paris shimmered. Because there was no reality left in the world. Reality was no more present than God was present in any cathedral. And now he, too, was shimmering.

"Nine," said the voice of NASA.

Ich bin der Geist der stets verneint. The only line of Goethe's *Faust* he knew in German had chimed into mind. But it was true! It was all a brief imperfection in Nothingness. Every infant was doomed to extinction, every leaf on every tree, every word, was lost. Consciousness was both a pretension and the punishment for that pretension.

"Eight."

But to believe that life was nothing was the greatest sin of all. And one that made all the others easy. How had he fallen so low, so swiftly? It had been fame, fame which was swift no matter how long you have been waiting for it, fame, swift by its very nature. It had propelled him around the nation like a jet pack. To Washington, all gossip and power; to honk-honk Manhattan, hawking stocks and superlatives; to Los Angeles, glitzy with skin cancer; to luncheons packed with admiring middle-aged ladies and dozing husbands; to television makeup rooms where fawning cosmeticians clipped his nose hairs; to the talk shows where they once broke for a Subaru ad before Blaine, who was reciting the invocation to his prize-winning poem, had time to quite reach the end, which meant that the visionary clincher would have to wait until the host reintroduced him for viewers who might have just tuned in.

He had forsaken the dignity of his calling. He had played by their rules, played their game, the American game of TV, success, new products.

Now the mystery of the Juicer was revealed to him. Of course, of course, of course. It was a profound symbol, and his mind had been right to use it. America was the Great Juicer. And he was just another fresh orange rolling down the belt. And he had been juiced. Juiced!

"Seven."

But was there not some great, strange luck in his being strapped to that blue-padded chair on his way to the moon where something so uncommon awaited him that he knew it could only be the vision he had thirsted for and the redemption he now so sorely needed. A lunar redemption! What brilliant and amazing luck!

"Six."

And sex was the only weightlessness we knew on earth, the weightlessness people had been seeking all through history, as if gravity were one of the punishments for Original Sin.

"Five."

Blaine looked over at the three others he could see. One of them moved his head slightly, his visor diffusing a patch of light. In a way, this was just another human experience; in something that was only a more powerful version of a jumbo jet; it was occurring in the presence of other people with their own lives, memories, personalities, and metabolism-scented breath. It was happening in Florida, on a Wednesday. But were there Wednesdays on the moon?

"Four."

The moon has its own days. They should have their own

names. He would name them, an Adam walking in a garden of craters.

"Three."

Now the seconds were once again quick measures of real time leading to a real event. Space flight, or space tragedy. Life or death. The funnel had narrowed to that. No room for any other possibilities. Only two now.

"Two," said the voice of NASA, as if their minds were one. But of course their minds were one. Their will and intent were one, and the rocket was a single vertical numeral, a—"

"One."

Blaine felt the shock wave through the immense cylinder at his back. Pressure Mongoloidized his face, and then there was no room in his mind for anything but the roaring.

CHAPTER 13

"Why wouldn't you cooperate, if only as a sign of solidarity?" asked Poplavsky.

"I didn't want to be involved in unreality when I'm feeling unreal enough as it is, if you follow me, Leonid."

"I follow you."

"So, you see, it has nothing to do with our working together."

"But it creates a certain general shakiness in the situation."

"Well, one sure sign of reality is that it's not what you would have wanted."

"That's true. Speaking of reality, you should know that tomorrow we go to the Kremlin."

"Tomorrow? What time?"

"Eight o'clock."

"I'm practically comatose at eight o'clock, let alone brilliant, and you can't even get coffee that tastes right in this country."

"See," said Poplavsky with a smile that was both warm and sad. "Reality again."

And it seemed like only a few seconds later that Poplavsky was shaking his shoulder and saying: "Time to get up, time to get up."

There was a slightly singed aroma of coffee in the air. Eliot Rabin unglued his eyes, blinking to dampen them for clearer sight, until once again they beheld that round and deeply homely face, that Slavic moon.

Drink me black, said the coffee, and Rabin, who usually took a little milk, realized it was a good idea. His brain would have to be pounding with blood that morning. Of course, he was a genius, but that didn't mean he was a perfect genius, or that he could always think of everything right on the spot. The real problem was that he could only give a brilliant answer to a brilliant questioner. At least Poplavsky had a sort of metaphysical *kopf*, that was part of his problem.

Still, unreal as it all seemed, Rabin's predicament did satisfy his first criterion of reality — that it not be the way you would have wanted. Reality reveals that we swim in a liquid of wishes.

But, as Poplavsky had put it, Rabin's stated desires were for respect and influence, and he was now being offered both in grand measure. So that meant reality sometimes was the way you wanted it to be, and your life became a wish come true.

In other words, thought Rabin, reality is not only not the way you would have liked it to be, when it is, it still isn't.

Rabin felt Poplavsky's eyes on him. Those eyes were chillier now, evaluating more than enjoying.

"We should be going," said Poplavsky.

There was no one in the corridor or in the courtyard, and Rabin could not help but wonder whether that was due to the early hour or whether Poplavsky had issued strict instructions as to his invisibility that day. It was unsettling to be so unseen.

But entering the small limo this time, Rabin caught a glimpse of the back of the driver's neck, which was clipped almost all the way up to his cap. It reminded him of Eisenstein movies, necks awaiting the axe.

Knowing it was stupid and utterly involuntary, Rabin rubbed the side of his own neck.

"Don't say anything unless someone asks you something," said Poplavsky who seemed concentrated elsewhere that morning.

"Who are we going to see?" asked Rabin.

"The General Secretary and anyone else he thinks should be there."

"Well, the head of the KGB will be there, won't he?"

"Why do you say that?"

"You must want his job, don't you?"

"How do you deduce that?" asked Poplavsky.

"You're making a move and in the universe of career there are only two directions — up and down. You were running things in America, so you were pretty high up already. And there's a couple of things that are pretty clear about you right away, Leonid. One is that you're very Russian, the other is that you're very KGB. And so that means you want to be home in Russia and you want a high, active position in the KGB. And I don't think you would have risked this whole business for a number two position."

"Very nice thinking."

"Thank you."

"And I fully intend to triumph, you should know."

"Well, listen, good luck."

But did he mean it? Did he really wish Poplavsky good luck? He still thought the best thing would be for the Politburo to take one look at the whole thing, pack Poplavsky off to a madhouse, and put him on the next plane out. They could have him back in San Francisco in less than a day, and there wasn't a chance in the world that anyone would believe his story. It was strictly the stuff of check-out stand tabloids, and, at best, would be seen as a pathetic cry for self-importance by a scholar who had gone off the deep end. His friends would say that Rabin had been very disturbed by his failure to achieve tenure. Howard would cry, and disown him. Janey would take him back. But what about the handwriting on the note to her, it could be shown to be a forgery. Ah yes, but could it be shown to be a KGB forgery, and not something a buddy whipped up for Rabin over a beer?

If Poplavsky's luck was good and he became the head of the KGB, Rabin would never get out of there. He'd be locked in that bear hug for the rest of his life!

It was sad in a way. Only one person in the world had ever really displayed a deep and accurate admiration for his genius, and Rabin had to betray him for the sake of survival. Once again the paradoxicalness of reality was revealed in all its deranging splendor.

"Here we are, right on time," said Poplavsky as the limo came to a springy halt. "I just wish the suit I ordered for you had been ready."

This courtyard was of green-blue brick, a lovely, some-how Old-Russian color.

Rabin had to admire the first two guards at the gate. So vigilant, so quick to become a barrier, pure attention, not a scrap of personality. Nor did they see you as a person, but as an identity to be committed to memory.

Poplavsky presented his papers, which were checked and returned.

The guard who took the papers turned to Rabin without saying a word; the demand itself was so obvious.

"He has no papers," said Poplavsky.

"I have a California driver's license," said Rabin.

"I remind you not to speak," said Poplavsky.

The guard now seemed slightly indignant in the way that only servants in a good house can be.

"My orders are to check the papers of every person entering here, without exception, Comrade Colonel," said the guard.

"Leonid, may I say something?" asked Rabin.

"Will it help?"

"Yes."

"Alright."

"Look," said Rabin to the guard, "I'm an American. We have our own kinds of documents. For example, this is a driver's license issued by the state of California, which is sort of an autonomous republic with beaches and Hollywood. And this is what we call a Sears card. With this card, I can walk into any Sears store in the entire United States of America — and there must be hundreds of them — and I can buy refrigerators, air conditioners, color TVs, Ping-Pong tables, and sofas, day or night," said Rabin feeling slightly guilty since he was well aware that his Sears card was far over the limit and would probably be confiscated if he tried to purchase anything larger than a hair dryer.

The guard took the two plastic rectangles and held them with a certain obvious respect and curiosity. He glanced from the face on Rabin's driver's license, going from the thumbnail-size technicolor image of Rabin to the full living face, each with a dark goatee and a scowl at being distracted from distraction.

Apparently, the Sears card was of more interest, mysterious in its space-age simplicity, and containing, like some wondrous economic microchip, the stored ability to buy and buy and buy.

"You may pass," said the guard, handing Rabin back his California driver's license and Sears card, souvenirs of another universe now.

"How could you forget that I would need some sort of papers, Leonid? You're in the check-your-papers business."

"I am reminding you that from this moment on, please do not speak on your own accord any longer."

Stifling an urge to point out the idiocy of that arrangement, Rabin preceded Poplavsky into a room that was dark except for a faint light around the baseboards. Machines whirred behind the wall. Rabin had the same feeling as when a dentist left him alone to x-ray a tooth from the next room.

Something that was clearly an "all right" signal sounded, and a door opened at the far end of the room, revealing a lit corridor, the entrance to which was blocked by two more guards.

Poplavsky's papers were checked and returned.

Rabin got out his license and Sears card again.

This guard took the cards but looked at them with much less curiosity. Cards still in hand, he walked to a small table on which there was a telephone and several color-coded clipboards. He picked up one of the clipboards, read what it had to say, and returned to Rabin, handing him the cards.

"I'm sorry, Comrade Colonel. According to my orders, in lieu of an American passport, I must see two forms of identification, one of which has to be a major credit card."

"Sears is not considered major?" asked Poplavsky.

"Not according to my list."

"Perhaps the list needs updating," said Poplavsky with a

sarcasm he knew to be useless, because the guard could do nothing but obey orders.

"May I say something?" said Rabin.

"Will it help?"

"I think so."

"Alright."

Rabin reached for his wallet and handed the guard his MasterCard, which had expired and had not been renewed due to irregularity of payment. "I think this should do it."

The guard took the slightly unclean, since unused, MasterCard and went back to the table with the clipboards.

"This is a valid second form of identification," said the guard, "but it has expired."

"What difference does that make? I'm not trying to charge anything," said Rabin.

"But the card loses its validity as identification when it expires," said the guard.

"That's one way of looking at it," said Rabin, "But it also acquires a new and different value."

"What's that?" said the guard.

"It now has the authority of a historical document. If someone had a copy of one of the earliest editions of *Pravda*, would you sneer and say it had no value because it's not to-day's paper? No, you would show proper reverence for that historical document, which is of even greater significance than today's issue of *Pravda*, which is cheap and plentiful. Isn't that so? And we do have an appointment with the General Secretary."

"I will make a call," said the guard, which was also an order not to move. He went to the desk and spoke on the phone very quietly with his back turned to Rabin and Poplavsky. Rabin thought he could catch the word *expired*.

Could you smoke there? Rabin wondered, but then decided not to ask. He sympathized with the guard who was in a very tricky position. They were inside; they had passed the first checkpoint; they clearly had an appointment, and one of them was clearly an important KGB official who would probably not be in the company of the wrong American. But, apparently, not many Americans came through that entrance. Still, just on the off chance that one might, instructions had been issued that were detailed and specific as instructions must always be. Having foreseen that an American entering the Kremlin through this passage might not be traveling on his passport, they had provided for alternative forms of identification. No doubt, they had chosen the forms of identification most common in America, which of course made good sense, except for those Americans with a poor credit rating like Eliot Rabin.

Dammit, if he had only kept up his payments they'd be in there with the General Secretary already!

But, as always, what counted was the cash of reality. Rabin could tell by the guard's face, perfectly blank though it might be, that an exception had been granted. Or maybe it was in the air, the aroma of approval.

"You will be received this morning in the New Room. I will show you the way."

They walked down a green-carpeted white corridor, which had a seventeenth-century feel to it.

As soon as the door was opened for them, Rabin could feel Poplavsky wince. It took him a second to realize why. There were only two men seated at the small oak table — the General Secretary and the head of the KGB, Edov. Rabin had never seen Edov on television and so knew him only from the airbrush and formaldehyde portraits issued by the Soviet press.

Edov had grey hair, combed straight back, and wore glasses with thick black plastic rims; he had the face of a man who made a point never to show it. His suit was a plain well-worn blue. Rabin felt as if he were walking into a circus cage where the great tamer and a tiger were already waiting. Poplavsky was the lion, and he, Rabin, some innocent tid-bit to stimulate their bloodlust.

Vigorous, neutral, amused, the General Secretary welcomed them with a nod of the head, which also indicated they should be seated. Poplavsky was to sit across from Edov, and Rabin at the long end facing the General Secretary.

The General Secretary took off his glasses and rubbed them with his napkin, using only a slight upward head motion and his eyes to point to the silver tray at the center of the table. The tray contained a pitcher of old-fashioned, black Russian tea and instant coffee in a curlicued silver holder, which Rabin guessed to have been commissioned by Catherine the Great or one of those other extravagant czarinas who mothered Russia a little after all Peter the Great's rough stuff.

Now Rabin became aware of the political meaning hidden in the choice. Old Russian tea could be a sign of your allegiance to the true Russia, but it could also signify insufficiently up-to-date tastes; the modern man, the man who would own all the tomorrows, would prefer instant coffee simply because it tasted of the future.

Rabin looked to see what Edov and the General Secretary were drinking, but they had both raised their cups the second before, a step ahead of him.

Poplavsky took tea as if to say, "Tea is what I want, and I take what I want." The General Secretary and Edov both registered the gesture but were waiting for something more than gestures to be impressed.

Now Rabin could feel the General Secretary's eyes and Edov's attention on him.

"Real tea is better than fake coffee," said Rabin in good Russian, making it sound almost like a folk saying. The General Secretary laughed to let Rabin know first that he was intelligent enough to appreciate the remark and, second, that he had in fact appreciated the remark.

Though Poplavsky had not turned in Rabin's direction yet, Rabin could feel silent imperatives streaming from him.

Having spoken somehow allowed Rabin to focus clearly on the General Secretary. And what Rabin saw was the Grand Duke of Muscovy in a business suit, the sadness of eyeglasses.

The General Secretary had allowed them a moment of ease and refreshment, but running one-sixth of the world was a demanding occupation, and it was time to get down to business: "If Comrade Poplavsky would state his case."

Poplavsky turned to face his leader and his back seemed impenetrable and menacing to Rabin now.

"This man is the Einstein of history. He is what Marx would have been if he had lived in the late twentieth century. His can be a powerful light in helping guide the ship of state. I offer him to you as a contribution and as proof that I have both the vision and the daring to lead state security into the next century."

By his expression, Rabin gauged the General Secretary to be interested though not wildly taken. "Can such a thing be?"

"There was such a thing as Einstein; there was such a thing as Marx," replied Poplavsky in the rapid monotone of catechism.

Edov moved back perhaps four degrees. Rabin caught that and knew that as of that minute Poplavsky was ahead.

Rabin wondered whether he should do something to disgrace Poplavsky. But somehow he couldn't. Somehow he was caught in the spell of that room, its slow magnetic whirlpool of liquid mineral.

It was only then that Rabin realized it was all going to be over very, very quickly. He had always assumed that his fate, if it ever came to that, would be decided with great and grave deliberation, and now he realized it would be all over in a matter of seconds. Because Poplavsky had stated his case, he had nothing else to say. Edov had been knocked back a few degrees but only a few. Now the room filled with the General Secretary's power, which would decide the fates of Poplavsky, Rabin, and Edov, all in one stroke. That power was dizzying, like a woman who is so much more beautiful then other women or a man who is so much richer than other men.

The General Secretary looked past both Poplavsky and Edov to Rabin.

"In principle I accept the possibility that such a thing as an Einstein of history could exist. But I am also a practical man. I will give you an opportunity to convince me."

Here it comes, thought Rabin.

"Since I have assumed the leadership," said the General Secretary with a tone that was not entirely free of selfcaressment, "I have had the same dream three times. The dream has something to do with Soviet history, and not only because it was dreamed by the leader of the Soviet Union. The dream preys on my mind. So, I will tell you the dream. If you can interpret it in a way that helps me, you will win both my gratitude and my belief in your mental powers. Are you willing?"

Could you say no? "Yes."

"The dream is simple. It's May Day. I'm reviewing the

troops and the marchers from on top of Lenin's tomb. Then a wizard who looks like Ayatollah Khomeini rises up against me, and the people follow him because of the magic word he says."

The General Secretary paused for a moment as if needing to gather just a bit of courage to continue.

"And that magic word, which is both a rallying cry and a curse, is . . . *Ushassar!*"

"Ushassar?" said Rabin to make sure he had it right.

"That's how he pronounced it," said the General Secretary, clearly not wishing to say it aloud a second time.

Ushassar, thought Rabin; it sounded Middle Eastern, very ancient, very Ur. So, it fit that it was coming out of Khomeini's mouth, but did it have something to do with the growing Islamic population in the Soviet Union? A fear of Islamization from within? But that was the wrong level of interpretation. All that mattered was the word itself. Ushassar. And it was hard to think his best in a room full of killers.

Suddenly, Rabin felt a distant synapse fire, and, to his horror, knew that he had the answer, but that it had gotten lodged en route, like the name of some movie star it takes a week to remember.

"I think I just got the answer," said Rabin, "but it's going to take a little while to work its way up."

"I will issue instructions that, as soon as it does work its way up, you are to be brought to me at once. In the meantime, I have not seen any reason to engage in any major rearrangements. So, until there is significant change in the situation, I will view this as a state security and not a political matter."

In plain English, thought Rabin, they were screwed.

"In my opinion, Comrade General Secretary," said Edov

who had not said a word yet, his voice reedier than Rabin would have expected, "this is a matter for our mental health unit."

"You could be right," said the General Secretary, leaning back and now regarding Rabin and Poplavsky with new eyes. "I would think the Gogol Institute of Higher Sanity could benefit by familiarizing itself with an American mentality."

Edov nodded and smiled slightly.

"As for Comrade Poplavsky," said the General Secretary, pausing, "perhaps he just needs to sit and think for a while, and no place is more conducive to thought than solitary at Lubyanka."

Edov seemed to be pleased and disappointed all at once.

"Any requests?" asked the General Secretary to Rabin who knew this was a genuine and final display of power.

"Cigarettes," said Rabin.

"He will have a pack a day, and in the event this so-called genius can tell me the true meaning of that word, I want to know at once and will be outraged if that is not absolutely the case," he said, now addressing Edov exclusively. As soon as he had issued those instructions, the General Secretary was magically no longer present in the room, even though he had yet to push his chair back from the table.

CHAPTER 14

SPACE JOURNAL

DAY ONE:

The first feeling I had never had before was of my pores giving off a mist of chemical sweat, an astringent dampness at the back of my neck.

The adrenaline doesn't stop either. Like an espresso jag.

Every few minutes the near perfect balance between terror and astonishment shifts in favor of one or the other.

In all the changing pressures and atmospheres, the body is like a confused dog. It starts one way, then another. It doesn't know where to go. Panic. Or happiness.

My thoughts have a tendency to jump from one topic to another as if there were no connecting links between them. Perhaps that is the influence of space on my mind. Ideas become like planets. I streak from one to another through the void.

Weightlessness: A hideous giddiness. Backflips in place-lessness.

Even the idea of center has not held.

DAY TWO:

But I started to love weightlessness as soon as I stopped feeling like a bagpipe hurled off a cliff. As soon as the bagpipe realized it could fly, a Scottish angel.

Oohing and aahing like a crowd watching fireworks, we took turns in the observation dome looking at the Great Wall of China, the only man-made object visible from space. The first tourist attraction in Disney's Tomorrowland. Earthworks on a planetary museum. The signature of our nature, a line, a wall, division. Beautiful earth, with tan deserts and green forests, studded with cities. Earth, provincial with life.

DAY THREE:

Today I am reading a book about the life cycles of stars.

On the one hand, that strikes me as odd — to be in space and reading about it.

But, on the other hand, it's no odder than sitting in a Paris café reading Baudelaire.

I don't think I ever had a desire that burned with a purer heat than my desire to see Paris when I was eighteen.

Now the stars are Paris, the place young men dream of going.

But what good is space compared to Paris?

In Paris you can stop at a café, have a red wine, smoke a Gauloise and look at a watermarked wall until your eyes become so clear that the red wool scarf of a passing woman literally tickles your sight.

But what is there here? How can you love atoms, gases, dust?

And how am I to reconcile those two images: sitting at a café in Paris, writing two lines on a napkin:

Some love is fated to renunciation
If it is to be remembered as love at all.

And floating here, pressing these words into vinyl with my stylus, a Phoenician of outer space.

But Baudelaire counseled: "Always be drunk — on wine, on virtue, or on poetry." And I am drunk on celestial champagne, the fizz of stars in pure being.

Africa is an elephant's head seen through clouds!

DAY FIVE:

I didn't write on day four. I couldn't.

Not so much that I couldn't, it just never occurred to me.

I was sitting in the observation dome watching the sun light the earth, a tide of white gold cresting to noon after noon.

I knew the answer: all there is is streaming time, dark in some places and bright in others.

DAY SIX:

There is constant background noise — keyboards clicking like distant mah jong tiles, the hum and whirr of systems, the staticky squawk of the open line to Houston which does not sound significantly better than a two-way radio in a suburban taxi.

Even space was unable to deliver irritationlessness.

Art took us to heaven, science took us to space. Now we

know all the centuries were the countdown. Jews, Greeks, all Romans, Medieval, Renaissance, Reason, Revolution, Blast Off!

DAY SEVEN:

Question: Does the poet have any place in the future, in space? Experiment: send one up and see what happens. Results: pending.

The crew has its experiments to perform and I have mine. The problem is that when we speak to each other of our experiments, we bore and irritate each other slightly, and feel embarrassed that we do. We polarize each other — they become plumbers with doctorates. Art becomes a hysterical diva who lives by astrology.

Of course, some of this is my weakness as a humanist. I only like the grand galactic generalizations, the Big Bangs and Black Holes.

And all they read is scientific articles and fat paperback novels riveted with technical details.

But it seems to me that if I cannot find the words to communicate with scientists, then poetry is doomed, because, in the future, everyone will be a scientist by the age of six.

So then how are we to communicate?

By the use of the simplest words, familiar to all. Words of one syllable. Words of one syllable are the realest. Sky. Food. Pain.

Words will always be with us. Words are crucial to us. We hang suspended over infinite space on a single adverb, the "still" in "I still love you."

DAY EIGHT:

I am experiencing an emotion possible only in space — I am homesick for Earth.

Space is supremely physical and supremely unsensual. Not like Earth, with its polleny air and grassy riverbanks. Earth, as gnarled and old-fashioned as an oak tree.

I miss congested sidewalks, bodies, trees, cars, the hair on forearms, exchanging glances with strangers that illuminate you both in a street of topcoats and drizzle.

I miss the smell of meat cooked by fire.

I miss the taste of air, October air, April air.

The air is not real here. Someday there will be people who have never breathed real air. Will they like it if they ever travel to Earth? Or will they find it too rich, biological, vulgar?

DAY NINE:

Weightlessness will make childbirth easier, offspring will slip from us as easily as they do from fish.

The first child not born of Earth. A Caesarian section done on the stratosphere.

We will not be free of the Old Adam until the New Adam is born in space.

A New Adam and a New Eve. A New Sexuality. A New Eden. Paradise Regained.

The New Children will preach to us from space. They will be born with a consciousness few on earth were ever able to attain. It will be their birthright. They will make us ashamed. All our ideas will seem like blood libels.

For them, Earth will be something they have looked down and seen.

From space its oneness will be self-evident. They will be shocked by Israelis and Palestinians. Irish and Irish.

DAY TEN:

We are orbiting the moon. We are under its sway. I can feel its stillness, its kinship with the grave.

DAY ELEVEN:

Thank God for logistics.

Time is structured by tasks again. And muddied by the confusion of all of a sudden having too much to do.

Drill on passing from the Command Module *(Conestoga 1)* to Lunar Excursion Module (LEM). There will be two passengers on the LEM: Astronaut Yates and myself.

Emergency procedures in LEM and on lunar surface.

The final schedule is still being worked out and depends on the arrival time of the Soviet craft. Numbers will be plugged in later. But its structure is known, and exists beforehand like a sonnet:

US LEM DEPARTS COMMAND MODULE.

US LEM ARRIVES LUNAR SURFACE.

MOON ORIENTATION.

NUTRIMENT AND RECUPERATION.

USSR LEM ARRIVES LUNAR SURFACE.

RUSSIAN BREAD AND SALT CEREMONY.

FRATERNIZATION WITH VIKTOROV (BLAINE). MOON-ROCK
RETRIEVAL (YATES).

SOVIET COVERAGE OF CULTURAL COOPERATION EVENT.

That last item, translated into normal English, means that
Viktorov and I will do a reading tomorrow. Tomorrow, on
the moon.

CHAPTER 15

"We are going to run a series of tests on you even though we have already diagnosed you as insane on the basis of your nationality," said Dr. Veer, the director of the Gogol Institute for Higher Sanity.

"You don't think that's a little rash?" asked Rabin.

"Either it is or it isn't. And it isn't," said Dr. Veer whose height was accentuated by his white lab coat and whose brown eyes sparkled with health, curiosity, and pleasure. Even when seated, he seemed in a hurry.

"Well, you won't convince me of that."

"That's exactly why you're here. If I succeed in convincing you of that, I will have done my duty as a doctor, I will have cured you."

"Cured me of what?"

"Acute subjectivitis. Living in the dream world of personality. Loss of contact with objective reality."

We can only know objectivity subjectively."

"You see, you see, the first and most typical symptom of the disease! The belief that objective reality cannot be objectively known. Therefore, everyone must have his own ideas, views, opinions, which become more and more individual until people can no longer communicate with one another, which, as you know, has already happened in America. Subjectivitis is the American mental illness par excellence. You're driving with your headlights off."

For a moment Rabin didn't say anything. He had to admit that in a way Dr. Veer was right — one of them was definitely insane and, who knew, it might well be on the basis of nationality. But now the important thing was to protect himself as he had never protected himself before.

"Alright, let's say there is one shining reality, and one shining truth," said Rabin. "I don't know it because I'm American and insane but, since you're the doctor, you must know it, so tell me, then, Dr. Veer."

"Well, this is a very favorable sign. You're only the second actual American I've had in here and so, as you can imagine, it's very interesting to be able to test the theory on a little human fact, so to speak."

"Yes, but the theory?"

"Yes, you're right, I digressed. Your mind remained on the point. Good, very good. The theory is my creation. It is based on many things but let me single out two of the more important. One is the discovery of the fourth dimension of geopolitics, which is mind. Mind as a dimension whose boundaries are as important as the Oder-Neisse. The boundary between reality and insanity must be as tight as the Berlin Wall. And so, especially in a historical period when everything is, as you Americans say, up for grabs, when even reality is up for grabs, it becomes extremely important who defines sanity, who defines reality. That is my First Principle: HE WHO DEFINES SANITY, DEFINES REALITY."

"But maybe reality is always eluding definition, and therefore sanity is always eluding us."

"It is one of the human imperatives to define reality. Human beings have been doing it uninterruptedly since they first appeared in the dawn of history. Not just in religions and philosophies, but what people saw through their eyes. People need reality; reality is the bread of the mind."

Resist him, Rabin told himself. Resist that dazzling hypnotic brilliance and ravishing confidence. "It's not reality unless it includes a certain dose of the subjective."

"True! But how much? That's the question."

"Well," said Rabin, "subjectivity can contain objectivity, but objectivity only has room for itself."

"An intelligent observation but one unfortunately skewed by your own subjectivitis with its constant need for self-exaltation. Watch," said Dr. Veer and leaned forward toward the large globe on his desk. He pulled a little ball and chain, and the globe not only lit up, but something swirling and white could be seen coming into focus under the continents and oceans.

"It takes a minute to warm up," said Dr. Veer with a certain technological shame. Rabin knew the feeling from other foreigners who always assumed you were technologically superior merely by virtue of being American.

Now Rabin could see that the white swirls were the folds of the brain, the names of whose parts he had always intended to memorize but never quite got around to and so his mind only echoed with vaguely gynecological terms, cerevellum.

"The world has two hemispheres and so does the brain. If the brain's hemispheres were totally uncoordinated, even you would say that the brain had to malfunction. Yes?"

"Yes."

"Good. The world has two hemispheres. Yours and ours. And here the two hemispheres are not just uncoordinated but actively hostile to one another. Two hemispheres of the same thing actively hostile to each other! Isn't that insanity? Don't we live in an insane world?"

"I concede the point," said Rabin.

"One side must be sane and the other insane."

"No, they could be in wrong relation."

"There are two kinds of wrong relations, wrong to wrong, and wrong to right. If one side is objectively in right relation, the side in wrong relation must change because the other one can only change from right to wrong."

"And who defines which one is in wrong relation?"

"The one in right relation, of course."

"He who defines sanity, defines reality."

"Exactly. Someone has to have the courage to take on the task. And it has to be us. Because you Americans prefer the backyard swimming pools of subjectivity to the stormy ocean of objective reality!"

Is this guy sincere? Rabin asked himself. Well, he's Russian and therefore he's sincere on the basis of nationality. But the problem with sincere people is that they can get so worked up when you don't agree with them that beating you over the head becomes nothing less than a duty.

"There is absolutely no punishment in our system here," said Dr. Veer with physicianly warmth. "There is only curative treatment. Though I should say that our system makes use of a great variety of human ideas and inventions, from, say, Zen to shock treatment, and we hardly limit ourselves to Viennese erotic schlag. And, by the way, your sexomania there in the West is yet another sign of rampant infantilism."

"Can I smoke?" asked Rabin.

"Certainly. By the way, I've received instructions that you are to be issued a pack of cigarettes a day."

"That could help."

"I think we are doing well for a first session. You have obviously learned to think objectively to a degree. And I think you may even be ready to hear the Second Principle. Do you think you could take two principles in one day? Or would you prefer to rest for a few hours?"

"No, I can take two principles in one sitting."

"The Second Principle is not, strictly speaking, mine. Although it was, of course, I who applied it to the science of higher sanity. In any case, you probably know that Goethe and Napoleon once had a little conversation about fate. Goethe was trying to write what he called a *schicksaltragödie*, meaning a tragedy of fate. Napoleon replied that in our time politics is fate.

"And he was right! Hundreds of millions of people have died because of politics in our century. Politics is fate. It makes wars. It sweeps people into exile. It blows up cafés. It makes a climate of terror that blankets the world.

"But everything hinges on the meaning of fate. Fate simply means forces that we cannot control. Whether or not those forces assume definite patterns is actually a subsidiary matter. The fact is that there are forces we cannot control; we can call them fate or we can call them reality.

"Thus, notice the syllogism:

> *Politics is fate.*
> *Fate is reality.*
> *Reality is sanity.*
> *Sanity is politics.*

"This is the mantra of sanity. Say it to yourself ten thousand times until it finally begins to penetrate the core.

"I don't want to see you again until you've said this to

yourself ten thousand times, and I want you to count and number each time you say it and keep a running count, as part of your practical training in objectivity," said the doctor with a sad smile, knowing his patient would never complete the therapy because his illness was, by definition, far worse than he could ever conceive.

It wasn't a bad room, which somehow made it more ominous. There was a man lying on one of the two beds, which were separated by a night table that had a reading lamp with a fringed shade. But was the man on the bed human company, or a booby trap that would take his unsuspecting arm right off his shoulder?

In his early thirties, the man had dark, curly hair and a clean-shaven face that was at once angelic and demented; he did not change the position of his head when Rabin entered the room.

Maybe this one is simply crazy, thought Rabin.

Or was there a certain wisdom here? Was he saying, Come in, get used to the place a little; then we'll talk. There'll be plenty of time to talk, but the moment when you first enter your cell comes but once.

They hadn't hit him over the head yet, so why not savor the moment. The walls were covered with square white tiles. There was a wooden table and two chairs. A chessboard had been set up on the table and, focusing on it, Rabin saw that a game was in progress. There were three thick books on the sill of a window that was woven with iron mesh and which probably could not have been broken by a three hundred pound longshoreman gone berserk.

"My name is Andrei," said the man on the bed.

"My name is Eliot."

"I can tell you some things. They'll never hit you. They will scream at you, but the screaming is done scientifically. It's a verbal form of electric shock treatment. More humane really, if you think about it. And cheaper too, of course. There can, however, be some fairly odd experiences."

"Like what?"

"In one cell there's a gigantic toilet, must be eleven feet tall. I don't quite understand it. They just put you in there with it. But after a few weeks alone in a cell with an eleven foot toilet very odd things start happening to your mind. The most ridiculous jokes start occurring to you. Hilarity alternates with helplessness and sadness. You touch the cool damp side of the bowl and you scream out for relief from something you can't even name."

"It may be some attempt to do a Freudian x-ray of the toilet-training layer of your development," said Rabin. "They can carp about Freud all they want, but the smartest ones have to have what is valuable taken from him."

"It's hard to figure them. The trick is to see how they think without getting caught up in their thinking. Very tricky."

"I can feel that already. I talked with the director, Dr. Veer, and I had to admit that a lot of what he said made sense."

"Be careful with him. He's invented a series of drugs that can cause specific hallucinations."

"Specific hallucinations?

"You'll see. Do you have a cigarette by any chance, Eliot? They only give me a pack a week."

"Sure, let's have a smoke. A pack a week, how do you stand it?"

"You can if you have to."

"Why not give up smoking to spite them?"

"Smoking's too good to spite them with."

"I can see that."

"Do you know what ward you're in, Eliot?"

"No."

"It's called ward one. It's for people who went insane by trying to understand Russia. And it's true. If you spend too much time trying to understand Russia you will go completely mad. I know. I know. That's what happened to me, that's why I'm here. I try not to think about Russia any more. But I can't help it. I love thinking about Russia. What could be better than just thinking about Russia!"

"They have a special ward for people like that?"

"Yes, but I don't know how many other people are in it. It may just be us two. It's a small institute, doing the most advanced experiments."

"Andrei, how did you end up in here?"

"I had a brainstorm. I understood Russia. I understood that all societies function like a swarm of bees, constantly in motion but constantly communicating position. But what was the formula of the swarm? Could the swarm of bees be represented mathematically? By the way, I am a mathematician. And I had even gone to work on this problem in the literal sense as well. But the real question was, how did Russia swarm? Then I got my second insight. Chess. Chess is in fact a ritual instinct dance like that of the bees.

I began to understand the workings of the system through chess analogies. The general secretary was the king. The KGB was the queen, able to strike anywhere. Ideology was a bishop, moving along the diagonals and ultimately expendable. The knights were conventional weapons, and the rooks were thermonuclear arms able to obliterate anything in their way, once a path opens like a missile silo. And the pawns are pawns!"

Rabin suddenly felt an urge to lie back on the bed, and, realizing he could because it was his, he did lie back on it, keeping his shoes off the spread.

He'd better break off the conversation pretty soon; he needed some time alone with himself, and Andrei might be one of those people who never shut up even when they're not talking.

"So," continued Andrei, with a certain emphasis, as if he had picked up a cool sense of his own coming reisolation, "I began studying the games of the great Russian chess masters throughout all of Soviet history and tried to establish a correlation between the moves of the grand masters and the moves of the state. And I was successful! I understood that AAAAAAAAAAAH!!!"

Andrei thrashed on his bed, stiffened, and then went limp.

An orderly wheeled in lunch. His attitude was one of perfect detachment and absolute vigilance. The only speck of human emotion he displayed was a slight irritated frown at Andrei.

Lunch was dark bread and processed cheese, which could only be called "cheese" and could never have a name of its own. But there was plenty of strong amber tea and more than a dozen pieces of lump sugar on a saucer.

Glancing anxiously at Andrei, Rabin ate the bread and cheese without appetite, a bored ruminant. But he did enjoy the tea and sugar.

He decided to drink the tea in old Russian style: the lump of sugar held between the teeth, the hot tea melting the sugar and washing it over the tongue, a spring flood of sweetness.

Before passing out, Rabin had time to realize that there must have been something in the cheese. Or maybe the bread, the tea, the sugar. But somehow he didn't think so. Somehow he knew it was the cheese in its terrifying blandness that contained the hallucinogenic spores.

In the white cube of the room, there was only an armchair and a dead seal that must have weighed eight hundred pounds.

He sat down in the chair. For a moment he wondered if he should sit down in the chair, if that was exactly what they wanted him to do, but he sat down anyway. It was better than standing or sitting on the floor.

He had the feeling that the ceiling of the cubic room was really a one-way mirror and Dr. Veer and his colleagues were standing above him and looking down from an amphitheater.

The stench was pungent, godawful. But what could he do about it? Breathe very shallowly. Try not to throw up.

Then the lights dimmed. Suddenly, images covered every inch of the floor. The walls, the floor, the ceiling, even his legs and hands and face were covered with beautiful images — sunrises, Rembrandts, women, icons, coliseums, seas. Celestial synthesizer music was everywhere and now was joined by a voice raptly whispering: "Know thyself . . . Our Father who art in heaven . . . To thine own self be true. . . . For all men are created equal . . ."

But the stink was horrible!

All the most beautiful, the best, and the noblest were as nothing compared to the stink of a dead eight hundred-pound seal.

It was so obvious.

Why hadn't he thought of it before?

Because he hadn't had the experience.

That experience had to be created.

Dr. Veer created it.

But an experience created by someone is an experiment.

Dr. Veer was only pretending to treat him. In fact he was a drugged guinea pig in a maze whose ceiling was a one-way mirror.

Of course, the smell of a decaying seal could overpower the beauty of the images, music, and ideas, thought Rabin, but the proportions were false. If the seal were at the far end of the beach, the aroma of its corruption might even enrich the air. I reject the very assumption!

"Could I ask you for another cigarette?" said Andrei from the chess table. "This is a very tense moment."

Shaking his head like a man coming out of the ocean, Rabin walked over to the chess table and handed Andrei a cigarette, which he lit voluptuously.

"It's coming to a very intense point. That's one advantage of Dr. Veer's Objectivity Therapy. You can really play both sides of a chess game."

"An important plus," said Rabin.

"I feel that this is an especially important game, one that's tuned into the swarm formula of the nation. I think the country is going to be divided on an issue quite soon."

"Any idea what that issue might be?"

"No, the game is perfectly abstract. It only tells you the structure of what is happening."

"Do you think it will cause any major shake-ups?" asked Rabin.

"The queens have done battle once. One drove the other away. But now it looks like the queens might do battle again, and this time the outcome will be more serious. That's what has me all keyed up. That's why I had that petit mal seizure."

"I was never very good at chess," said Rabin.

"But you remember what the queens stand for in my system?" asked Andrei.

"The KGB."

"Very good. You see, there are certain kinds of wisdoms that must be acquired at the right time, when your mind is strong enough to bear the knowledge. People under thirty weren't allowed knowledge of the Kabala. You know what the Kabala is?"

"I do," said Rabin, wondering if Andrei were trying to determine whether he was Jewish.

"Russia is pure Kabala. You shouldn't try to understand it too soon. I understood it too soon! About three weeks too soon! Three lousy weeks!"

"Don't get excited, Andrei."

"How can I keep from getting excited! I understood Russia, but three weeks too soon. I understood there had to be some means of collective coordination, like the bees have. Russia is a swarming chess game that can be represented mathematically as AAAAAAAAAAAAAAHHHHHH!!!"

Andrei went back over in his chair, his knees slamming against the table on the way, upsetting nearly all the chess pieces.

The door opened. The attendant, detached and vigilant as ever, wheeled in a tray of food, casting a glance of irritated disapproval at Andrei who was thrashing on the floor like a fish on a dock.

Rabin lifted up the tray and saw the usual bread and cheese. Then he noticed that there was something in the cover. Small, it had grille work like a microphone.

"No, this is not a crude bugging device," said Dr. Veer's voice, "but an ordinary speaker. I just wanted you to know that all the food we serve here is perfectly normal and contains no hallucinogens whatsoever. If any hallucinogenics are used, they are used exclusively through the air-conditioning system.

★   171

Think of it. If a person could invent a hallucinogen that creates specific hallucinations, and if it could function in an air-conditioning system, well, to put it in political terms, the minister of higher sanity would be a more important figure than the minister of defense."

Just then the air-conditioner surged. Rabin could feel the added coldness in the room.

"Now I am going to tell you the Third Principle. If reality is political, then insanity must be political. The Soviet Union is thoroughly political. Ergo it is thoroughly real. To the degree that your mind is proreality, it will be pro-Soviet." Click.

Rabin suddenly became aware of the aroma of dead seal issuing from the teapot which he opened and found to contain a steamy grey liquid.

Andrei struggled to his feet, looking glazed but determined. "Could I ask you for another cigarette?" he said. "You can't imagine how good that first cigarette tastes after an epileptic fit."

CHAPTER *16*

At the end, the LEM did not so much fly to the moon as let itself fall, braking its way down in long smooth stretches punctuated by quick jolts.

But the final jolt, arrival, reminded Blaine that whatever else the moon might be, it was quite definitely a thing, with all the bone-rattling density that matter alone possesses.

Yates, the commander of the LEM, his short hair beginning to turn the distinguished grey of airplane pilots, turned to Blaine and said: "Take a second to let it sink in, then we'll begin procedure."

Yates seemed to want a response to indicate that all of Blaine's systems were functioning.

"Yes. Let's give being on the moon a few seconds to sink in," said Blaine, his voice three inches left of center, as it can be during a bad head cold.

"I don't know why they gave the Russians the TV rights on this one," said Yates, to make conversation, humanize the environment.

"Well, economically speaking," said Blaine, "it's not the world series or anything."

"Naw, it's all politics."

Blaine was momentarily dumbstruck by that sentiment,

★ 173

which had the hollow clang of a locker door slamming in a locker room.

"We begin moon orientation in ninety seconds," said Yates, speaking to Houston now.

The chummy static of Houston filled Blaine's helmet. But he didn't have to listen. Yates was in charge of communications. And thank God he was scheduled for two hours of "poetic" solitude. Houston would break radio contact with him and only monitor the bio-sensors in his suit.

Yates checked the line that would connect them in Phase One of Lunar Orientation. The line was secure, the tug was tight. Blaine felt a second tug, the first-time parachute jumper's tug of regret, no less keen for being irrelevant.

At first, it was nothing. Eight steps down thin strong stairs toward white-yellow dust.

Keeping in step with Yates.

Coordination.

But then Blaine felt the first buoyant ripple of a lighter gravity, familiar from running down snowy hillsides as a boy.

It was only when both his feet were on the moon and he had aligned himself with Yates that Blaine looked up and saw the December night of the universe.

"Don't stare at it," said Yates.

"That's right," said Blaine, "they told us that."

"Time for coordinated bounding practice," said Houston, clearly audible now but thinned by distance. "Remember to enjoy yourselves. Enjoyment helps take the edge off."

At first they kept knocking into each other with all the slap-happy clumsiness of people in a three-legged race, but then, getting the hang of it, they whooped each other on through their helmet phones as they went bounding, bounding, Waltzing Matildas bounding over badlands of pure chiaroscuro.

When Houston informed them it was time for directed movement toward a goal, Yates said: "You see the slope I'm pointing to?"

"Yes."

"We're going to head there. You know what's there?"

Recall was effort. "The first footprints?"

"That's right."

The boot prints serrating the grey-yellow dust, the second tourist attraction of space, were as insipid as anything else viewed out of obligation.

With a sinking spirit, Blaine knew that some day in the not too distant future a railing, like the one at Plymouth Rock, would be built around those footprints.

The moon was going to be a stop off point, like Frankfurt.

They would mine the moon. A lot of it was probably useable. Environmental groups would protest. But people would say it was pretty beat-up anyway and you couldn't tell the difference without a telescope.

"Holy cow, look at that!" yelled Yates.

Blaine looked up at the black sky.

Huge, blue with sea and white with cloud, and a hundred times brighter than the moon, the earth was rising over the smaller but purer horizon of brightening craters and exact rock shadow.

His house was up there! His books and papers! Davis was up there! Five billion people were up there doing everything people had ever thought of doing! He should never have come here! The naked mind had no more chance in space than the naked body!

"You know what?" said Yates in a voice that was momentously even.

"What?" said Blaine, not sure that he had spoken.

★   175

"I think we should go in for a while. They say the first time you get certain feelings, you should go in for a while. You know what I'm talking about?"

"I do."

"You see why it's important to maintain conversation, perform tasks, take food?"

"I do."

Once inside the LEM, Yates became crisper. "Steak or chicken?" he asked from the galley.

"Steak," said Blaine, settling himself at the hard black plastic table. The padded interior now seemed wonderfully man-made, a hi-tech cocoon.

Smelling the beautiful aroma of a steak being grilled, Blaine asked: "Are you cooking real food?"

"No," said Yates. "It's what they call a sizzulator. It simulates sizzle."

"Now why would they bother to do that?"

"To create memory sensations, to help us maintain our mental equilibrium."

Yates sat down at the table, handing Blaine a brown tube and keeping one for himself.

"Not that bad," said Yates.

"I haven't really had much of an appetite since we left earth," said Blaine after his first slurp of steak concentrate which even seemed to have strands of synthetic gristle in it.

"One day," said Yates, looking past Blaine into the future, "one day they'll have everything up here. Restaurants. Stores. Enclosed malls. Even sports. There'll be new low gravity sports. Somebody's going to make a fortune on that one."

For a moment Blaine said nothing, as he summoned the energy to challenge that offhanded vision of a lunar Cincinnati. It was Yates and people like Yates he must communicate with if poets were not to become interior decorators of the mind. "I hope there'll be something else, too."

"For instance?"

"A Renaissance. That was what my poem was about, the one I won the Apollo Prize for. The whole planet one Renaissance court. 'With Columbuses returning from Americas of space, Shakespeares when telling their adventures to the queen', to quote myself a little."

"You'll have to excuse me but I never did get around to reading it. I'll tell you one thing though. The Columbuses are all going to be machines unless we can figure out a way of living hundreds of years. The distances out here are longer than our lives."

"But at least the Shakespeares will be human."

"Not if they want to talk to the Columbuses, they won't."

All human society had been reduced to two people and Arthur Blaine still felt alienated.

To break the awkward pause, Yates said: "I'll bet the inside of the Russian craft isn't as nice as ours." Then he glanced at the instruments and fittings that looked the way the future should.

"They're no slouches either," said Blaine.

"If they would just go away, what a nice place the world would be. Them and the Arabs."

"But they're not going away. In fact, four of them will be arriving here pretty soon."

"Right, and that means it's rest time," said Yates. "See if you can get some real sleep."

While Yates informed Houston that they would be taking their scheduled rest and rechecked the estimated arrival time of the Soviet LEM, Blaine lay down on the padded bench by the table. His eyelids closed like snails sliding on their own liquid.

In flight all his sleep had been clear and empty like space itself. There had been no dreams, only rushes of after-images, as after a long day's driving. But now Blaine dreamed he was on the MTA coming into Boston through a suburban woods of pine and birch, New England's only color, green, shaded in a thousand tones. The profiles of perfect strangers were minted on the instant in the other passing trolleys. At the last stop before the tracks went underground, his eye was caught by a man on the platform wearing a business suit and holding a briefcase. But his skin was pink-blue, he had no nose and there were gills on his throat.

"Look, everybody, they're here!" cried Blaine, opening the window. "Look, they're here!"

The creature on the platform flushed maroon with indignation and brandished a finny fist, gurgling: "It's time you humans finally woke up!"

Blaine woke up, Yates shaking him by the shoulder.

"Did you sleep?" asked Yates.

"Yes. You?"

"I got a few winks in. OK, let's get our helmets on," said Yates.

"I had a strange dream," said Blaine. "I can't remember it, but I know it was strange."

"Speaking of strange, you know what's happening to me?" said Yates, his voice reaching Blaine through the helmet phones which they were now testing. "Every time I close my eyes for a second, I see the same thing."

"What's that?"

"I'm driving along at night and I see a little league night game. Just enough light to the light the field."

"Sounds nice enough."

"It is. I just don't like the idea of knowing it's going to be there every time."

Unlike the last pause, which had been the one that comes after a failure to communicate, this was the pause of reluctance to proceed to the matter at hand.

"I always loved baseball," said Blaine, sharing Yates's need for the anesthesia of the mundane. "I always loved the Red Sox."

"The Sox always look like they're going to make it, but then they never do."

"Boston loves a loser."

"Not in basketball."

"How about wrestling, do you ever watch wrestling?"

"Naw, it's all fake. We better go."

This time the first sight of the white-yellow dust was both familiar and more rawly itself.

"Help me get the golf cart out," said Yates.

They went around to the back of the LEM where a small four-wheel vehicle had been built into the side. The vehicle opened like a bridge table and looked like something that might come hurtling over a dune in California.

"It's electric," said Yates.

"A good thing," said Blaine. "The nearest gas station is 250,000 miles away."

Yates pressed the red start button. The vehicle shuddered then came to rest. Yates pressed the button again but this time the shudder was even weaker. He pressed it a third time and it seemed on the verge of catching when it clattered to a halt.

"The fucking thing won't start," said Yates, turning down the volume on his microphone so he could vent expletives without Houston's knowledge.

"Give it a minute," said Blaine.

"I always forget this stuff goes to the lowest bidder," hissed Yates.

"What if it doesn't start?" asked Blaine, suddenly worried that he might not get his two hours of solitude. And suddenly relieved as well.

"They can send a fucking poet to the moon, but they can't make a fucking moon-rock-retrieval vehicle that will fucking start when you press the fucking start button!"

"It'll start, it'll start."

"And so what if it does. Now I can't trust the fucking thing not to conk out on me."

"Give it one more try."

"Alright."

It started perfectly.

"Now it fucking starts perfectly," said Yates with the last of his ire, switching the volume back up and feigning ignorance of the glitch as he cheerfully informed Houston that the golf cart was GO.

"What's the speed limit up here," said Yates with a laugh as he settled himself behind the wheel, happy to be driving something again.

"It's a blinking yellow, I'd say," said Blaine.

"Are you secured to the LEM?"

"I am."

"Remember, don't go near the dark craters. Some of them are so cold you put your hand in them and two seconds later your fingers won't be there when you pull them out."

"But didn't they say the length of the line had been measured relative to our position and so there shouldn't be anything to worry about?"

"And the check is in the mail."

"Good luck," said Blaine.

"Take care now," said Yates, pulling away and waving back over his shoulder like an officer in a jeep.

When Yates was out of sight, Blaine felt a familiar aloneness, that of a host returned to himself after the last guest is gone.

As soon as he requested and received Houston's permission to proceed with Solitary Lunar Orientation, he was acutely aware of a second severance from that world of houses, streets, and people.

All that was left now was the landscape of astrophysics where man is never so much as mentioned. Slopes of ash and yellow chalkdust, space rich with its own emptiness.

Then even that was gone and Arthur Blaine was alone on the planet of himself.

Now he saw that there were two ways to go out of your mind, one by going over the edge, and the other by going to its very core where you could see the mind's workings from the inside out.

And there he saw that the nucleus of the atom of consciousness was composed of pronouns bound by the strong force of human relationship — the He and She of sex, the Us and Them of society and war, the ultimate I and You of being. There were two I's. The I that related, and the I that did not.

When he was the I that did not relate, he would be ready for the vision.

But I am that I, knew Blaine. I am.

I.

Then there was only the light of being, and the light was in ecstasy with its own being, and the ecstasy was light.

And the light took form, and the form was that of a human being.

And that human being was capable of thought and speech, and that human being said:

"Hello, and welcome to Channel Vision's Championship Wrestling. I'm your host, Gil Allen of Integrity Marketing. Let's take a quick pause for a unique double-product commercial break, and then it's back to today's match."

"Hello, I'm Arthur Blaine. After a long day in the old wordsmith shop, I like to relax with a beer and a smoke. And no bottled beer is quite as poetic as Heineken." Sips, puffs. "I like the classical forms in literature, the sonnet, the ode, and I like a classical smoke which is why I choose Camels. For that, ah, classic taste."

"Alright, thank you, Art, and welcome back to ringside, ladies and gentlemen. Referee Carmine Fuccelli will now introduce today's contenders."

"Ladeeeeez and gentlemen, today's first contender for the undisputed champeenship of American culture is the bearded wonder of Camden, Mr. *Leaves of Grass*, WAAAAAAALT WHITMAN!!"

In trunks of bath-mat green worn over grey long-johns, his beard permanently blowing in the wind, Walt Whitman danced out into the center of the ring seemingly oblivious to the weakness of the cheers for him.

"And his opponent tonight, Ladeeeez and Gentlemen, is America's favorite artist, the Michelangelo of animation, our architect of tomorrow, the most creative creator in creation, the one, the only, WAAAAAAAAAAAAAAAAALT DISNEY!!!!!"

"When You Wish upon a Star" played as Disney, damp-haired, mustached, wearing a light grey suit, walked smiling to the center of the ring where he shook hands with Whitman.

Fuccelli motioned for the crowd to quiet down but people's hearts and hands were too delirious with ovation. He started three times before he could finally say:

"Today's match will be ten rounds. The winner will be the undisputed champeen of American culture. He will receive the official Champeen of American Culture Wrestling Belt, and his aesthetics will be declared the official American Waltanschauung. And so may the best Walt win!"

Silent except for isolated pockets of rowdiness, the stadium reverberated with the bell for ROUND ONE. His shoulders bobbing, Whitman moved cautiously out of his corner to cries of "Hey nature boy" and "Forget it."

You're back at ringside with Gil Allen.

"Whitman and Disney are circling each other, no one's making the first move here. No, here comes Whitman, he slaps a bearhug on Disney, lifts him up, Whitman's got Disney off his feet in the opening moments of round one, he's pounding the soles of Disney's feet against the canvas, and Disney is stunned, Ladies and Gentlemen. Whitman bounces Disney off the ropes then shoulderflips him over his back and Disney is down. But Disney slips free and he's back on his feet, sports fans, and he's got Whitman by the beard. Disney is spinning Whitman dizzy by the beard and now it's Whitman that looks stunned. Disney is rotating on his heels and Whitman is spinning, Disney lets go of Whitman's beard and Whitman slams into that turnbuckle like a ton of bricks. But Whitman is back on his feet, you got to hand it to him, he's back on his feet and on the attack. Whitman ankle-tackles Disney and Disney is down. The referee Carmine Fuccelli is on one knee and count-ing. One, two, three . . .

And it's the bell, Disney saved by the bell at the end of round one. We'll be right back. After this."

"Hello, my name is Arthur Blaine. You may not know my work but you've heard of me, because I was the first American poet on the moon. I always use American Express. Never leave Earth without it."

"It's round two and Whitman's out, looking like he wants to finish what he started at the end of round one. Whitman is taking charge right away, he's got Disney in an Alaskan finger lock; he's twisting Disney's arm behind his back and Whit-man's got Disney in a half nelson. Disney is down on one knee and there's a look of real pain on his face here in the wild opening of round two. But Disney does a sudden collapse and roll, and he's back on his feet. Whitman's running from Dis-ney, no, he's going to bounce himself off the ropes. He's com-ing right at Disney, but Disney sidesteps and it looks like Whitman may be going through the ropes and into the press corps. But, no! Whitman's straightened up in time and he's going to rebound off the ropes with tremendous force, Ladies and Gentlemen, tremendous force, and Disney's not ready for it! Disney has taken a tremendous blow here and Disney is going down. This could be it — that was a tremendous blow by Mr. *Leaves of Grass* here in round two. Carmine Fuccelli is beginning the count for the second time in two rounds, both times with Disney down. One, two, three, four, but wait, Fuccelli is slipping something to Disney. It's a foreign object of some sort. It's Disney's magic wand and Disney's waving it, and here they come Ladies and Gentlemen, the Seven Dwarfs fresh from their winning tour on the Midget Wrestling Circuit, and they're all over Whitman pinning him wrist and ankle, he's down dazed and dumbfounded, this could be it!"

"It's all fake, it's all fixed," said a husky, streetwise voice deep within Blaine's helmet and mind. "Did you see the ref slip him the wand? And you wanna know why? Because Fuccelli works for the Godfather, God the Father. And Disney is the Godfather's number-one all-time favorite. This whole thing was fixed from the very top. Your boy Whitman never had a Chinaman's chance."

Fuccelli was just handing the red-white-and-blue, gold-encrusted, and jewel-studded belt to Disney when Blaine bounded over the ropes, snatched the belt, and cleared the other side of the ring, all in a single, fluid M-shaped motion. The audience laughed, thinking it was part of the show, but only until Fuccelli grabbed the swaying mike and shouted: "Cream that son of a bitch!"

The fans climbed over each other in pursuit of Blaine who was racing for the EMERGENCY EXIT, already imagining hands snapping him apart like a lobster. Just as the first fingernails were stropping his back, he shoved open the double doors and was stopped cold by the moon's perfect silence, a translucent bell rung once by his solitude.

CHAPTER *17*

"I told you to kill Rabin," said Stalin, "Living people are nothing but one problem after the other."

"I have not lost entirely yet," said Poplavsky.

"No, your defeat will take a while. As the proverb says, the first pancake's always a flop."

"There are other proverbs — Pray to God but keep rowing to shore."

"God's too high and the tsar's too far away."

"Even the grave won't straighten the hunchback."

"That's not true," said Stalin, "it straightened me. Do you want me to tell you what it's like here? Do you want to know the secret of life after death?"

"Yes."

"There is something. But it's only you. You as you always really were."

"That's all?"

"It's too much as it is. I would have preferred extinction. Nothing we ever do is ever perfect. Not even dying."

"I wouldn't have guessed."

"But there must be others here somewhere. Maybe it's different for them. I don't know. Wait, there goes something. I'm sure I saw something moving."

"Who was it?"

"It may have been Zinoviev. Or it may have been nothing."

"What do you advise me to do now?"

"It's getting harder for me to concentrate on your world. It's becoming like the old country."

"Your spirit is fading from us, Comrade Stalin?"

"Yes. And do you know why? Because of the most important event that happened in Russia in the twentieth century."

"The Revolution? The Second World War?"

"No, you fool, I mean the day my body was removed from the mausoleum and buried in the ground like any shitty drunken shoemaker."

"That was more important than the revolution or the war?"

"Of course, because that was the day Russia lost its tragic essence."

"I will reinvigorate Russia's nervous system with good old-fashioned terror if I reach the top."

"No, it's too late now, everything's gone modern. But I will give you one last piece of good advice."

"Thank you, Comrade Stalin."

"My advice is — kill."

"Who?"

"Anyone who has caused you grief, is causing you grief, or might cause you grief in the future."

"But how can I kill anyone when I'm all alone in a cell?"

"Precisely. You have proved to be your own worst enemy. Therefore, if you are willing to live by the iron logic of the terrible truth, you must kill yourself."

"Maybe you're right. Maybe I have failed. Maybe this is only a stay of execution."

"But of course they won't really execute you. They will

only kill you symbolically through humiliation. None of you is capable of anything but symbolic existence. None of you has the balls for the literal like I did. And so your suicide only has to be symbolic, performed here in your heart of hearts, no razor or arteries involved."

"Maybe I should."

"No maybes."

"But I love life. My own especially. Even symbolically."

"Leonid Nikolaevich Poplavsky, you are pathetic."

"So are you! You told me so yourself. You told me the terrible truth behind the terrible truth. So why shouldn't I be a little pathetic, too. I've got a right."

"You failed to kill Rabin, and now you're failing to kill yourself, what's become of Russia."

"I'm glad I didn't take your advice and kill Rabin. I still say I'm right about him. The man is a genius."

"His genius landed you in here."

"Everything can still work out fine if he can interpret the dream in time."

"What dream?"

"The General Secretary's dream."

"Ah yes, I remember. He had that dream three times."

"Do you know what it means?"

"No."

"But Rabin will crack it, I know."

"If he doesn't crack first."

"Oh, they're so weak, Americans, so untempered."

"Wait! I think I saw something again. Way to the left. The darkness got darker in one place, and then it shifted position. No, no it was nothing."

CHAPTER *18*

If he could burp he'd be sane.

Rabin burped.

But he still wasn't sane.

Because it was the wrong kind of burp, with the wrong taste and the wrong resonance.

It tasted of kasha, black bread, and seal tea.

A Soviet burp.

He wanted to burp an American burp.

If he could burp an American burp he would be sane.

But he needed American food to burp himself back to sanity.

Or perhaps to even think those thoughts proved that he was insane.

No, no, if he could just have a pepper steak sub or a cheeseburger or a hot dog with mustard and relish; some ribs with a side of cole slaw; a thin, slightly overcooked cheese omelette in a diner; a pork chop, mashed potatoes and green peas in a bum cafeteria; a slice of oily pizza on a piece of waxed paper; a jelly donut and a cup of bad coffee in a donut shop with locals slumped by the napkin dispensers. Oh, how he'd burp then. Oh, how sane he'd be then!

Rabin suddenly felt cold and thought that the air-conditioner must have surged with hallucinogens again.

He opened his eyes.

Four attendants entered the room.

Without a word being spoken, it was clear which two Rabin was to obey and which two Andrei was to obey.

They were marched down a well-waxed corridor on which the attendants' rubber soles squeaked to a room marked: NEWS THERAPY.

The four attendants stood by the wall with their arms folded as Rabin and Andrei took seats in front of the wall-sized TV screen.

"Andrei," whispered Rabin, "is this really happening?"

"Try to get out of the room and you'll find out."

"I know that. But what I mean is are you here, sitting beside me?"

"Yes," said Andrei in a tone that suggested complete sympathy with Rabin's very need to ask the question.

"Touch my hand," said Rabin.

Andrei touched his hand. Rabin felt the distinct oddness of another person's flesh and knew that this at least was real.

The news could help him. It could tell him what the date was. Sanity was built on the sense of time and place, and of course that had been the first thing they had tried to destroy. As if *who* were intimately tied to *when* and *where*, as he had suspected as a schoolboy learning those owlish adverbs.

Rabin even began to relax as his reflective powers returned to him.

"Look," said Andrei, "it's their new logo."

Rabin looked. The room had dimmed but not quite darkened. The screen was runny with color. Yes, Andrei was right, the Soviet evening news had a new logo.

The anchorman, who had not quite mastered the teleprompter and seemed to be looking in two directions at once, said: "Good evening. This is the news of the day. The Soviet spacecraft, *Tsiolkovsky I*, is within hours of landing on the moon. The renowned Soviet poet, Viktor Viktorovich Viktorov, will read his commemorative poem, "Path To The Stars," live from the moon tomorrow."

"Wait!" said Rabin. "Now I understand!"

"Shhhh," said Andrei. "Understand later."

"I can't help it, it's so obvious—the logo. Don't you see? Don't you see? The very fact of wanting to have a new up-to-date logo tells you everything you need to know. It is not the choice of the particular logo that matters, but the very spiritual fact of choosing one. Technology has led mankind to a momentous choice—annihilation or banalization. And, of course, man with his ratlike instinct for life has chosen banalization!"

Now Rabin was on his feet, pointing at the screen, his face grotesquely creased and awash in red and blue.

Andrei looked up sadly at him, as if having been through all this too many times before. The flight into the abstract. Chess. Grand theories.

"Everything is going to be fine! There's not going to be any nuclear catastrophe! We're safe! We have a thousand years of banality, happiness, and technology ahead of us. Banatechnohap! Banatechnohap!"

"Give him an injection of Trotskyzine!" said Dr. Veer's voice over the intercom, the third person once again suggesting invisible anatomy theaters, attentive students.

Three attendants grabbed Rabin and thrust him back into his chair. He struggled, but six weight-trained arms were stronger than two, and he was strapped thrashing in the chair before he had even lost his breath.

Two of them began bending his head to one side, making

him hideously aware of the vulnerability of his neck. They had bent his head toward Andrei who cast him a quick glance of encouragement and resignation before turning to watch the rest of the news, which he knew was exactly what he was supposed to be doing.

The pain was quick. The image was immediate. He was at his desk in Mexico writing a furious polemic against Stalin. He looked out the arched window and over the red tile roof to the courtyard where cactus and gaudy flowers grew. A donkey piled neatly with slats of firewood was led down a cobbled street by a man in a tatty sombrero.

He went over to the mirror and pulled at his grey goatee. He was getting older. Women still found him magnetic, but what good was that? What good was all that unless he could return to Russia, return to power, unless Trotskyism vanquished Stalinism.

There was a knock at his door, the little bird knuckles of his secretary, the believer.

"Yes?" he said.

"It's three o'clock, Comrade Trotsky. The assassin is here to see you."

"I thought that was tomorrow."

"No, today. It's on the appointment calendar."

"Show him in."

The assassin came to the door.

"Come in. I'd like to sit down if I may. I don't want to see it coming."

"But you should have seen it coming."

"Yes, probably. I'll be writing. You come around in back of me, alright?"

"Fine."

He began writing, caught in the pleasure of watching an autonomous hand draw Russian in black ink on lamp-lit paper.

Any second now, any second now. Now he could hear the air whistling, stirring the hair at the nape of his neck.

The ice axe shattered his skull like safety glass held together only by the wire of agony.

For an instant he could see Andrei in his chair wincing, wincing for him. Then he was looking out the window again at the cactus and the gaudy flowers and the donkey neatly piled with slats of firewood.

There was just time enough to understand that it would happen again and again. Then he tugged his goatee, and his secretary knocked at the door.

If he could get underneath it somehow, if he could dive deeper than it went, he could be free of it.

But that was too deep to dive; he couldn't stand the pressure on his eyes and lungs.

It was too dark down there. Luminous monsters lived down there. It was better in the world of color and light, better in the study in Mexico with the view of the garden and the street and himself, standing before a mirror, sad at the evidence of age.

"It's three o'clock. The assassin is here to see you."

He could hear the donkey bray some donkey sadness of its own.

No, he had to get out of that room.

He had to get to the one place where no assassin could find him. The place that ran deeper than pain.

Now when he looked down at his desk he saw that his initials and an arrow-pierced heart had been carved into it. He opened his desk top and for a moment he was away from the class in a little tent of privacy. He could smell his sandwich through the brown paper bag. His mother had made him tongue salad with mayonnaise and piccalilli, and he was glad, and he loved her.

His third grade home-room teacher, Mr. McHenry, came in, wearing his too tight Air Force blue uniform, his usual baffled look on his face.

He hated stupid teachers. He hated teachers who said "er" and "um" a lot and whose breath smelled like egg yolks and tobacco.

"Open your books to page 107," said Mr. McHenry.

He opened his DLIWC Russian textbook to page 107.

"My military unit is now stationed at the outskirts of a major industrial center," translated the first student in the first row where Mr. McHenry always began.

"Quiet! American spies are everywhere!"

Mr. McHenry looked up to see if the class thought that was funny.

Who could think that was funny.

The classroom door opened.

In came Principal Poplavsky with the new superintendent of schools, the General Secretary dressed in blue and gold.

"Do you always call on the students in order?" asked the General Secretary.

"Yes," said Mr. McHenry.

"Bad idea! You've got to keep them on their toes. I've got a question. We'll find out how good a teacher you are and how smart these brats really are!"

Mr. McHenry turned pink as a pencil eraser then grey as an ink eraser.

"Alright, which of you knows what Ushassar means?" asked the General Secretary.

"Perhaps Eliot Rabin would like to answer that question," said Mr. McHenry.

Eliot Rabin stood up in the aisle by his desk. The other students were looking at him but not directly, just with one eye.

"Well?" said the General Secretary in a way that made the answer slip away from him like a minnow from a fist. From behind the General Secretary's back, Principal Poplavsky was begging Rabin to answer the question fast and right.

"Can I write the answer on the board?"

"Alright," said Mr. McHenry who was now bracing himself with one hand against the desk.

His heart beating so fast it was making his ears pop, Eliot Rabin strode to the blackboard and inhaled the smell of chalk dust.

Now he was in the center, and the whole room radiated from him, revolved around him—even the grownups.

He picked up a piece of chalk and wrote the word. "In English that would be USASSR. The pronunciation 'Ushassar' may be a slight Persianization caused by fear."

"Yes, but what does it mean! What does it mean!" shouted the General Secretary.

There was a soft knock at the door, and the room became very quiet.

A woman's voice said: "It's three o'clock. The assassin's here to see you."

Rabin awoke to darkness with the answer on the tip of his tongue.

Where was he? In a bed. He could hear Andrei's rattling snore. In his room. But he had no paper or pen. The walls resisted scratching; he had already tried with a spoon.

He had to do it fast. It was dissolving. The slightest wrong jiggle of his body and the answer would be gone.

His hand reached out into the darkness touching something angled and wooden. Then something glass and round. Then something square and sealed in cellophane. His pack for tomorrow!

He peeled the opening strip very smoothly and carefully. Then he undid the foil as slowly as if he were defusing a buzz bomb.

He pulled out one cigarette, then two, then four, then seven, until he had all the cigarettes out and in one hand. They felt like soft, light pieces of chalk. The dark floor was the blackboard.

Making stick figures he spelled out: USASSR.

By the two left in his hand, he knew that it had come to exactly eighteen cigarettes.

A donkey brayed.

He tugged at his grey goatee.

He was getting old, old.

A knock at the door woke him to peace and morning light.

But he could not keep his eyes open for another second.

There was a pinpoint of pain with a tingling radius at the back of his neck.

"I'm so glad to see you're alright," said Andrei. "You don't know how upset I was. I had fit after fit."

"I'm sorry to hear that," said Rabin.

"Forgive me!" the words came bursting from Andrei in a shrill sob.

"For watching the news when they stuck the needle into me?"

"For that, too."

"Too?"

"I smoked the rest of my cigarettes after the first fit, and I told you how good that first cigarette after a fit tastes."

"Yes?"

"It was fit after fit, Eliot. I already told you that."

"And?"

"I had to have a few cigarettes after each one, or I would have gone out of my mind and never come back, never, do you understand me?"

Rabin understood all too well. For a moment he did not even have the courage to open his eyes and stare over the edge of his bed to the floor.

But he had to look, and he had to look fast.

Maybe there was still enough left to make sense of it.

He looked. Floor and nothing but floor.

"The whole pack!"

"Forgive me!"

"I'll never forgive you!"

"In the name of God!"

"Never!"

"What could matter more than forgiveness?"

"Freedom! Mine!"

"You value freedom more than forgiveness?"

"You're damned right I do!"

"I'm only human."

"What do you think I am?"

"Forgive me, please."

"Shut up for a minute! Listen, when you started taking my cigarettes was it dark in here?"

"No, the fits started at daybreak."

"So, you saw the order I had arranged the cigarettes in?"

"Yes, I wondered what that word meant."

"What word?"

"USASSR."

"I know what it means."

"What?"

"There's someone I promised to tell first," said Rabin, sitting up in bed. "And besides it might not be good for your condition to know."

"I understand," said Andrei sadly, "you don't trust me anymore. You hate me."

"No, not at all, Andrei, now I forgive you. And I'd forgive you even more if you had left me at least one smoke. Doesn't matter. Dr. Veer, I know you can hear me. I know that the General Secretary left instructions that I was to be brought to him immediately if I could interpret his dream. And I can. And I would think it wise to obey the General Secretary's instructions."

There was a pause, blank as the floor had been, and Rabin suddenly felt foolish. He had assumed their room was monitored at all times, but perhaps he had become paranoid. Perhaps he had ascribed too much power and diligence to Dr. Veer. Perhaps Dr. Veer was really like everyone else, basically sloppy and indifferent.

But then the door opened and two attendants appeared.

Just as he knew they were there for him, he could also sense a shift in their attitude toward him. He had gone from being utterly powerless to potentially exceedingly powerful, but with no change in status.

Rabin decided to launch a probe.

"I want to dress," he said.

The attendants did not react in the slightest, as if made of pure muscle.

Rabin walked over to the wardrobe and opened one door

of it, creating a little tent of privacy that seemed oddly familiar.

He put on his clothes then closed the door. Now, when he turned to Andrei, he felt the power freedom gives, or the freedom power gives—he could not be quite sure.

"I won't forget you. Don't worry," said Rabin.

"You forgive me?"

"I do. I really do."

"Let me give you one last word of advice," said Andrei. "You're going out of here into Russia, the real thing. And so you have to be very careful. Believe me, I know. You have to be careful because Russia is . . . Russia is RussiAAAAAA!"

One of the attendants frowned then took Rabin by the arm with a grip that said, "Although you might be a prisoner with a dangerously ambiguous status, you are still a prisoner and come with us."

Rabin was glad of the strong hands holding him by the arms. He felt like a man whose legs had grown used to a swaying deck and are then stunned by the sudden stability of dry land. The dry land of real time.

He assumed that he was being taken directly to the General Secretary and reminded himself to note the means of conveyance as a sign of his standing. It all seemed so long ago, those rides with Poplavsky in the limo with the blue windows, memories of other trips to Russia returning to mind. But Poplavsky, how was Poplavsky? What had been done to him in the meantime?

All it took was the opening of a single door to refute his assumptions because he was in Dr. Veer's office, the same office he had been in the first day but which he entered from another door this time.

Dr. Veer eyed him evenly.

The attendants took up positions by the door.

Dr. Veer nodded to the chair facing his desk.

"I'd like to get going," said Rabin.

"We need to talk first."

Rabin understood—it was war. To the death. He sat down.

"It would be professionally irresponsible for me as a doctor to allow every lunatic who thought he had a message for the leader to be whisked over to the Kremlin."

"The difference," said Rabin, "is that the General Secretary has specifically requested that I be brought to him if I was able to interpret his dream. And I can."

"Fine. I'm very glad to hear that. It can only reflect well on our institute. After a *relatively* short period of therapy, a patient suffering from acute subjectivitis is able to interpret our leader's dream on the deepest level, the level of objective political sanity."

"I'm glad," said Rabin with a hostile flatness to his voice, "that this has all worked out well for you, too."

"Simply tell me the dream and your interpretation, and if I find it within the limits of objective political sanity, I'll sign this release for you, and you'll be on your way."

"Tell you the dream and the interpretation? Not on your life!"

"How about on yours?"

"You would take the responsibility of killing the one person able to interpret the General Secretary's dream?"

"People die here all the time. Especially weak foreigners."

"But some people already know that I can interpret the dream."

"Like who? Andrei, that madman?"

"How about the two attendants right here in this room?

They might be more loyal to the General Secretary than to you," said Rabin, making his voice louder.

"Yes, loyalties are a shifting thing, but, fortunately, Mitya and Vitya are both deaf as posts, not to mention mute. So, objectively, only three people know that you've interpreted the dream: Andrei, myself, and you. Can you perceive the reality of the situation, where the power lies, what the politics of sanity are in this particular case? Think of it as a last oral exam. You are being given a very basic and direct problem to solve in objective reality. It takes the form of a choice: either tell me what I want to know or you'll be dead within fifteen minutes," said Dr. Veer with a glance at his watch.

In a flash of fear, insight, and adrenaline, Rabin realized that the sincere could only be defeated on their own terms, otherwise they wouldn't even know they had lost. And that meant that now he had to enter Veer's universe of mind entirely if he was ever to be free of it.

But he could not enter that universe fully because he did not believe in it as sincerely as Dr. Veer did. Dr. Veer's total sincerity gave him total power in that universe of his own creation. But, by the vertiginous law of paradox, every power was a weakness, and there was a special pleasure in killing your assailant with his own weapon.

"I'll tell you why I can't tell you," said Rabin in a gentle voice.

"Yes, do that," said Dr. Veer with another glance at his voice.

"Because your therapy was a brilliant success. You cured me of my subjectivitis. And I'm very grateful to you."

"Apparently the course of therapy I applied was not entirely successful if you have not achieved the objectivity to save your own skin."

"No," said Rabin, "that is not the real choice here. The greatest objective force at work in this room is the force that brought me to the General Secretary in the first place, the force that hurled me here, the force that liberated the meaning of the General Secretary's dream. That was not your force, Dr. Veer. Because you had nothing to do with getting me to Russia. Because your destiny is not as great as the General Secretary's—he heads the Soviet Union and that is the most political of destinies. And so the true choice here is not mine but yours. Either renounce your theory or let me go!"

A green vein leaped into bas relief on Dr. Veer's temple as both hemispheres of his brain engorged with blood. Rabin watched the doctor's brown eyes dim with indecision. Once again, it would be over in seconds. He had made his move. Now there was nothing he could do but pray that Dr. Veer would find the inner courage to remain true to himself, and, to help him achieve that highest of integrities, Rabin intoned: "Politics is destiny. And destiny is reality. And reality is sanity. And sanity is politics."

"It is, it is," hissed Dr. Veer, clutching his head with one hand and signing the release with the other. "God help me, it is."

CHAPTER 19

For several minutes Blaine stood as motionless as a toy left in a sandbox.

Then he slowly raised his hands over his head to display the victory belt to the stars in defiance of truth and God the Father, the Godfather.

When he looked up between his outstretched hands, the victory belt had, by some evil magic, vanished. What he saw instead was an immense blackjack hurtling through the dark to punish him for his Luciferian defiance, his Promethean theft.

No, up-to-date and scientific, God had chosen a meteorite to obliterate him.

But then that meteorite slowed and began jolting downward like a jack handle on an invisible jack.

Then he could see that it was not a meteorite but a large gun-metal grey object that could only have been made by human beings. And not just any human beings, but the ones who put a red hammer and a red sickle on everything.

Blaine could not remember just who those people were or why they were here; nor could he fathom why God the Father, the Godfather, had not taken his vengeance.

Then he was suddenly and hideously lucid.

The Russian poet had arrived. The traditional Russian

hospitality ceremony with bread and salt would be followed by fraternization.

The door of the Soviet LEM was hinged at the bottom and became an extendable walkway as soon as it was opened. The first three cosmonauts backed out; all of them held cameras. Viktorov emerged carrying a silver tray on which there was a hefty loaf of dark bread and a rococo salt cellar.

Viktorov looked to the cameras and then past them to Blaine.

Blaine felt relieved. He was not alone. Viktorov was with him now. There were two of them now.

Holding the tray in one hand, Viktorov began to gesture with the other. Blaine could tell he was reciting poetry. But why couldn't he hear it? He was supposed to be able to hear it, in the original and in translation; that was part of the schedule.

Press the yellow button on your wrist, he reminded himself.

But how could pressing a little yellow button help him hear?

Press the little button, said his own voice with the nagging insistence of a buzzer.

To shut it up, he pressed the little yellow button.

Now he could hear Viktorov's voice, distant Slavic thunder. The interpreter's voice seemed closer and slightly British as it said in a concluding tone:

> Here, on the same moon Adam saw,
> Here, on the stepping-stone to Mars,
> Here, in the name of Russia and Earth,
> I offer bread and salt to the stars.

Now Viktorov raised the tray, offering Russian hospitality to the entire universe, turning and bowing to all the four corners of space and time. At moments, the silver tray became a bar of light.

Then, to Blaine's surprise, Viktorov began heading toward him; the three Soviet cameramen slowly panned in his direction. Of course, of course. He was not only part of one media circus but of two.

Blaine raised his hand in a greeting that sought the severe dignity of a Massachusetts Indian. Viktorov was trying to maintain his dignity too, but the moon's gravity was too bouncy and slippery for that.

Now Viktorov was in front of him. At first, when he tried to catch Viktorov's eye through the face shield, all Blaine saw was a reflection of his own face, the space between nose and lip now both simian and extra-terrestrial, but then, turning his head, he could make out Viktorov's eyes, their grey-blue pushed to the edge by the pupil's dilation, blacker than space.

He wondered if he looked like that.

A Soviet cameraman was now passing Blaine on his right to get a shot of Viktorov from above and behind Blaine.

Viktorov bowed and extended the tray to Blaine who bowed in return, trying to remember if the schedule had called for any symbolic taking and tasting of the bread. Feeling suddenly illiterate in the language of gesture, Blaine bowed again, trying to make his helmet bob in a way that expressed both gratitude and acknowledgment.

Suddenly, Yates's voice came through Blaine's headphone. "It conked out again!"

"Give it a minute," said Blaine.

"Do you require emergency assistance?" asked Houston.

"I will if the thing won't start back up," said Yates with infinite thin-lipped exasperation.

"Attempt a reactivation," said Houston.

In the staticky cosmic silence Blaine thought he could hear a wordless curse, muttered abstractly for decency's sake.

"Negative," said Yates. "Like a doornail."

"Contact Soviet LEM Commander Bardakov for emergency assistance," said Houston.

"It'll look terrible," said Yates.

"Contact Soviet LEM Commander Bardakov for assistance."

"Affirmative."

Blaine felt that his entire head had become a telephone on which he was overhearing a conversation that, though boring in itself, was fascinating simply because it was between others.

"How can I be of assistance?" asked Soviet LEM Commander Bardakov.

"What I need is a jump or a tow," said Yates.

"Our battery is not equipped for jump starts. But we can try a tow."

"Great."

"We'll locate you by radio position. Over and out."

Blaine felt sorry for Yates. There was always something vaguely humiliating about being towed, in heaven as it is on earth.

The three-man Soviet crew, who seemed to possess a variety of skills, was now busy assembling their own lunar vehicle. It started at once, which caused Blaine a surge of automotive shame—compounded when he realized that they were taking their cameras with them to film the incident.

When all three crew members were on board the vehicle, Bardakov came on again, and now Blaine thought he could detect the faintest shade of malicious triumph in his voice. "We should return in under two hours, in plenty of time for the reading. Viktorov, you may proceed with fraternization, but better in their LEM."

"Yes, Commander Bardakov," said Viktorov.

The Soviet lunar vehicle pulled away with what would have been a dashing squeal on earth.

Inside the American LEM, Blaine and Viktorov removed their helmets and saw each other directly for the first time. They both looked permanently startled, the skin on their cheeks and forehead pulled back and too tight, like a woman who has just gotten her first facelift.

"It's strange, isn't it?" asked Blaine.

"Very strange," agreed Viktorov, setting his tray down on the table.

"I could probably defrost that bread in the microwave," said Blaine, reaching for the tray.

"Don't touch that bread!" cried Viktorov, covering it with his hand.

"Is there something wrong with it?" asked Blaine.

"No, it's perfectly good bread. Better than most," he said, his broad Slavic lips rising into a private grin. "I'll show you. Do you have something to cut with?"

Blaine went over to the small galley that had been Yates's exclusive province so far. All he could find was a pair of tongs for extracting the food tubes from the microwave and a screwdriver.

"Will either of these help?"

"What do you call that thing?" asked Viktorov pointing to the screwdriver.

"A screwdriver."

"Those are the kinds of words you never learn in a foreign language," said Viktorov. "Alright, I think the screwdriver will do the job. This must be a careful operation."

Viktorov began pecking chunks of bread from where the loaf made its fullest curve. Each time he twisted the screwdriver in a little further, like a surgeon probing for the spongy resistance of a tumor. "Good, good, I can feel it now."

Viktorov moved the screwdriver in expanding concentric circles. Blaine thought he heard a clink of contact.

"And now for the extraction," said Viktorov, inserting his thumb and forefinger into the dark brown aperture. "And here she comes!"

With obstetric care, Viktorov slowly withdrew a bottle whose label, though in Russian, was instantly recognizable as Stoli, the sole Soviet export ever to enjoy popular success in the American market.

"I haven't had a drop for eleven days," said Viktorov. "I never go eleven days on earth without vodka, not to mention space. And just look how beautifully chilled it is." He leaned forward and kissed the bottle.

Blaine thought the gesture rather wonderful and grand but then concluded that Viktorov was overdoing it, since after a few seconds, his lips were still pressed to the bottle. Viktorov was whispering what sounded like endearments to the vodka. But, leaning closer, Blaine could hear that he was saying: "My lips are frozen to the bottle."

"Give it a minute, maybe it'll melt by itself."

"Think of something!"

He couldn't use the screwdriver, it might take off chunks of Viktorov's lips in the process. But he had to think of something fast. Viktorov could hardly appear to all mankind with a vodka bottle frozen to his face.

"I've got an idea," said Blaine.

"What?" muttered Viktorov.

"I'm going to put salt on top of your lips. We use it in America to melt snow on the roads."

"Try it."

Blaine unscrewed the top of the salt cellar on the ornate silver tray and began sprinkling pinches along Viktorov's upper lip.

"Give it a minute," said Blaine.

Viktorov's head began bobbing. He was trying to say something, but Blaine could not make it out because Viktorov seemed to be breathing the words in rather than out.

The sneeze, when it came, was epic.

Except for two scraps of red and gold label that were still stuck to Viktorov's lips, the bottle tore free and sailed with lazy grace toward the wall and catastrophe.

"Grab that bottle!" commanded Viktorov with his labelled lips.

Blaine caught the bottle with one hand, the slow motion instant replay having at last become the reality.

"Are you alright?" asked Blaine noticing a trace of blood seeping through the scraps of label.

"Nothing a drink won't fix," said Viktorov.

"I could use one myself. I'll get glasses," said Blaine who remembered noticing two black plastic tumblers in the galley section. "But first . . ." He draped his helmet over the LEM intercom. Houston's protests were only an annoying fly, buzzing in a far corner of the room.

The tumblers' magnetized bottoms sucked hold of the table.

"Good," said Viktorov. "I'll teach you the proper Russian way to drink vodka. There are five steps. First, one person proposes a toast from the heart. That itself has a certain uplifting effect. Second, expel all breath. Third, take vodka in one shot. Fourth, take what we call *zakuski* meaning appetizers, meaning anything you can get your hands on, but preferably black bread, pickles, smoked fish, that sort of thing. Fifth, breathe. You understand?"

"I understand. Toast, expel, gulp, eat, breathe."

"Correct."

"Who should make the first toast?"

"I should," said Viktorov, "because I am an expert in such matters." He did, however, say this with a knitted brow, perhaps because a man with blood-tinged labels frozen to his lips automatically loses the better part of his authority.

Viktorov broke off a piece of bread and sprinkled it with salt, and Blaine followed suit. It made sense, to have the bread all ready.

Viktorov poured a healthy slug into each of their glasses.

"Arthur, to poetry, which took so much and gave so little. But that little got us to the moon."

Viktorov was right. Warmth sped through Blaine's chest.

They expelled their breath and did not so much drink the vodka as pour it shimmering and viscous as quicksilver down their gullets.

The bread, which still had a touch of moon frost on it, made Blaine think of Halloween.

The first breath they took after the food had all the desperate gasping sweetness of the first breath you take after having been underwater a little too long.

"Good," said Blaine.

"Yes," said Viktorov, "good."

"I feel warmer."

"Good. It's funny, you know. The colder the vodka, the hotter you feel. Wait a second, I think the vodka has warmed my bloodstream enough to melt some parts of the label. I'm going to try to remove them."

"Careful, careful."

Viktorov's face grimaced with the anticipation of pain, then with the reality of pain as he manfully ripped both strips off his lips, wiping the blood on the arm of his space suit where it left only a faint brownish smear.

"I want to drink to poetry too," said Arthur Blaine, nodding at the empty tumbler which Viktorov needed no further prompting to refill. "I want to drink to the death of poetry. Poetry which has been killed by cartoons and physics. To the death of poetry! Long live poetry!"

"Long live it!"

Viktorov's eyes smiled to Blaine over the black tumbler. "So," said Viktorov with a mouth full of bread, "you really think poetry is dead?"

"The Godfather of the new universe loves Disney best."

"Hello?" said Viktorov.

"What I mean, Viktor, is that you and I are soldiers in an army that's been routed. And we only have two choices—run for our lives or turn one more time and fire."

"What are you exactly suggesting?"

"What I'm exactly suggesting is that while we're here, we have to do something. They're using us, but we can use them, too."

"How?"

"I don't know."

"Let's keep drinking. We're bound to think of something," said Viktorov in a pragmatic tone, pouring another round. He tried to exert more of a sense of measure this time, but at the end an extra slosh or two escaped his control. He waved dismissively at it.

"Your turn for a toast," said Blaine.

"I want to drink a toast to Russian proverbs," said Viktorov, raising his tumbler, "which are the greatest proverbs in the world. They are the true art form of Russia, cupolas and proverbs. And I want to drink to the simplest and most Russian proverb of all. And let's not only drink to it, let's live by it. That proverb is—'Eat bread and salt and speak the truth.'"

"Eat bread and salt and speak the truth," echoed Blaine.

This time they both slammed their tumblers down onto the table.

"The salt hurts my cuts," said Viktorov, a wince in his voice.

"That sounds like the truth."

"I'll tell you some other true things," said Viktorov reinvigorated by anger. "You heard Bardakov tell me to go to your LEM, didn't you?"

"I heard him."

"See!"

"See what?"

"They're everywhere."

"Who?"

"The state, the committee on state security, the KGB, whatever you want to call them, the sons of bitches are everywhere."

"The cameramen are KGB?"

"Of course, what did you think they were?"

"I thought they were cameramen."

"Of course, they're cameramen. They have plumbers, dentists, everything. It even saves money."

"But why are they here?"

"For the same reason they always are—to control the situation."

"I envy you."

"You envy me? I pity you."

"You pity me for envying you? I envy you for pitying me."

"Wait, stop, I can't follow it anymore. What was the point?"

"The point, Viktor, was that I envy you."

"Why?"

"I envy you because in your country poets are taken seriously enough that three KGB men had to accompany you to the moon. That could never happen in America. Poetry is of no consequence in America. It doesn't even have the weight of the paper it's written on."

"And in Russia everything weighs too much," said Viktorov. "Russia weighs a hundred million tons. I never knew how much Russia weighed until I floated weightless in space. Then I understood everything. How can I say it? The heart is like a dog. It only has one truth. It only wants to run free."

"I'll drink to the truth of the dog's heart," said Blaine in a pirate voice as he nudged his black tumbler across the table.

"We must," said Viktorov, pouring with no sense of measure at all this time, if only because that would have been out of keeping with the toast itself. "To the truth of the dog's heart."

Blaine threw back his head and bayed like a a hound: "Aaaaaooooooo!"

"Aaaaaaooooooooooo!" responded Viktorov, laughing out the vowels.

This time Blaine felt like a robot drinking antifreeze.

"But still," said Viktorov, wiping his lips, "I still pity you for envying me, you, who can just hop on a plane to Paris like it was a number 6 bus."

"Of course you can do what you want when nothing you do matters. I want to live in a place where poetry matters. I hate America."

"So, go to Paris."

"Paris, you think Paris is something. It's nothing anymore. The existentialists were its last dying gasp. It's just its own reflection now."

"Don't say that. I haven't been to Paris yet. I've only been to East Germany and the moon! They're not all that different either."

"Alright, alright, Viktor, let's drink to Paris."

They drank to Paris, then to Moscow, and finally ended their three-city tour with Boston.

"I also want to drink to garter belts," said Blaine, with a faraway look.

"Goethe belts?"

"No, garter belts."

"Yes, I know what they are. All women in Paris wear them, just waiting."

"And to women, their sadness and their humor!" said Blaine.

After taking bread, they both lapsed into a momentary silence, thinking of women, their sadness and their humor.

Snapping to, Viktorov quickly refilled their glasses and rose. "You know, I have drunk hundreds, maybe even thousands of toasts in my life, but I have never drunk a toast to vodka itself. And so now I want to toast vodka with vodka. . . . Vodka, I love you. Vodka, you have never failed me. Everything in life has failed me, Russia, poetry, women, but you, Oh Vodka, have never failed me. Never once did I drink a bottle of you that something marvelous and extraordinary did not happen. Never once did you fail to deliver me from the world of toothaches and puddles. Vodka, you are the true poetry, vodka, you are the last wildness, you are the one great love of my life and I thank you with all my heart! Vodka! Vodka!"

The toast alone was dizzying and, when combined with actual vodka, consumed in an atmosphere where the two men together weighed barely fifty pounds, the upsurge they experienced was much like the one that had torn them free from Earth freighted with a billion graves.

"What we need now is a concrete plan," said Viktorov.

"Yes," said Blaine. "We will have the world's attention for an hour. We have to know what we're going to do."

"We won't have it for an hour. They'll pull the plug as soon as we do anything funny."

"Alright," said Blaine, "now we know one thing. It'll have to be quick. What else do we know?"

"We know that you envy me and that I envy you for being able to hop the number 6 to Paris."

"That's true. That's important. That's key."

"But I pity you for envying me."

"Wait a second!" said Blaine. "We have proverbs, too. And I just remembered one, 'Actions speak louder than words'."

"I like that! I like that! Poets take action, which speaks louder than words, to save words from the world of constant action. Is that right? Is that what you're saying?"

"Yes, that's right. That's what I'm saying."

"I'll drink to that."

They drank to that.

"So," said Viktorov, "now we know everything but precisely what action to take."

"Yes," said Blaine, "but it'll come to us."

"A last tongue-wetter," said Viktorov shaking a few drops into each tumbler. "To the first bottle of vodka drunk on the moon, and to the idea it will unfailingly deliver!"

This time they did not bother with bread, instead savoring the arctic aftertaste that made their molars feel like icebergs drifting toward some Titanic.

"I am convinced," said Viktorov, "that the answer will come

to me as soon as I smash this bottle. My best ideas come to me when I'm smashing bottles."

"Not in here! We'll be cut to ribbons!"

"Yes, not in here, very practical."

Then, with the exquisite attention that only the profoundly inebriated can bring to detail, Blaine and Viktorov redonned their helmets and checked their air supply.

Ignoring ground-control's anxious calls for communication, they walked a distance from the LEM that Blaine perceived as the length of a football field and Viktorov as a hundred meters. Coming to a stop, they both looked up and saw China in the sky.

Viktorov threw back his head and howled: "Aaaaaaaaaa-ooooooooo!"

"Aaaaaaoooooooooooooo!" bayed Blaine, like a hound at the other end of a field picking up a cry.

"Aaaaaaaaaooooooooooooooooooooo!" they bayed in unison, for everything that is, for everything that had already come and gone, and for everything that would never come to pass.

Then Viktorov lofted the bottle end over end glinting with Earth light in the black air.

CHAPTER *20*

The General Secretary placed a finger to his lips as the doors closed behind Rabin and the room went from silent to hushed.

For a second Rabin was not sure whether he should move from where he stood. With the same finger the General Secretary had placed to his lips, he now beckoned Rabin to where he was standing at his desk.

The plush carpeting aborted any sound of footsteps in that office whose length far exceeded its height.

The General Secretary's third command was a slight but absolute nod. Rabin obeyed it as smoothly as he had the other two and looked down at the desk.

On the desk, grey against green baize, was the sort of magic disappearing slate Rabin had played with as a child, but which had never been one of his favorites.

The General Secretary took the wooden stylus, and, with his face displaying the concern of both a fellow man and an investor, he traced out: "Are you alright?"

Rabin used both hands, holding them in front of his chest and shaking them slightly to mean that he had been significantly better many times in the past, but was functioning pretty well just the same, thank you.

The General Secretary lifted the page briskly, and the words disappeared. He paused, as if giving a moment's thought to the wording, then wrote: "Have you understood the dream?"

Rabin had an impulse to take the stylus, but then thought better of it, certain that his hand would be trembling, at least somewhat, and he did not want to advertise that vibration.

He nodded.

"Follow me," said the General Secretary softly.

They went through a door upholstered in black leather that led to a large, dark-paneled dressing room with brass hooks and wooden benches.

The General Secretary sat down on a long wooden bench and began removing a shoe.

As soon as Rabin slipped off one shoe, he turned to stone. He could not take off his clothes with the General Secretary. It was not that he was modest or ashamed; it was just somehow absolutely impossible to be naked with the leader of the Union of Soviet Socialist Republics.

But when Rabin remembered himself conducting the cloud of silvery fish at Pacific Grove, his body became a stone statue that could move, a Golem in the Kremlin.

Ghosts of steam escaped the glass door which the General Secretary held open in impatient invitation. He had the shoulders of those who are born strong but whose bones are more fragile than they appear.

Inside, the steam made Rabin cough as it moistened his nicotine-stained mucous membranes and smoke-dried cilia. After the General Secretary had taken what seemed to be his usual place, Rabin sat at his left at what seemed the proper distance.

He could make out the General Secretary's form but not his features through the steam.

"We can talk in here," said the General Secretary.

"We couldn't out there?" asked Rabin.

"You never can tell," said the General Secretary. "In any case, I didn't want anyone else to hear what you're going to tell me. That's why I used the slate. It's a trick we learned from the dissidents. And so it cannot be said that they had no influence on Russian history."

Rabin peered through the steam, trying to read the General Secretary's expression, so to gauge the exact blend of humor that remark contained, but the air whirled with humid ectoplasms, and he saw nothing.

There was a pause, because the next subject of conversation would be the point.

Rabin took a little gasp of air for oxygen and luck then said: "Alright, I'll tell you what the dream means. I'll tell you the meaning of that Persian-sounding word, Ushassar."

Even through the steam, Rabin could feel the General Secretary recoil.

"Ushassar," he repeated taking pleasure in the power of that word, "is the letters USA and USSR melded together into USASSR.

"It represents your greatest fear, which is convergence. The fear of the USA and USSR merging into a single political corporation."

For a moment the steam was silent.

"That is absolutely right," said the General Secretary in a voice gentle with relief.

Rabin did not respond.

"And that means Poplavsky was right," continued the General Secretary. "I need a moment to think."

Now Rabin was only flesh, sweat stinging his eyes, a thimbleful in his navel. Even his shins were sweating.

The General Secretary's head seemed to rise as if he were going to begin to speak, but perhaps that had been a mirage in the steam.

"B-l," said a voice that Rabin thought the General Secretary's only for a moment. A voice from a distant room.

"B-l," the voice repeated.

Rabin saw the General Secretary reach over and press something. They would not be hearing that voice again.

"Let's get a quick shower now," said the General Secretary, rising and heading directly for the door.

Taking advantage of the comradeship of the showers, Rabin asked: "What happened?"

"We have a B-l emergency," said the General Secretary, soaping his arms vigorously.

"Is that bad?"

"No," said the General Secretary. Then, as if reaching a conclusion, he continued: "A B-level emergency is a secondary emergency. But a B-l emergency is the highest category of secondary emergency. A B-level emergency is an emergency on the level of prestige, not power." That's A-level."

"Well, at least it's not an A," said Rabin.

"Still, I have to call a partial Politburo meeting. All A-level emergencies require a full Politburo meeting. But B-level emergencies only require myself and two or more members."

"Are there C-level emergencies?"

"Yes."

"What are they?"

"Personal."

"Are they broken down into numbers, too?"

"Of course. We instantly know what level to worry on."

"Makes a certain sense," said Rabin.

"It will take a few hours for people to assemble. It's a Sunday. No one is too far away but some people might be out fishing. In the meantime I will get a report, and you can tell me your opinion."

By then they were done drying themselves. Rabin was about to reach for his pants when he saw the General Secretary take a fresh bath towel from a pile and wrap it around himself. And the very fact of the action was itself a command.

He followed the General Secretary into a small room whose lighting was a dim blue-white. Leather chairs and footstools were arranged in a semicircle around a large television.

Rabin didn't particularly like the feeling of leather on his still damp skin, but the footstool was a pleasure.

Leaning back in his chair, no more than a shadowy imperial profile, the General Secretary pointed the remote control at the set.

Looking like a combination newscaster and desk sergeant, a duty officer came on screen.

KGB-TV! thought Rabin, wondering at what exact point history had become an interactive television program.

"Comrade General Secretary," said the KGB duty officer, "we have had a B-l emergency in connection with the poetry event on the moon."

"Is there any footage?" asked the General Secretary.

"Unfortunately, there is. As you know, Comrade General Secretary, the two poets were scheduled to appear on world television today. And they did. For about three minutes. Then it happened."

"Let's see the tape," said the General Secretary.

There was a distant electronic squawk; the screen went white, and then an image locked in—the moon over the Kremlin.

"Speed up through the nonsense!" ordered the General

Secretary, and the images began leaping past. But Rabin's eye, honed on jump cuts, multi-image TV commercials, and avant-garde film, had no problem in distinguishing the American and Soviet LEMs landing on the moon, the Soviet poet offering the universe bread and salt, and three Soviet cosmonauts driving away in their lunar vehicle. The screen then became a triptych of lunar landscapes that must have been made by all three cameramen shooting at once from their vehicle. Craters raced by, conicular streaks of rusted sand. And then a tri-umphal rescue-tow operation was performed in a matter of seconds.

Rabin wasn't sure whether the two poets were having difficulty maneuvering on the lunar surface or whether everything seemed herky-jerky at that speed. The Soviet and American poets planted the flags of their countries side by side then reached over the flags and shook hands, to mean—what separates us is small, and what connects us is large and good.

Now the squeaking blur of the voice track slowed into the speed at which human speech is understood.

The American poet said: "To shame America for not honoring poetry, and because Russia is a country where poets are still taken seriously enough to punish, I, Arthur Blaine, hereby defect to Russia."

The American poet hopped over the imaginary boundary between the American and Soviet flags, landing beside the Russian poet who now spoke: "Simply because the heart is dog that wants to run free, I, Viktor Viktorovich Viktorov, hereby defect to America."

Baying like a hound dog, Viktorov sprang to the place beside the American flag that Blaine had occupied a moment before.

The face of the other American astronaut filled the screen, shouting: "Blaine, you stupid motherfu—"

"Enough," said the General Secretary.

The KGB duty officer came back on screen.

"And the current situation?" asked the General Secretary.

"The current situation is that Viktorov made a successful dash for the American LEM. The other American astronaut, Yates, is in there with him. We have taken the American poet Blaine into our LEM for three reasons."

"Let's hear them."

"First, our people could not gain access to the American LEM. Second, they could not remain on the surface of the moon much longer without recharging their oxygen supplies and they could not leave the American poet out there to die. And third, if they've got one of ours, we should have one of theirs."

"And what are our people saying to the American?" asked the General Secretary.

"Commander Bardakov is not saying anything. He's waiting to know what to say."

"Very good. Can I speak with him directly if I need to?"

"Yes."

"Good. For the meantime inform him that a decision on policy will be communicated to him as soon as it has been made."

"Yes, Comrade General Secretary."

"Has there been any report on world reaction?"

"Reports are still coming in. It's a Sunday, and there are important soccer matches in England, Belgium, and Italy. Not that many people were actually watching when it happened, but it'll be big news on Monday."

"Have the Americans issued a statement?"

"Nothing so far."

"Beep me on channel eleven if there are developments," said the General Secretary, clicking off the set, firing the remote like a space gun.

"Absolutely the most unnecessary . . ." hissed the General Secretary, his face crimped by anger and disgust. "What do you think?"

"Definitely qualifies as a B-1," said Rabin.

"No, I mean, what do you think happened up there?"

"It looks like reduced gravity or something caused their psyches to repolarize. They each overenvied what the other had. And this character defect caused them to defect."

"Is it solvable?"

"It doesn't seem absolutely impossible, though it's quite a snarl they've got up there."

"You stay here!" commanded the General Secretary in his last and most authoritarian command. The cords of muscles distinct in his calfs, the General Secretary sprinted from the room before Rabin had even formulated what would have been his reply—what does "here" mean? This chair? This room?

At first, Rabin decided to obey the order in its most absolute and fullest form. There was an odd peace in that chair, that room, the relief that comes when you are no longer dealing with Russians of any sort.

He gave a moment's thought to the lunar situation which he did not find particularly more outrageous than his own. Yes, Dr. Veer was probably right—there was some interaction between the hemispheres of the world and the mind. Energies were flashing back and forth, abduction, defection. Opposites were in dramatic alignment: Earth-Moon, East-West,

USA, USSR. Fear of convergence. But was the problem solvable? He'd need more facts.

Then, perhaps simply because Rabin was tired of sitting in the chair, he reasoned that the General Secretary could not have meant either the chair or the room when he said "You stay here." What he had of course meant was the general area which included the dressing room.

There was a towel on the dressing room floor, clearly not dropped but thrown aside.

As soon as Rabin was dressed, he was hungry. Then, without intending to, he perceived that his hunger was composed of an objective need for food and the subjective craving for a cheeseburger. Any other food would only fill his stomach like a pail. His very being cried out for the eucharist of the cheeseburger!

Perhaps, he thought, if he closed his eyes, he could at least subjectively satisfy the subjective part of his hunger. He pictured the white dust and glow of charcoal, the hiss of fat in fire, the seared stripes on the burger as it was turned and the cheese carefully placed on it.

But it was no good! It didn't work! There was no masturbatory equivalent of lunch!

And, if that weren't enough, when Rabin opened his eyes, there was Leonid Poplavsky holding a bundle bound in brown twine.

CHAPTER *21*

"Thanks to you," said Poplavsky, "I have been released on the General Secretary's personal orders. And I will be at today's Politburo meeting with you."

"Do you have power?"

"More than ever, but not total."

"Edov is still in charge?"

"Still."

"Leonid, do you have enough power to get me a cheeseburger?"

"You want a cheeseburger?"

"Yes. Badly."

"I can understand the nostalgia for national cuisine; I experienced it often myself in America."

"So?"

"Strictly speaking, there are only two places in Moscow where you can get anything resembling a cheeseburger," said Poplavsky. "One is the American embassy, but I'm sure you realize there is no possibility of you setting foot inside there."

"Maybe we can get one to go?"

"On one condition," said Poplavsky.

"Namely?"

"Namely that you don't try anything."

"Like what?"

"Like never mind."

"So, let's go."

"You can't go to the Kremlin in those clothes."

"Leonid, I already am in the Kremlin."

"I mean you can't go to a Politburo meeting in jeans, it's disgraceful."

"What's in the package, Leonid?"

"A suit. For you."

"What kind of suit?"

"A nice Russian suit. Dark blue. A serious suit."

"Let's have a look."

"I warned you the first day you might have to wear one," said Poplavsky, tearing away the twine to reveal a suit, so blue it was almost black. "So, what do you think?"

"I was never much for suits, Leonid. That's one of the reasons I stayed in California."

"This is not Love Beach! It's a meeting of the Soviet leadership!"

"Don't get excited. I'll try it on. If it's comfortable, I'll wear it. But like I told you before, I do my best when my stomach is happy and my clothes feel right."

Poplavsky stood back like a tailor, lacking only a yellow tape measure around his neck, a chunk of chalk in his hand, and a row of pins bristling between his lips.

"Not bad," said Rabin, buttoning the jacket and feeling a rich darkness surround his bones. "Not bad at all."

"Suits you," said Poplavsky.

The Kremlin proved to have many secret passageways, most of which were heavily guarded though some were not guarded at all, and Rabin could not tell if those were the passageways that everyone used, or whether they were so secret that even guards could not be allowed to know of their existence.

The limo's pale grey upholstery was puffy but firm. Its windows were also a sight-defying blue.

After a few stops, they began racing down what must have been one of the lanes reserved for the most important of the most important.

The next time the limo stopped, Rabin heard the left front door open and close.

After what seemed too long a time even for international relations, Rabin heard the front door open and close again and yet another intercom click on.

"Comrade Colonel," came a brisk young voice from the front seat, "they would be glad to provide us with a cheese-burger but, apparently, someone in our organization cut off their electricity overnight in retaliation for some heating problems that our UN mission in New York experienced, and, to make a long story short, the meat went bad and they threw it out."

"Threw it out!" cried Rabin.

"However," continued the voice in the front seat, "they do have egg salad, tuna salad, and chicken salad."

Rabin considered chicken salad for a second. Chicken salad could hit the spot on certain occasions, but this was not one of them.

"Didn't you say there were two places you could get a cheeseburger in Moscow?" said Rabin.

"Yes. Gatchina is the other," said Poplavsky.

"Gatchina has cheeseburgers?"

"You have heard of Gatchina?"

"Yes."

"What did you hear?"

"I heard that it was a special language school designed to look like America. And I seem to remember something about it being first outside Leningrad then moved to Moscow."

"Who squealed?"

"I don't remember the author's name."

"There is a McDonald's at Gatchina. It's top clearance but that shouldn't be a problem. And for me it will also be something of a sentimental journey—Gatchina was my alma mater."

Rabin smiled and nodded, as if to say, These things mean more as you get older.

"To Gatchina, and kill the intercom," ordered Poplavsky leaning slightly forward, then falling back as the limo sprang into motion.

"Is is far?" asked Rabin.

"Gatchina's location is a state secret."

"I just want to be able to time my appetite."

"The problem is that not only is Gatchina a state secret but you are a state secret as well. If I tell one state secret to another state secret, that immediately creates an entire new dimension of state secrecy to worry about."

Rabin did not reply. But it couldn't be far because they both had to be back for the meeting. Shouldn't he be listening for every factory whistle and train crossing, amassing the little pieces that could be fitted together later on? No, he told himself, he wasn't the type. He always had trouble remembering where he parked.

After about twenty minutes, the car stopped, its brakes squeaking with newness, not age.

But it was only to let something pass. Something that took a while to pass.

What could be more important than their Politburo limo? thought Rabin suddenly hating the blue blindfold of the window glass.

Then he had a definite intuition of titanic presence.

A nuclear missile was going by! Or a few of them.

And a missile would have the right-of-way over a limo involved in a B-l emergency.

"Won't be long," said Poplavsky in a confidential whisper.

Now they were moving at a slow, even rate as if they had already arrived at their basic destination and were only seeking some specific portion of it.

This meant that Gatchina was located near a missile site, which of course made sense since both were top secret.

Poplavsky flattened his hair with his left hand then tugged at an ear lobe with his right.

They stopped. A door opened, making a corrugated sound, which it repeated behind them after they had advanced twenty feet.

"We're here," said Poplavsky.

"Can I get out?" asked Rabin.

"The driver will open your door."

Rabin took a deep, gasping breath and braced himself.

The driver opened the door, Rabin slid himself out, and he was in America. If America was a nameless town, a cluster of franchises located less than a minute away from an off-ramp. The McDonald's shared a parking lot with Bud's Esso. There was a Holiday Inn just past the traffic light.

Green-haired punks lounged maliciously on the concrete picnic tables in front of McDonald's, radios blaring.

"Leonid, I have to ask you a question. I have to know if my intuition's working. About five minutes ago we stopped to let something go by. Was it a missile?"

"I couldn't see, but it well could have been."

"It made sense to me that Gatchina would be located near a missile installation."

"Gatchina is not only located *near* a missile installation. Gatchina *is* a missile installation. There are forty warheads under this artificial turf," said Poplavsky, lifting up one end of the grass in front of McDonald's to reveal smooth concrete. "In the event of nuclear war, the Gatchina model of America will be the first to go."

Rabin instinctively looked up to the sky, and it was only then that he realized he was inside something vast, probably a hangar, but one that could have easily housed a dozen 747s, which meant that the blue of the sky and the interstate in the distance were frescoes by some Giotto of visual disinformation.

As they walked up the heavily-puddled flagstone walk to the McDonald's, Rabin caught sight of a man reaching furtively into a blue dumpster.

"Is that man Russian or American?" asked Rabin.

"Russian, of course," said Poplavsky.

"No, what I mean is, is he supposed to be American?"

"American, of course."

Hungry as he was, and now even able to smell meat grease on the air, Rabin came to a full stop.

"You are not going to deny the presence of the homeless in major urban centers?" said Poplavsky playfully.

Noticing that he was being looked at, the bum began striding toward Poplavsky and Rabin.

His filthy beard was specked with twig-like scraps. Long hair fell across his bruised face. He had a half-pint wrapped in a brown paper bag in one pocket.

"Got any spare change?" he asked.

"Don't even touch his hand," said Poplavsky to Rabin who had automatically reached for his change.

"I used to be a prominent eye surgeon," said the bum. "You heard me, an eye surgeon. Then I started taking just that one little shot before going into surgery. Just to steady my hand. That's how it all got started. Leonid, is that you?"

"Grisha! I didn't recognize you! How long have you been working here?"

"After the Americans kicked us out of the UN, I spent a little time in Sri Lanka. Then I developed lumbago and they transferred me home. I've been here three years now. I like it. How have you been?"

"Fine, Grisha, fine, but we're in a rush now."

"Stop by when you get a chance," said Grisha over his shoulder as he walked off toward the teenagers listening to their radio on the concrete picnic table.

As he and Poplavsky approached the glass doors, Rabin could hear Grisha asking plaintively: "Got any spare change?"

"Fuck off," said the teenagers. "Get lost."

"Your American youth today has no heart," muttered Poplavsky with indignation.

The blonde at the register looked a little too old and sophisticated for the McDonald's productive-teen uniform. As he approached the counter, Rabin saw that she was the petite-yet-vital type, the hair piled on her head exposing her neck and ear. His eye went right to the striations of her neck where it met her hair and suddenly all he wanted to do was kiss that throat and breathe in her hair. When he looked over and into her cougar-grey eyes, they were already laughing.

"Nothing for me," said Poplavsky as they reached the counter. "Or maybe a tea."

"I'd like a Big Mac, fries, and a large Diet Coke," said

Rabin not knowing what else to say and sure that this at least needed saying.

"I'm sorry, Comrades, neither of you are on the photo list of today's customers."

"Listen very carefully, darling," said Poplavsky moving in front of Rabin at the counter.

"My name isn't darling. My name is Lieutenant Valentina Borisovna Gurev."

"Valya, I am Colonel Leonid Poplavsky, State Security. This man with me is himself a state secret. We are here on Politburo business. And so the burger, fries, and Coke you are immediately to serve him should be considered a direct order from the General Secretary."

"I am sworn to obey my orders," said Valya. "And my orders are to serve no one not on the photo list. If you care to speak with my immediate superior, we have a direct line to him here."

Now Rabin hated her. She was a Soviet company girl.

But hating her made him desire her more. Now he wanted to shake her every bit as much as he wanted to stroke and embrace her.

"And who is your immediate superior?'

"Edov."

"I knew it!" exploded Poplavsky.

"Valya, listen," said Rabin, leaning onto the counter. "I'm an American, I'm not here to practice my English."

"I have to say that your English is almost perfect."

"What do you mean almost perfect? It is perfect."

"No, it isn't," she said matter-of-factly. "I have heard bet-ter pronunciation."

"Alright, I slur things a little, I admit it. But that's because I'm a native speaker."

"If you're an American and you wanted a burger, why didn't you go to the embassy?"

"We did, we did," interjected Poplavsky. "The meat went bad in their freezer."

"I'd love to help," she said coquettishly, melting Rabin for a moment until he realized that the subjunctive meant that the bitch wasn't budging!

"Go out and look at the license plate on our limo," said Poplavsky.

"No."

"Why not?"

"You'll run behind the counter and grab a burger. And I could be held accountable for deserting my post."

"Didn't you ever hear of civil disobedience? Didn't they make you read Thoreau in your classes on American life?" yelled Poplavsky. "Don't you know that sometimes rules have to be broken so that higher laws can be obeyed?"

"Everyone knows that," said Valya. "The only question is, when?"

"Now!"

"No."

Poplavsky puffed up his chest, tucked in his chin, then to Rabin's surprise he ran out the front door.

"Listen, I'm sorry," said Valya when they were alone. "I really am. But this is top clearance here and they test you all the time. Someone came in last week. All he wanted was a small Seven-Up to go. I almost gave it to him. And a good thing I didn't because he turned out to be doing a spot check."

"The difference is that this time there's a risk in refusing," said Rabin.

"We'll see about that," she said turning her face away, refusing to speak with him either as an official or as a woman.

Now he saw that her lips were slightly puffy in profile.

"We're taking over!" shouted Poplavsky, bursting through the floor door followed by Grisha.

Valya pressed an alarm button that sounded immediately, and, in the same motion, grabbed a large kitchen knife which she brandished professionally enough to slow Poplavsky's momentum substantially.

"I'll cut a Big Mac out of you!" threatened Valya with heroic sincerity.

Grisha grabbed two trays, handed one to Poplavsky, and, using them as shields, they began slowly approaching her.

Rabin looked out the window. The attendants from Bud's Esso were charging toward the McDonald's wielding tire irons and monkey wrenches. But apparently some plan of defense had been worked out between Poplavsky and the teenagers, who were now lining up and whirling chains over their heads.

Poplavsky had Valya backed up against the fries machine.

Two cooks ran out of the kitchen and tackled Grisha from behind.

Poplavsky lunged forward, ducking almost to one knee, moving the plastic tray to take Valya's slashes. Reaching behind him, he grabbed a burger with one hand and tossed it to Rabin, then disappeared behind the counter with a howl.

Rabin ran to a table and tore off the wrapper. Just as he bit in, the attacking force from Bud's Esso overpowered the punks, and they all imploded the plate glass in a single tumbling mass of overalls, black leather, wrenches, green hair, and chains.

His teeth had bitten through the burger to the bottom bun, but for a moment Rabin had lockjaw. What had stunned his mind was not that he was wearing a Russian suit in a top-secret-KGB-language-school-missile-site McDonalds, but that he no longer found any of this improbable in the least.

"Stick the burger in your pocket and let's get out of here!" yelled Poplavsky over his shoulder as he slid himself feet first over the counter. "That bitch fought like a tiger, but I grabbed a Coke for you."

"Is she alright?"

"Is she alright? Look at this!" puffed Poplavsky displaying a cut that ran above four knuckles. "The Kremlin! Immediately!" he yelled as soon as they were in the limo. "We can't be late. Do you have any idea how bad it is to be late for a Politburo meeting?"

As Poplavsky sucked blood from his fingers, Rabin finished the burger, alternating bites and sips, but leaving himself enough Coke to wash the meat grit from his cavities at the end.

Wincing, Poplavsky wrapped his handkerchief around the four fingers, watching in dismay as the red wet through.

Rabin burped, a sharp carbonated burp that reminded him of solitary lunches on the grassy hill overlooking Monterey Bay, the air pocked by artillery and the barking of seals.

As if looking down from heaven, he smiled at that memory of himself. He had thought that was unhappiness, and it had only been life.

"We may make it yet," said Poplavsky with a nervous glance at his watch. "We just may."

CHAPTER 22

They made it, they made it. They even had a couple of minutes to spare.

As they entered the conference room, the General Secretary paused in a conversation and flashed Rabin a quick smile, half in greeting, half in apology for his sudden departure from the TV room.

A rectangular mahogany table had already been set with mineral water, pencils, pads, and ashtrays.

A man was drawing the shades as if performing a military operation. Four others were checking the TV cameras, one in each corner of the room.

Scanning the scene as if he were at any gathering, checking to see who was alone or which little group was joinable, Rabin saw that the little groups in that room were in fact political units, molecules of power in Soviet suits. He and Poplavsky were one such unit. Not the worst one either. The others had noticed the special smile. Now Rabin could feel at least two of those molecules emitting beams in their direction, beams that could result in mutual attraction and bonding into larger and more powerful units.

Rabin swung around to face Poplavsky and to let the interested atoms know that he was not particularly interested, which would of course make them more interested.

"Who's here?" Rabin asked, flicking a shred of lettuce off Poplavsky's lapel.

"Edov isn't," said Poplavsky. "It looks like a meeting of the Central Committee of the Politburo."

"The Politburo has a central committee? I thought only the party had a central committee."

"Everything has a central committee. Even the Central Committee."

"So who is the General Secretary talking to?"

"That's Petrov. He used to be head of propaganda. Then we switched to the new policy of openness, *glasnost*. The two merged, and now he's head of *propaglasnost*. The man by himself is Ermilov, the General Secretary's interpreter. He doesn't count. In the far corner, the head of the space program is talking with the head of the Writers' Union. They're both in trouble. The man with the medals is, of course, Marshal Minomyotov, head of defense, speaking with Revanzhnadze, the Minister of Foreign Affairs. Those two and Petrov have all the weight. Revanzhnadze is the ideological enemy of the head of the space program, a high-tech neo-Trotskyite who favors beginning socialist colonies in space before there is communism on one planet first."

"But isn't that Edov?" asked Rabin.

Edov's arrival sent ripples of electro-magnetic terror through the air.

Both the allusion to Trotsky and the entrance of Edov had reminded Rabin that, for all the suits and cameras there, that room was a jungle, and the loser would end up just as the loser always ends up in nature—eaten alive.

As Edov approached, the groups of molecules began to

bunch and densen. Energy was withdrawn from the air until the entire atmosphere had gone into suspension.

But that only lasted a few seconds until the General Secretary clapped his hands and the room aligned in a dynamic silence.

The host was about to assign places.

The General Secretary paused long enough to give the matter a moment's executive thought, and to brandish his power to pause at that moment. The heads of space and the writers' union were to sit at the far end of the table, indicating both their remoteness from favor and the negligible role they were to play in the discussion. The next pair were Petrov, the head of Propaglasnost, and Ermilov, the interpreter. "Ermilov, you will come to my side if we need to communicate with the Americans," said the General Secretary. Defense and Foreign Affairs were last, and closest to the head of the table.

Everyone was seated now but the General Secretary, Edov, Poplavsky, and Rabin. There were only three chairs left: the one at the head of the table and the two at the end.

"Edov, you will sit at my right," said the General Secretary.

Edov took his seat quickly, even a little too quickly, thereby losing a bit of what he had just gained.

"Poplavsky, you will be on my left."

Poplavsky took his seat less quickly than Edov, but he was not projecting unassailable confidence either.

"I will now introduce Professor Eliot Rabin, here as a specialist in Soviet-US relations."

Rabin nodded slightly, and all those seated at the table nodded slightly.

"A chair for the professor!" the General Secretary ordered the man just drawing the last of the curtains.

The timing, Rabin noticed, was balletic. There just happened to be a chair by the last curtain. It was whisked from that position to one behind and slightly to the right of Poplavsky, as if the spot had been marked with invisible chalk.

The chair drew Rabin right into its firm blue plush, and he was seated before he knew it, his view now that of Poplavsky's ear, the General Secretary's profile, and Edov's eyes, bright blue with hatred.

"Everyone has been briefed?" asked the General Secretary.

The table rippled with nods and unhappiness.

"This is the most serious B-l crisis we have faced in several years, and it is extremely important that it be resolved in our favor. First, we will review the existing material, and then the floor will be open for discussion. I require frank presentation of position, comrades, and I'd like to hear a few good ideas for a change," said the General Secretary picking up a microphone the size of a thumb from his blotter. "Lights."

The lights went out, plunging the room into a darkness so absolute that Rabin touched the back of Poplavsky's chair to ground himself.

"Ours," said the General Secretary.

The question—Our what?—which automatically arose in Rabin's mind was immediately answered by a wall-sized freeze-frame close-up of an American astronaut whom Rabin recognized from the previous screening as Yates.

"You have all seen the segment of our live broadcast that has unfortunately also been seen by millions throughout Russia, I mean the Soviet Union, and the rest of the world," said the General Secretary. "However, in the best Soviet documentary tradition, one of our cameras continued filming after transmission to earth was cut off. Watch carefully. Go!"

". . . cker," said Yates as the freeze frame instantly thawed into movement and speech.

For a few seconds the screen was a turbulence of yellow dust whose color reminded Rabin of Wyoming. Viktorov emerged from the cloud jabbing the American flag at the camera like a bayonet. Two Soviet cosmonauts hit Viktorov from either side like a pair of linebackers, but the moon did not allow the brutal impact of earth and they only spun and tumbled like clothes in a drier. Yates was pounding Blaine's helmet with a moon rock.

The sound track was composed exclusively of clunks and curses.

Now Viktorov was on the stairs of the American LEM and had one foot in the door. He was gesturing toward the camera with the thumb of his space glove sticking up between the index and middle finger of his space glove.

Funny how giving someone the finger that way has no meaning, thought Rabin, made immediately wary by the inappropriateness of the thought.

Suddenly, but with one-sixth of earth's suddenness, Blaine stopped beating a cosmonaut and bounded away toward the Soviet LEM. One Soviet cosmonaut started after him but then hesitated as if unsure whether it was more important to regain Viktorov or to prevent the American from entering their LEM.

Here, apparently, the Soviet cameraman who was still filming experienced something exceedingly rare among photographers in the twentieth century—his ethics overcame his professionalism. Real life suddenly mattered to him more than anything else. Rushing to join the fray, do his duty, serve his country, help his friends, he let his camera fall. It tumbled gently downward sliding along a curved rink of black space, and came to rest pointing at earth. Edges of South America could be seen through the clouds.

The lights came on, startling optic nerves.

The General Secretary shot a double-barreled beam of disfavor toward the far end of the table.

"I do have one piece of new information," said the head of the Soviet space program.

"Namely?"

"According to the biosensors in Viktorov's suit, by the time of the incident, he had far exceeded the scientific norms of sobriety."

"You mean he was drunk?!" roared the General Secretary.

"Yes, to put it in nonscientific terms, he was sloshed to the gills—on vodka, apparently."

"How did he get the vodka to the moon?" asked the General Secretary.

"It may have been baked into the bread used in the opening ceremony," interjected Edov.

"Has the baker been arrested?"

"The baker has been arrested," said Edov. "I was a few minutes late arriving here because I was personally interrogating him."

"And what did he say?" asked the General Secretary.

"He hasn't cracked yet," admitted Edov with a downward glance that he tried to resist but could not.

"You blockhead!" roared the General Secretary. "Who cares if he baked it in or not? What good does that do us now? And besides, those were your men there on the moon with Viktorov. They should have known better than to leave him alone."

"They went to help the American astronaut. They thought it was a great opportunity to gain prestige by filming a Soviet crew performing a lunar rescue."

"Prestige, prestige, I'm sick of prestige!" said the General Secretary pounding the table with his fist. "Who invented it in the first place!"

Regaining his self-control, the General Secretary switched his eyes from space to literature. "And how was it that you selected an alcoholic poet to send to the moon?"

"Comrade General Secretary, they're all drinkers. And our information indicated some correlation between political loyalty and heavy drinking."

"Apparently, that information was incomplete."

"I have a concrete suggestion," said Revanzhnadze. "One, that the propaglasnost department get right to work on creating a new video version of events that will mix actual and staged footage to document the fact that Viktorov was abducted against his will. Two, that we inform the American president that if Viktorov is not returned to us on the moon, we will take drastic and immediate action. I believe that Comrade Minomyotov is better equipped to take the scenario from here."

Minomyotov, whose old head seemed magnetically attracted to the decorations on his chest, threw that head back and said: "If Viktorov is not returned on the moon, we can send Soviet craft into the upper atmosphere and force the American reentry vessel to land on Soviet territory or else be blasted out of the sky."

"And what about the American in our LEM?" asked the General Secretary.

"Bring him back then kick him out. Or arrest him as a spy. Or shoot them down."

"We can't kill an American citizen."

"He's asked for political asylum," interjected Revanzhnadze. "The Supreme Soviet can confer citizenship on him in two minutes. Then we can do whatever we want to him."

"That's a little formalistic," said the General Secretary, the corners of his mouth tucking inward.

The room became still except for the inevitable creakings of chairs and clearings of throats. After a few seconds it was apparent that this silence could only be broken by the General Secretary himself.

Rabin could see that the General Secretary had not been very taken with what he'd heard so far. And besides, those really weren't very good ideas, just updated versions of hit and lie.

Poplavsky's head was down like a horse waiting out a rainstorm.

"We will now take a brief look at the way the American networks are covering the incident. Which one do you suggest we watch, Petrov?"

"On the basis of last week's Neilsens, we should watch the one who wears the sweaters and makes eyes at the camera, what's his name?"

The General Secretary whispered into his mike, and the room went dark again.

"In what some are considering a sort of Keystone Cops in space, the double defection of the two poetnauts has disrupted an otherwise peaceful Sunday here in Washington. The President is in a prayer brunch with representatives of the American Ophthalmologists Association and cannot be reached for comment. Those of you just tuning in may want a look at the little footage of the incident we have."

As soon as the image of Viktorov and Blaine standing by their respective flags appeared, the General Secretary yelled, "Kill it!" and the lights came back on.

His eyes directly on Rabin, the General Secretary asked: "What does 'Keystone Cops' mean?"

For a second Rabin had no voice in his throat. Then he said: "Keystone Cops means crazy comedy."

"In other words, at this stage the American media is treating the incident as a farce?"

"Yes."

"Bad. Comedy takes away all prestige. Tragedy at least has dignity. But it may get tragic yet," said the General Secretary, "At least for some people in this room."

There was another silence, a very tense and brittle one. "Any other ideas?" asked the General Secretary.

"I have one," said Minomyotov. "Invade Iran."

"What good is that?"

"First, it will eclipse this foolish affair. Second, it will cause enormous confusion in the western camp, which hates Iran. And third, we might get Iran out of it."

"We'll have to do it sooner or later," said Revanzhnadze, backing up his ally Minomyotov.

"I'm against the idea," said Petrov. "Openness is a good policy, but openly grabbing a whole country might be stretching it too far. Geopolitically, of course, there are great advantages, but who wants to try and rule Iranians? Too much energy is required."

"I tend to agree with Petrov," said the General Secretary. "Still, it's an idea. Let's hear more."

"I have another idea," said Minomyotov.

"What?"

"We could invade one of the socialist countries. Bulgaria, for example. They wouldn't mind."

"But there's nothing happening in Bulgaria," said the General Secretary.

"No one in the West has the slightest idea of what's happening in Bulgaria," said Revanzhnadze. "And besides, the very fact that nothing is happening there will make an invasion all the easier and all the safer for our troops."

"Or, if you want a fight, we could hit Poland," added Minomyotov.

"Can't you think of anything but invasion?" asked the General Secretary irritably.

"Yes," replied Minomyotov, with soldierly dignity, "defense."

"But there's no one attacking us."

"I know. That's why I thought of invasion."

"It's a last resort," said the General Secretary in a tone indicating that the idea was being shelved and that they had better come up with something better.

"Terrorists could blow up some monument, the Eiffel Tower, Big Ben?" proposed Edov.

The General Secretary did not respond to the suggestion but said: "We have a link-up with our LEM. I'm going to speak with them now to learn if there have been any further developments that might influence our thinking." He paused as if to give ironic emphasis to the last word. Then he spoke into the mike: "Connect me to our LEM."

"Lieutenant Colonel Bardakov here," said a voice from a quarter of a million miles away.

"Has there been any change in the situation?" asked the General Secretary.

"The American astronaut Yates is demanding the return of Blaine."

"And what are you doing?"

"Demanding the return of Viktorov."

"And what does the American astronaut say?"

"He says that the three of us should grab Blaine and then

bring him back to the American LEM and, while we're there, grab Viktorov."

"What do you think?"

"The problem is, Comrade General Secretary, what if we drag Blaine back and then we can't grab Viktorov?"

"But it will be four against one."

"But Blaine will fight with Viktorov, and that makes it four against two. And who knows if Yates will really fight for us? And so that could make it four against three, and it's hard to hurt people up here."

"I see, I see," said the General Secretary. "For the time being do nothing. And keep that Blaine. It's all we have that the Americans want."

"One other point, Comrade General Secretary," said Bardakov.

"Yes?" said the General Secretary with a short sigh, knowing without the least uncertainty that it would not be good news.

"For various technical reasons, we can only spend another hour and twenty minutes here, and then we have to return to the command module."

"So now there's a time limit, too!" said the General Secretary, slamming the mike against the table, causing genuine pain a few seconds later to Bardakov's already throbbing head.

There was a long silence, heavy as a winter dusk.

"We could release fifty thousand Jews in one day!" cried Edov, propelled to his feet by the force of his idea. "We could flood Vienna and Rome with Jews. It will be like an exodus. The Jewish-controlled media, meaning nearly all of it, will forget all about those dimwits on the moon!"

"No! Never!" bellowed Poplavsky as if gored. "Jews are

more precious than roubles or prestige. There might be two Einsteins and a Rabin in the batch!"

Poplavsky's eruption stole Edov's thunder and caused all eyes in the room to focus on Rabin.

The General Secretary flashed a quick smile of official encouragement as he said: "Yes, we have yet to hear from you on the subject, Professor Rabin."

Clearing his throat, Rabin said: "There is one little section of the videotape that I would like to see again."

"Very good," said the General Secretary. "I'll have them fast forward it. You say when to stop."

The fast-forward made it seem all the more like Keystone Cops. But amending his old definition, Rabin now preferred to think of the incident as a space comedy by Plato adapted for television by Hegel and Groucho. "Stop!" said Rabin just as Blaine's lips were opening. Blaine said: "To shame America for not honoring poetry, and because Russia is a country where poets are taken seriously enough to punish, I, Arthur Blaine, hereby defect to Russia."

Groans and indignant gasps could be heard in the darkness.

Joined on his side of the Soviet flag by Blaine, Viktorov said: "Simply because the heart is a dog that wants to run free, I, Viktor Viktorovich Viktorov, hereby defect to America."

"Drunken swine!" hissed the General Secretary.

"That's all I need," said Rabin.

"Kill it."

"Mind if I smoke?" asked Rabin.

"Not if it helps you think," said the General Secretary.

"It does."

"So, smoke."

"I don't have any cigarettes."

"Who has a cigarette?" asked the General Secretary.

"I do," said Minomyotov pulling out a crumpled pack of Marlboros from his rear pants pocket.

"Can I take a couple?" asked Rabin.

"Keep the pack."

"Before I start, General Secretary, there's one thing I want to say. At the beginning of the session you asked for frank positions, and, frankly, I'd like to remind you that I am here under duress."

"Yes."

"I'm asking for a deal."

"Yes?"

"It's simple. I do my best for you here, and then I go home."

Rabin felt Poplavsky wince, and not from the pain in his fingers.

The General Secretary did not have to think long. "We agree."

"Good," said Rabin. "Alright, both Blaine and Viktorov stated their motivations quite clearly. Blaine is defecting because he wants poetry to be treated seriously and Viktorov because he wants to run free."

"Yes," said General Secretary.

"Because of various complex historical reasons that we won't go into here, Blaine comes from a society that doesn't value literature and Viktorov comes from one that values it too much."

"Yes," said the General Secretary.

Edov was squirming with fury. Poplavsky had become very pacific, smiling reverently up at Rabin.

"We can't change Blaine and Viktorov, at least we can't change them quickly enough," said Rabin reintroducing the time-element factor. "And we certainly can't change American and Soviet society in an hour and twenty minutes."

"With all due respect, the professor is stating the obvious," interjected Revanzhnadze.

"So are you!" said the General Secretary.

"So," continued Rabin, gladdened that the General Secretary had exerted power on his behalf, "we cannot change the poets and we cannot change their societies. But . . . but we can change *their* relationship to society."

"How?"

Rabin paused, exercising his right, and his need to do so. His eyes dimmed momentarily then laughed with light.

"We need a four-way linkup. Us, the Soviet LEM, the American LEM, and the President of the United States."

"We can have it as soon as we want it," said the General Secretary, "but not until I know why you want it."

"We need to take the broadest historical view for a moment," said Rabin. "For example, what stage of historical development is the Soviet Union at, developed socialism or communism?"

The General Secretary said: "We do not claim to have entered the phase of communism yet."

"But that's the goal isn't it?" asked Rabin.

"Of course," said the General Secretary, almost as if Rabin had suggested something indecent.

"And what is the ultimate goal of communism?" asked Rabin.

"The withering away of the state," said the General Secretary.

"Exactly!" said Rabin. "The most mysterious part of the doctrine! The Holy Ghost of communism!"

"And what does this have to do with the case at hand?" asked the General Secretary in a voice whose patience was wearing thin.

"At this very second," said Rabin, "you are facing a choice between two roads, one which leads to convergence, a convergence of the USA and USSR that might be represented as Ushassar, and another road which leads to communism."

"I choose communism."

"I was somehow sure you would," said Rabin. "The current situation is one of convergence, is it not? A Russian poet wants to become part of America, and an American poet wants to become part of Russia. First, it's the poets who, as the American poet Ezra Pound said, are the antennae of the race, and then it's everybody else. In thirty years you won't be able to tell Kharkov from Portland."

Rabin paused to let the effect of the comparison sink in.

"The only force strong enough to withstand convergence is real communism which you, General Secretary, can personally launch in history, not by any mere Khrushchevian bluster but by a genuine, concrete, and specific act."

"Namely?"

"By giving Viktorov exactly what he wants. The state grants Viktorov the privilege of perfect freedom and does so proudly, holding up this act for all the world to see as the first atom of the state withering away. And don't worry, the second atom doesn't have to wither for a good long time."

"The propaglasnost value would be immense!" said Petrov, smelling a winner.

"We can't have Viktorov setting an example like that!" yelled Edov with an edge of angry desperation to his voice.

"The thing about freedom," said Rabin, thinking how wonderful it would be to have a little of his own, "is that it's like everything else—not as good as you might have imagined. Why else have an imagination."

The General Secretary gazed off into a distance, which

only he, because of his political elevation, could see.

"The state must not surrender one iota of its power," objected Minomyotov.

"Convergence is the only other choice," reiterated Rabin.

"Comrades," said the General Secretary, "I propose that we assume the great and awesome responsibility of leading Russia, I mean the Soviet Union, from the stage of developed socialism into actual communism. All those in favor, raise their right hand."

Only Minomyotov and Edov failed to raise their right hands.

Although it was the same room, and the same people in the same suits, everyone knew everything was different now.

"And your idea for the American?" asked the General Secretary?"

"Just as good," said Rabin.

"Time is short. Just tell me where the American poet ends up."

"In the American LEM."

"Get me a hook-up with our LEM, the American LEM, and the American President," said the General Secretary into the mike.

As the technical arrangements, audible as squawks on the conference room's sound system, were being made, the table went into momentary recess. Some people merely stretched and yawned, proof that even a cosmic crisis could have its tedious side. Others buzzed and whispered. At the far end of the table, Space and Literature stared blankly at each other. Edov and Minomyotov, the lone dissenters, were looking at each other across the table without speaking, yet messages seemed to be streaming back and forth from their eyes.

Could they be planning something? wondered Rabin. After

all, those two were in charge of the bullets, the final oratory of the submachine gun.

He stole a glance at the General Secretary who seemed to be pleased both by the solution Rabin had proposed and the terms in which it had been couched. Thank God, he's afflicted with the vanity of modernity, thought Rabin, knowing that he wouldn't have stood a chance with an old-timer like Minomyotov.

"Good morning, Mr. General Secretary," said the President of the United States, his face filling the wall screen. "At least it's still morning over here."

"Ermilov, come over here. Interpret for me," said the General Secretary. "Good morning and good day, Mr. President."

"You're looking well, Mr. General Secretary."

"Thank you, and so are you. The surgery was a complete success I take it."

"Never felt better."

"We have a sort of complicated situation on our hands, Mr. President."

"To put it mildly."

"It's even a little more complicated than you think."

"How's that?"

"For reasons that really do not matter now, I have an American, Professor Eliot Rabin, here with me in the Kremlin."

"You've arrested him?"

"No, not at all."

"Then what's he doing there? Has he defected like that stupid poet?"

"No, he hasn't defected at all, he's . . . he'll explain it all when he returns to the United States."

"Mr. General Secretary?"

"Yes?"

"I've just been handed a computer printout that indicates that no US citizen by the name of Eliot Rabin is currently traveling on a US passport in the USSR."

"This is true. He came here without a passport or a visa."

"Now how the hell could that be?"

"He was forcibly abducted here, transported in a special compartment in the cargo hold of an Aeroflot plane," said the General Secretary.

"You mean you abducted him and you're holding him hostage?"

"No, no, no, we don't want anything for him."

"I can't stand it when Americans are taken hostage. Do you know what happened yesterday in Pittsburgh?"

"No."

"An Islamic splinter group abducted an unemployed steel worker."

"Abducted him to where?"

"If we knew that, we'd have a tactical squad on the way there right now."

"I'm sorry to hear of this misfortune, Mr. President, but I can assure you, and so can Professor Rabin himself, that he is not being held hostage. I will give you him right now."

The General Secretary handed Rabin the mike.

"Good morning, Mr. President."

"How are they treating you?"

"Fine, Mr. President, fine. It's an unusual situation."

"So, you're right there in the Kremlin?"

"Yes, Mr. President."

"And you can leave at any time?"

"Any time!" yelled the General Secretary before Rabin even had a chance to respond.

"I guess you have the General Secretary's word on that."

"There's one thing I don't understand, Professor."

"What's that, Mr. President?"

"What the hell exactly are you doing there?"

"Well, at the moment, I'm trying to help unravel the problem up there on the moon. I think I've found a solution to getting the Russian back into his own LEM."

"You have? What is it?"

"It doesn't matter. Only a Russian could understand it. The important thing is to get Blaine back into our LEM."

"How?"

"By offering him what he wants. I mean if you give a person exactly what he wants, how's he going to complain?"

"People always complain."

"That's another story."

"So what are you suggesting?"

"You see, Blaine is unhappy because he lives in a society where poetry is not important."

"So what are you saying I should do?"

"Give him what he wants! It's the only solution. He wants literature to be important enough to punish, so punish him! Your precedent can be the Ezra Pound case."

"Could you refresh my memory on that one?"

"Ezra Pound was an American poet who lived in Italy during the Second World War and collaborated with the fascists by speaking on the radio."

"The son of a bitch! What did we do to him?"

"We put him in a mental hospital."

"What the hell kind of punishment is that?"

"Believe me, it's a punishment."

"So are you saying that I should throw Blaine in the nut-house?"

"No, Mr. President, I have something different in mind. You remember Thoreau?"

"Refresh my memory on that one."

"He was the guy who went to live in the woods."

"Of course, of course."

"Well, he also said that there is a higher law that we some-times have to take into account."

"Yes?"

"What I think you have to do, Mr. President, is use your moral authority as president of the United States to morally exile Blaine to Alaska. It won't be a legal agreement; it will simply be a moral and historical agreement between you and Blaine. The agreement can be broken at any moment with no legal consequences for either party. That way you can keep the lawyers out of it."

"You mean you think he'll agree to be exiled to Alaska?"

"I'm sure he will. Poets love to be exiled. It makes them feel important."

"I would like to get this whole thing over with. It's loused up the weekend, and it's putting a serious strain on US-Soviet relations just when they were starting to get good again."

"The Russians aren't happy about it either."

"Let's give it a go."

Ermilov hesitated over this idiom then said: "OK, let's proceed."

"Mr. General Secretary, we're going to link you in to our LEM so you can talk with Viktorov," said the President. "And could you please link us in to your LEM so we can talk with Blaine?"

"You can have both image and voice contact from our LEM," said the General Secretary.

"Good," said the President. "Sorry we can't return the favor."

"My technicians inform me that link-up has occurred on our side. You may speak with Blaine."

"We have link-up, too. You may speak with Viktorov."

"But who should go first?"

"What does it matter?"

"Let me think, let me think," said the General Secretary. "If the one who goes first fails, that takes all the pressure off the one who goes second. But, but if the one who goes first succeeds, that puts tremendous pressure on the one who goes second."

"Sounds like a toss-up to me," said the President.

"So, let's toss, Mr. President," said Rabin.

"In whose room?"

"How about here, I'll keep an eye on it."

"Alright, let's stop wasting time. Flip a rouble there. I call it heads."

Everyone began fishing in their pockets but the General Secretary was already holding a commemorative Lenin rouble up to the camera. He paused, then flicked it, gleaming end over end.

It landed Leninside up. The camera zoomed in on Lenin's face, which seemed to radiate special pride and confidence now that the USSR was on the verge of concretely entering communism.

"Heads it is, Mr. President," verified Rabin.

"Let them lead off," said the President.

"Us first," translated Ermilov.

"This is Astronaut Yates speaking."

"Hello, Astronaut Yates," said the General Secretary. "I have your President's permission to speak with our cosmonaut and citizen, Viktorov."

"He passed out, sir."

"He what!"

"Yes, sir, about five minutes ago. He was yelling and singing, then I looked over, and he was out like a light."

"Wake him up!"

"I don't take orders from you. Sorry, sir," said Yates.

"Wake him up! Wake him up!" said the President.

"Yes, sir! Wake up you stupid . . . Sir, is this a closed system?"

"Yes."

"Wake up, you stupid motherfucker. Wake the fuck up before I . . ."

"What? What?" said Viktorov. "Oh my head, don't hit my head. It feels like nails are being driven through my forehead."

"Shut up!" roared the General Secretary in Russian.

"Who said that?" said Viktorov, invisible because there was no camera in the American LEM. The image of the American President remained on the Kremlin screen. Tilting to his right, the President bent toward the interpreter, who was visible only as a chin, lips, and a scant prickly mustache.

"I said it. The General Secretary!"

"Oh my God, these are the worst D.T.'s I ever had!" moaned Viktorov.

"No, it's really me. Tell him, Astronaut Yates."

"That's right, we're linked up with the Kremlin and the White House now because of you two assholes."

"We are?"

"Listen, Viktorov, everything that caused you to defect no

longer exists for you. We've decided to begin the withering away of the state with you. You're going to be the first Soviet citizen to experience communist freedom."

"That sounds even worse than socialist freedom."

"It isn't, it isn't. It's much better."

"How? Could I have a permanent visa to France?"

"Yes."

"You mean I could just hop on a plane to France?"

"Yes."

"And come back, too?"

"Of course."

"But will my books be published in Russia?"

"Certainly."

"I don't believe it. You'll never publish a line of me again. I'll have to live out my life in Flushing, New York and publish in pathetic emigré journals."

"You won't, you won't. One moment."

The General Secretary and Rabin conferred in whispers.

"Listen, Viktorov, as the General Secretary of the Communist Party of the Soviet Union, in the presence of witnesses, including the President of the United States of America, I promise you that in the event any State publisher turns down your work, which they of course have the socialist freedom to do, I promise you that you will have the right to start your own publishing company. You won't be able to publish anyone but yourself, of course, because yours will be the only communist publishing company and you will be the only full communist poet."

"Could I call it the Withering of the State Publishing House?"

"Of course, of course. That would even be a very appropriate name for it."

"You can't fool me. You'll let me have my own publishing house, but you won't let me have any paper or distribution."

"As General Secretary, I guarantee distribution. But, to be frank and open, paper is sometimes a problem, like thread or meat."

"I don't know, I don't know. I think I'm going to be sick."

On the screen, the President's larger-than-life face crinkled in distaste as the sounds of human retching reached the earth.

"Now you've stunk up the whole fucking LEM!" cried Yates.

The only reply was additional gurgling spasms.

"Yates!" said the President.

"Yes, Mr. President!"

"Give that bozo one of those instant anti-spacesickness pills. That may bring him around."

"Yes, Mr. President!"

There was an expectant pause in the capitals of both hemispheres as they all listened to the hopeful sound of liquid coursing down rather than up.

"Better?" asked the General Secretary.

"Better," said Viktorov.

"So?"

"Freedom? Paris? Publication?"

"Yes."

"I miss Russia already."

"And Russia misses you."

"Alright, I accept."

"One down," said the President, clapping his hands.

The General Secretary began clapping, too, Russian style, more like a chant than a cheer. He was looking directly at Rabin. Everyone stood, even Edov and Minomyotov.

Rabin rose, nodded in acknowledgment, saying: "We're only halfway home."

"You can speak to yours now, Mr. President," said the General Secretary.

"It's a trick, it's a trap! What am I, a sucker, a pigeon?" shouted Viktorov expunging all celebration from the air.

"Viktorov, we made an agreement!" said the General Secretary.

"How do I know what's really going on? All I can hear is voices. For all I know they're being transmitted from the Soviet LEM to this one. I know KGB tricks."

"Viktorov, you heard the President of the United States."

"You can do anything with machines."

"Ask the American astronaut."

"Why should I believe him? He wants me out of here, too."

"Viktorov, there comes a time when, as a last resort, you have to trust people."

"How can I trust people? They're all so crummy. Me too, I'm crummy too. I've botched the whole thing. My life disgusts me!"

"Does your eight-year-old daughter Katya from your second marriage disgust you, too?" asked the General Secretary referring to a piece of paper he had just been handed.

"Katya is the only beautiful thing in my life."

"Then how can you abandon her?"

"I can! I can! That's how low I am!"

"But you won't just be abandoning her, you'll be condemning her to a life of humiliation and oppression as the daughter of a turncoat."

"Are you threatening to make my beautiful little eight-year-old daughter pay for my sins? That's truly vile. That's something only a Soviet leader would do. Wait a minute! Now I believe I am talking with the real General Secretary. Does the old deal still hold?"

"It still holds."

"Alright, as a last resort, I'm going to trust you."

There was a long pause on the moon and on the earth, but no further outbursts were forthcoming from Viktorov.

"I'd like to speak to Blaine now and wind this up," said the President.

The image of the President slid to the right, and Blaine's face filled the left half of the screen.

"Never, never, never," moaned Blaine, his head swaying, "never drink vodka on the moon."

"I'm sure it's a very wrong thing to do, Arthur," said the President. "And I'm sure that's the main reason you've been acting the way you have. Did the Russian force the vodka on you?"

"No, sir. I wanted to drink after Whitman lost the Waltanschauung match to Disney."

"Arthur, Arthur, pay attention, son. Do you remember the case of Thoreau who went on the air for the fascists during World War II?" asked the President.

"Thoreau went on the air for the fascists?" asked Blaine.

Whispering lips appeared at the President's ear.

"Excuse me, Arthur, I misspoke. I meant to say, do you remember the case of Ezra Pound?"

"Of course I do, of course. He didn't like Walt Whitman either."

"Now, Pound was sentenced to a mental hospital."

"I didn't know Americans sentenced writers to mental hospitals, too," whispered the General Secretary to Rabin. "When was that?"

"Late forties, I think," said Rabin.

"Very early. Very advanced. I didn't know."

"Of course I remember all that," said Blaine. "Pound spent years in St. Elizabeth's."

"Arthur, I'd like to propose an agreement, a moral and historical agreement, that will exist just between the two of us."

"A moral and historical agreement between a president and a poet? What?"

"I will exile you to Nome, Alaska."

"Nome. I like the sound of that. 'The Nome Cantos,' 'The Nome Exile Cantos.' "

"He's still pretty drunk," said one of the Soviet cosmonauts as Blaine's head disappeared from the screen.

"Arthur," said the President, "get ahold of yourself."

Blaine returned in profile, staring at the three Soviet cosmonauts. "Whose hoods are these? I think I know!"

"Arthur! Listen to me! You will be exiled to Nome. It won't be a legal agreement but a moral one. You can leave any time you want. This is America, after all."

"Can my poems be smuggled into the rest of America?"

"Yes."

"Can they be printed?"

"Of course."

"I don't want them to."

"I thought poets liked to get published."

"It's too easy. Everything's too easy. Nothing matters. Nothing counts."

"Arthur, I promise you that I will use all my persuasive powers to keep you from getting published."

"Yes, but what can you really do, it's a free society."

"Arthur, we are not going to turn America into a totalitarian country just to make you happy."

"Even I wouldn't ask that," said Blaine with a melancholy that may have heralded the return of sobriety.

"So, what do you say?"

"Say to what?"

"Say to being exiled in Nome."

"All roads lead to Nome. There's no place like Nome. All the world is sad and dreary, everywhere I Nome" sang Blaine. "Isn't that the most beautiful line in any American song, Mr. President? All the world is sad and dreary."

"The world isn't sad and dreary, Arthur," said the President. "It's full of wonderful opportunities."

"You have to believe that because you're the president, but I know it's sad and dreary."

"But just look at yourself. Just look at the marvelous opportunities you've been given. First American poet on the moon, first American poet to be morally exiled to Nome, Alaska. Who knows what's next!"

The pause that ensued lasted long enough for Eliot Rabin to feel emboldened to speak. "Mr. Blaine, if you accept the President's offer, you will become more than well-known, more than famous. You will achieve utter glory."

"Utter glory," repeated Blaine pensively.

"Yes, the name of Arthur Blaine will live as long as the English language lives."

"That's not long enough. People can't even read Chaucer in the original anymore, and that's just a few hundred years. There's no such thing as undying glory."

"Is Dante a great poet?" asked Rabin.

"What a question! Dante is one of the immortals."

"And how's your Italian?" asked Rabin.

"My Italian?"

"Yes, your Italian."

"Largely nonexistent."

"So then how do you know he's one of the greats?"

"Alright. Proving what?"

"Proving that a poet can gain immortality even if no one reads him."

"I want people to read me."

"They will. There will always be that select few."

"Yes but who are they? Who are they really? Do you have any idea what those people are like?"

"Dante was exiled, too."

"Yes, but to a beautiful Italian city."

"Nome has its charm. And it hasn't been done before."

"That's true."

"So?"

"I can't do it."

"Why not?"

"I'd feel like I was betraying Viktorov."

"Viktorov is going back to Russia."

"Is he crazy?"

"No, it's true. He's going to be allowed to travel and have his own publishing company."

"I won't believe it till I hear it from him," said Blaine with blurry belligerence.

"Astronaut Yates, can you contact the Soviet LEM?" asked the President.

"Yes, sir. We have contact."

"Arthur," said the President, "you may speak to Viktorov. And thank you for your help again, Professor Rabin."

"Viktor, you're going back?"

"Why not? We've succeeded. We stopped the world. And I've got everything I ever wanted."

"Me too."

"What did you get?"

"A presidential exile to Nome, Alaska."

"Perfect!"

"It's too perfect. Maybe I should still go to Russia."

"Don't be crazy. Don't go to Russia. It's hard enough for us. You could never take it. I'll come visit you in Nome. It will be another historic occasion—the Russian poet traveling freely to visit the American poet in exile. We'll drink vodka. We'll reminisce about the old days on the moon."

"The old days on the moon . . ." said Blaine pensively. "How do you like 'Luniad' for a title?"

"Excellent! Perhaps you should try rhymed verse and I'll try free," said Viktorov.

"Listen, fellas," said Yates, "everybody likes to talk shop, but we're running out of time and oxygen here."

"So?" said Viktorov.

"In for a penny, in for a Pound."

There was silence in heaven and on earth. Whatever it exactly was, it was over. There was a stunned, letdown feeling in Washington and in Moscow. Everyone shared the spiritual state in which the inner being becomes a simple question: "That's it?"

The world of logistics and consequences went into operation. Bodies and machines began to move. All that remained was to wind up the conversation.

"Well, nothing quite beats getting off the hook," said the President.

"Very true," said the General Secretary.

"I'd like to speak to Professor Rabin for a moment if I could," said the President.

"Of course."

"You did a bang-up job today, Professor," said the President.

"Thank you, sir."

"We could use a person with your brains and experience on our team. Say, as special consultant on Soviet affairs?"

"I accept."

"You're on the payroll. However, since you're working for me now, I do have something I'd like done."

"Already? I mean, yes?"

"I want you to return to America the same way you left it, in that special compartment in the cargo hold."

"May I ask why, sir?"

"Well, I'll be damned if I know how, but word about you has already leaked to television. Not only that, an Islamic splinter group has already threatened to abduct you. They're calling you the Jew Satan of the Kremlin. And if you've been abducted once, who's to say it won't happen again. One of our staff psychologists even thinks you might be abduction-prone."

"Alright, Sir, I'll go back in the hold."

"It's perfectly safe," said Poplavsky speaking with the confidence that he was already the new head of the Committee on State Security.

"I'm sure your Soviet hosts will be glad to help with any arrangements," said the President.

"Anything Professor Rabin desires is his," said the General Secretary. "And it has been a pleasure cooperating with you, Mr. President, in averting this crisis."

"See you at the summit," said the President, signing off.

The screen darkened, the lights brightened, and they were all back in that room again.

Poplavsky looked toward the General Secretary who nodded anointment.

"Don't worry, Edov, your career isn't over," said Poplavsky to Edov who was holding his head in his hands. "We could use a good man in Tadzhikistan."

"But wait a second! Wait a second!" cried Edov. "Your Jew has tricked us! The Americans are starting to act like us, and we're starting to act like them! That's not the beginning of communism! That's the road to convergence!"

Hostile electricity tensed every muscle in every suit.

"Well?" said the General Secretary to Rabin who was suddenly terrified that the last moment had not in fact passed, that there was still ample time to fail miserably. But he was sick of the tears-and-dishwater taste of misery, which he knew all too well from the Defense Language Institute, and the Gogol.

"What we always forget," said Rabin, "is that nobody ever knows what's really going on at the moment. Who knows, communism might look like convergence for a while. Why not? It's looked like plenty of other things. And, unlike Mr. Edov's, my job is secure."

"Once again, Professor Rabin's logic is invincible," said the General Secretary with the finality of a gavel.

EPILOGUE

The plane with the special compartment, which brought Rabin to Moscow in the first place, had taken off for San Francisco an hour and ten minutes before the final resolution of the crisis, and, given travel time, refueling, etc., could not return and be ready to leave in less than twenty-four hours. Viktorov and Blaine were already en route to their destinies and destinations, and Rabin, now not only a Soviet state secret, but an American one as well, couldn't even go out for a stroll on Red Square.

"You like my new office?" asked Poplavsky, gesturing at the high, banked windows.

"Very nice," said Rabin. "It bespeaks . . . authority."

"It does, it does. But you know," said Poplavsky wistfully, "I would have loved it even more when I was still a Stalinist."

"You're not a Stalinist any more?"

"No."

"What are you then?"

"Nothing. Like everybody else. A success."

"Beats Tadzhikistan. Listen, Leonid, there are a few arrangements I'd like to make."

"Whatever you want, within reason."

"Within reason hardly defines the recent situation, but never mind. The first question is, What's that compartment on the plane like?"

"Small, padded, good for sleeping."

"Sounds like a coffin. That gives me something to think about. I'll let you know when I decide. In the meantime, you've got to get Andrei out of there."

"Who out of where?"

"Andrei was in ward 1 with me at the Gogol Institute."

"He's probably crazy then."

"Maybe he is and maybe he isn't. If he can't take care of himself, at least have him put in a normal institution."

"I will take it under advisement."

"None of that, Leonid. Say you'll do it. For me."

"Alright, for you, I'll do it. Consider it done."

"Now I'd like to put a call into McDonald's."

"You're hungry again?"

"No, I want to talk to Valya."

"Aha, you scamp. In the middle of everything . . ."

"It sometimes happens when you least expect it," said Rabin with a shrug.

"She said they had a direct line to Edov, now which phone would that be. Here it is, here it is," said Poplavsky handing Rabin a yellow receiver.

"McDonald's," said a deep male voice sounding somewhat dazed.

"Is Valya there?"

"One minute, I'll see. Valya!"

There was a pause in which Rabin thought he heard the sound of broken glass being swept up.

"She wants to know who's calling," said the man's voice.

She would, thought Rabin. "Tell her it's the American

who was in earlier and who she wouldn't serve, which started the brawl there."

He heard the phone clunk against a surface, followed by an abstract dialogue of voices, one male, one female. Quick light footsteps approached.

"What do you want now?" said Valya.

"I'd like to take you out to dinner."

"When?"

"Tonight."

"Tonight? I can't. I'm busy. I have to work late, cleaning up this place."

"What time will you get through?" The questions never vary, thought Rabin. And always just that little touch of high school.

"It doesn't matter when I get through. I'll be so exhausted, all I'll want to do is go to sleep."

"I can get you off work early."

"Why should I let you. Don't you think I take my work seriously? Are you one of those men who don't consider a woman capable of serious work? I'll have you know that I am the first woman in the Soviet Union to combine a career in state security and fast food, and I'm proud of what I've accomplished here. And I won't go out with any man who doesn't treat me with respect. Period."

"It's not that at all," said Rabin. "I have tremendous respect for the way you held your post today. I admired that greatly even though I did find it inconvenient."

"I hope I didn't hurt your friend too badly," said Valya, her voice softer now.

"By the way, you should know that my friend, Leonid Poplavsky, is now the chairman of the Committee on State

Security, meaning, he's your boss. But don't worry, I'll put in a good word for you."

"Are you telling me the truth?"

"How else do you think I'd be calling you on the direct line?"

There was a moment of silence on Valya's end. Rabin knew that she was running a complex equation. She was a career woman, and that meant she was necessarily involved in both career maintenance and career advancement. Great connections never hurt. Not to mention the fact that through overzealousness she had done serious injury to four fingers belonging to the person who was now her boss. But, practical inducements aside, he didn't want her if she didn't want him, the more wanting on both sides the better, he had always found.

"What time?" she said.

"The sooner the better."

"I need at least an hour and a half." This was a statement of pure femininity and therefore indisputable.

"Fine," said Rabin. "So, let's say seven thirty at the Holiday Inn."

"The Holiday Inn in Gatchina?"

"Yes."

"The food's terrible there!"

"It's supposed to be."

"And I spent the whole day in Gatchina. Can't we go somewhere else?"

"Gatchina is the only place I can go."

"Why?"

"Because I'm a state secret."

"Well," said Valya with a sudden flirtatiousness, "I'm very good at keeping secrets."

"Look, I know it's no fun to go out so near where you

work, but with enough wine we might both forget where we are."

"That sounds nice."

"So, I'll see you there at seven thirty."

"Bye."

"Got a date?" asked Poplavsky, who was busy tossing Edov's effects into a large cardboard box.

"Yes."

"She's a cute one, that Valya. But trouble."

"That I noticed. And, by the way, don't you think she deserves something for the fight she put up today, a medal, a promotion?"

"That would make you happy?"

"It would."

"Then tell her that she is now lieutenant colonel and has been awarded the Order of Gatchina, which is too secret to exist as an actual, physical medal but will be so noted on her record."

"Speaking of promotions, Leonid, I really feel that the Polish general who leaked the secret to the West in the first place should be restored to his rank. I mean, after all, if it weren't for him, you wouldn't be sitting at that desk."

"Very true! A very brilliant insight into the actual mechanics of development. Still, I hate to do anything good for a Pole."

"Make an exception in this case. I think it would be bad luck not to. Asymmetrical."

"If that's what you think, that's what I'll do. I might as well get a little more use out of that wonderful brain before it goes to work for the other side."

Suddenly, Rabin felt a chilling visual ray on him. It was the murderer in Poplavsky taking a quick peek out his eyes.

But it was only a second later that Poplavsky was smiling at Rabin with love, and sorrow.

"And even apart from your brain, I'm going to miss you," said Poplavsky. "We've been through so much together. Our lives are linked forever. I can't believe you're going to desert me for a woman, a woman, on our last night together in Moscow!"

"I didn't know it meant so much to you. It's just that I felt a tremendous attraction to her in the McDonald's, and, after all I've been through, to be naked with a woman—"

"Stop! It's bad enough that you're going to spend your final hours here with a stranger, I don't need to hear all the details. Do you think I'm not human? I'm probably more human than you are. I'm probably more human than anybody should ever be. That's my true tragedy, if anybody cares," said Poplavsky swiveling in his high-backed chair toward the window to conceal his emotion.

Rabin rested his head on one hand. Why was it that, if there were two elements in any situation, they would immediately take the form of a conflict?

"You know, Leonid," said Rabin when Poplavsky had swung a third of the way back around. "There's always one person who loves more, and in this case it was you who abducted me as I recall."

"And was I so stupid either?"

"No, you were the only one who saw me with innocent eyes. And who wouldn't love you? Probably the most frightening thing about you is that you're lovable."

"Ah! Edov has a good bottle of cognac in his desk. Let's have a farewell drink."

Glasses were found, filled, and clinked.

"To having met," said Rabin.

"To meeting again," said Poplavsky.

The cognac turned Rabin's chest into a fireplace where the kindling has just caught.

"Good," he said, "good."

"Yes," said Poplavsky, "life is good."

"I have an idea," said Rabin.

"Another one?"

"A simple one. You remember your friend Lunin who had the Mexican postcards?"

"Of course, he's in the building."

"I want those postcards now. I want to write them."

Poplavsky ordered the postcards brought at once, his first order as minister.

The postcards arrived by messenger, accompanied by an apologetic note saying that only two were left. They were clipped to a file containing photocopies of all the previous postcards sent and replies received.

A quick check of the photocopies revealed that Rabin was involved with a Mexican painter who made Frida Kahlo look demure, and that he had quarreled bitterly by mail with his friend Howard over the direction Rabin's life had taken—down.

One postcard was of a flowering cactus and the other of the Paseo, the Sunday ritual in which boys and girls walk counter-clockwise to each other in concentric circles.

The Paseo was for Janey, the flowering cactus for Howard, Rabin decided, accepting another cognac and taking pen in hand for the first time in a long while.

Dear Howard,

I trust you will still be happy to hear that I am abandoning Mexico for a position as Presidential Consultant on Soviet Affairs and have not, to use your words, suffered "mañanaization of the moral sense."

Your ex and future friend
Eliot Rabin

Dear Janey,

I ask your forgiveness for leaving you, and for staying longer than I should.

But I still love you in the way that survives the love of men and women.

Eliot

"Done?" asked Poplavsky.

"Done," said Rabin.

"I'll have them put with the diplomatic mail to Mexico, or would you rather have us postmark them ourselves and hand deliver them in the US?"

"Hand delivered if you can make it inconspicuous."

"Believe me."

"That's best then. I don't want to trust the Mexican mails. And ours can be a little quirky, too."

"Let's have one more, and then you should probably get going," said Poplavsky with a doleful glance at his watch.

Few words were exchanged over this drink. They simply sat with each other, and looked at each other as men rarely do—easily, just wanting to see each other.

"There is one thing I'd like to ask of you," said Poplavsky.

"Anything within reason," said Rabin, with a grin.

"Maybe it's too petty to bother with," said Poplavsky with a dismissive flick.

"No. It's alright, ask."

"But don't laugh."

"I won't."

"What exactly is the difference between 'a' and 'the'?

Rabin laughed.

"You said you wouldn't laugh."

"Sorry. I didn't mean to."

"Well?"

"Oh. The difference between 'a' and 'the'. Let's see."

Rabin took a puff on his cigarette at one side of his mouth while squinting in the other direction. "Well, you could say that everything is an 'a' until you look at it and see it; then it becomes a 'the'."

"But why does it become *a* 'the' and not *the* 'the'?"

"It's because . . . Wait . . . It's such a fine point, it keeps disappearing . . . No, I don't know."

"Even you?" said Poplavsky, with a snow-just-stopping hush of wonderment.

"Anyway, I'm sick of solving problems," said Rabin pushing his glass toward Poplavsky. "I'd just like to live for a while. Be outdoors in the heat. Swim. Eat shrimp, drink beer."

"Oficially speaking, that's all you've been doing."

"But now I could use it. Well, I guess this one's for the road," said Rabin, raising his glass in acknowledgment of Leonid and life.

At first they drank slowly, regarding each other over their glasses then polished them off, drawing the line on sentiment.

"I will see you to the limo," said Poplavsky, casting an anxious look about his office, a man behind in his work.

Standing by the open passenger door, Rabin said: "There is one more thing I would like to ask of you, Leonid."

"Anything, anything," said Poplavsky.

Rabin bent to Poplavsky's ear, and there in that most secret of buildings and in the most confidential of whispers, Rabin imparted a final desire.

Poplavsky's face expressed perplexity, displeasure, astonishment, glee, and agreement.

Then they hugged Russian style, rib cage to rib cage.

"Leonid, I can't believe we're not going to take any more limo rides together," said Rabin as he slipped into the limo like a letter disappearing down a mail chute. "I can't believe it's over."

"I know, I know," said Poplavsky. "Time is the true tyrant."

Valya was late. He should have figured. What good was seeing into the very workings of reality if you still arrived early for dates?

But what if that bitch stood him up? He'd have to spend the evening alone in that Holiday Inn, a funeral parlor that served after-dinner mints.

Poplavsky would laugh at him when he found out. Poplavsky would laugh at him for not knowing one essential truth of life—that women were another tribe, another religion, and the great moments should be marked among your own.

But that truth vanished instantly from mind as soon as she breezed in, all scarf, fresh air and apology.

"I shouldn't have tried to go home, but I had nothing good to wear in my locker," said Valya opening her coat, turning slightly to each side.

She was wearing a dark-blue knitted dress with a Scandinavian snow-flake pattern above the breast line. Her earrings, thin, dangly, and gold, caught the light and reflected it to her hair.

"Valya, you look smashing," said Rabin, punning for himself.

He helped her off with her coat and into her chair, both of them freely enjoying the intimacy that courtesy prescribes.

"I'll order champagne," said Rabin resuming his seat and his cigarette.

"I adore champagne."

"You'll adore it more when you hear what we're drinking to. Waiter!"

"Yes, citizen consumer!" said the waiter springing to the side of the table and coming to an abrupt halt.

"We don't say 'citizen consumer' in America," said Rabin with professorial irritation.

"Sorry, it's my first day."

"Alright, just bring us your best champagne."

When the champagne was poured and the waiter had backed away into the darkness, Rabin raised his glass and said: "To you, Lieutenant Colonel, congratulations on being awarded the Order of Gatchina."

Her eyes went from wary to merry. She laughed: "Yes, I'll drink to that."

The clearness of the clink their glasses made was itself a good omen.

"I liked you as soon as you walked in," said Valya. "Did you know that?"

"Yes."

"Good."

"It happens every so often."

"Not often enough."

"Who's to say?"

"Not often enough," repeated Valya. "But, who cares, the champagne is so cold."

Over the oysters they argued if he was really American. It was only well into the roast beef that he finished his story and, with some slight reservation about certain details, she believed him. She asked him questions about America during coffee and dessert, saying she would love to see Manhattan, the Grand Canyon, and Disney World some day.

A pause set in after he had stubbed out his after-coffee cigarette. Frank, amused, respectful, his eyes tendered a formal invitation.

Pushing out her lower lip, she said: "Eliot, you shouldn't smoke so much."

"My compliments to the chef," said Rabin to the waiter as he rose from his chair. "The roast beef was a perfect uniform grey."

In the room, quickly naked, they toyed with each other's nipples, teasing the dial toward pain.

And in the next five hours they were only apart twice, Valya hiding in the bathroom when the waiter rolled in his cart of caviar and champagne, Rabin, a poker-faced Indian wrapped in a patterned blanket, muttering: "I'll pour, I'll pour. Go."

Although, when Rabin's sleep finally came, it could not have been any deeper, it took but a single knock at the door to wake him.

"Your package, Professor Rabin," said the room service waiter. "If you could just sign here."

"Who is it?" asked Valya sleepily from bed. "Is it time for you to go?" she asked, sounding more awake.

"Not quite," said Rabin, answering only the second question.

"Good," she said, "I hate hurried goodbyes."

"The instructions are inside," said the waiter.

Valya was sitting up in bed when he turned from the door. "What's in there?"

"You'll see in a minute," said Rabin, heading for the bathroom.

"No, tell me now."

"You'll see, you'll see. Just don't laugh."

She laughed when Rabin came out of the bathroom.

"I know it looks ridiculous but it's important to me," he said, pointing a finger at the velcro headband from which a wire ran to a small device on his right buttock held in place by a holsterlike strap around his right thigh.

"What's it for?"

"You remember I told you how they abducted me in the first place?"

"I remember."

"Well, the little box back there will shoot a dart into me when the electrode sensors on my head tell it that I'm . . . experiencing maximal distraction."

"And you expect me to have any part of that?"

"Valya, please, for the love of God, I can't fly all the way back to America wide awake in that little compartment. I'll go out of my mind. If you've come to care for me at all . . ."

"And if you've come to care for me in the least, you would never think of asking me to denigrate myself in a manner that is not only offensive but absurd."

"Valya, please, what's the difference, it's still me."

"I'm sure you don't need me to make that thing operate,"

she said, turning away to pretend to look for something on the night table.

"You'll do as I say!"

"Or you'll tell my boss?" she said.

"No. You'll just do it!"

"Alright, climb aboard."

"No, I'm sorry, Valya. I don't want you like that."

"Oh you don't. You want this. You don't want that."

"Valya, if there's one thing I've learned it's sometimes, as a last resort, you have to trust people. So trust me when I say sure, I want this, but only if you can want it, too."

"Very nicely said."

Though initially somewhat crimped by the technology, they soon found a rhythm that was fiery, yet touched with the sadness of a farewell that could arrive at any moment, and finally, suddenly, did.

The only way to travel, thought Eliot Rabin forty-eight hours later. Bending to admire a rose on his way to work, he could feel that his dark blue suit was too heavy for steamy D.C. and that the souvenir tingle of pain in his hip had still not entirely faded. The red of the rose was like a sudden kiss at a crowded party.